SAVAGE SNIPER

A World War II Thriller

DAVID HEALEY

INTRACOASTAL

SAVAGE SNIPER

A World War II Thriller

By David Healey

Intracoastal Media digital edition published 2023. Print ISBN 979-8-9872808-2-9

Cover photo by Deny Howeth

Cover design by Streetlight Graphics

Editing by Castle Walls Editing

BISAC Subject Headings:

FIC014000 FICTION/Historical

FIC032000 FICTION/War & Military

Savage:

1. (adj.) Wild and ferocious; extremely cruel

— WEBSTER'S DICTIONARY

... I still wish with you that Pikes could be introduc'd; and I would add Bows and Arrows. Those were good Weapons, not wisely laid aside.

— BENJAMIN FRANKLIN

CHAPTER ONE

STILL AS STONE, Deacon Cole stared through the rifle scope at the ravine directly across from him.

His eye had caught a flicker of movement in that ravine, indicating that Patrol Easy might be walking into an ambush. Maybe it had been only a bird, or some small jungle animal, but his gut told another story. Trusting your gut was the best way to stay alive.

"What is it?" Philly whispered.

"I think I saw something."

"When you're nervous, then I know I ought to be nervous."

"I ain't nervous," Deke said. "I'm just trying not to get shot."

"If that doesn't make you nervous, then I don't know what does," Philly replied.

"Hush now and let me think."

Philly had his own sniper rifle to his shoulder, peering through the telescopic sight at the tangled vegetation ahead. Though useful, the scope amplified just a small circle of greenery.

It didn't help that the dense vegetation could have hidden an entire Japanese company, let alone a single sniper. Deke stayed on the scope and waited, staring in hopes of catching the smallest flicker of movement, confident that Philly was watching his back.

Although Philly also carried a sniper rifle, there was no doubt about which of the two men was the better shot. In situations like this, Philly defaulted to being the spotter, keeping an eye on the big picture so that Deke could stay focused on whatever he saw through the narrow field of the rifle scope.

After all, it had been Deke who had spotted something in the ravine. He seemed to have a sixth sense about these things. When Deke said something didn't feel right, nobody argued.

During their months of fighting, starting with their arrival on Guam, some men had simply survived, but Deke had somehow grown more comfortable in hunting men with a rifle. Philly had also sensed this about Deke, and it sometimes made him wary of the former farm boy, the same way you might watch out for a dog that liked to bite even after you had scratched his ears.

They were in the countryside on the outskirts of Ormoc. The transition from residential areas back to forest was abrupt here, northwest of the city. To the northeast lay vast rice paddies that, in their own way, would likely prove more hazardous than the jungle.

Ormoc had finally fallen to the US Army after fierce street fighting. The port city and its nearby airfield were a vital cog in the wheel that was Leyte. Now that American forces held Ormoc, they were one step closer to taking complete control of Leyte. Of course, that was just one of the Philippine islands, but it was a key Japanese stronghold. Nobody even wanted to think as far ahead as capturing Manila.

This fight came down to one day at a time, one step at a time. That was how you eventually won the war. That was how you stayed alive.

The Japanese had been defeated at Ormoc, but they were far from beaten elsewhere in the jungles and mountains of Leyte. In one of those twists of fate, it was the Japanese who had traded places with the Filipinos, who early in the occupation had fled their villages and homes to shelter in the hills, growing whatever meager crops they could encourage in the rugged soil. Now those refugees were returning to their homes, and it was the Japanese who were taking to the hills to make their last stand.

Patrol Easy's task was to probe this area, determining where all the enemy units were hidden. It was a job that was easier said than done. It was also a job that was necessary, hard as it might be. The last thing they needed was a clutch of enemy holdouts so close to Ormoc, giving them an easy place from which to launch insurgent attacks.

The enemy was out here, all right. Deke was certain of that. Probably closer than anybody knew. Like maybe right in front of them.

But where?

Deke set aside his rifle and took out his binoculars to scan the jungle. There was nothing but trees and bushes. He continued to look, searching for any sign of movement. Suddenly he spotted the greenery shifting as something pushed through it. He couldn't tell what it was, but he knew it was the enemy.

"Did you see that?" Philly whispered. "Movement at your two o'clock."

"I see it," Deke replied in a barely audible whisper.

He signaled to the others, pointing in the direction where he had seen something moving through the trees. He held his fire, hoping for a clear target.

The rest of the squad took up positions, their weapons at the ready.

Lieutenant Steele edged closer. Steele commanded their small sniper patrol. He carried a twelve-gauge shotgun, and one eye was covered by a patch. He'd lost the eye at Guadalcanal, and it should have been the lieutenant's ticket home. However, he claimed to have some unfinished business with the Japanese. Deke understood.

"What have you got?" Steele asked.

"There's something up in those trees."

"How many?"

"Don't know yet."

"All right. Go check it out. We don't want to bite off more than we can chew."

Deke nodded and began to move toward where he thought the enemy soldiers might be hidden.

The dense vegetation seemed to swallow him whole as he crept forward, his senses on high alert. He could feel his heart pounding as he searched for any sign of the enemy. Every sound seemed amplified, every rustle of leaves a potential threat.

Despite his efforts at stealth, he heard a twig snap beneath his boot. He froze, his eyes scanning the trees ahead. Sweat ran down his face, but the hands holding his rifle remained steady as ever.

Waiting, he held his breath.

But there was nothing. No movement, no sound. Just the oppressive silence of the jungle. Even the birds and ever-present insects seemed to have fallen silent.

Deke felt a moment of doubt. Had he been wrong? Was there really nobody there?

No—he had seen something. He was sure of it.

Just then he saw movement out of the corner of his eye. He spun sideways, his rifle at the ready.

A Japanese soldier was charging at him, a bayonet reflecting in the dappled sunlight under the canopy of trees. The man burst from the greenery, shouting some sort of foreign battle cry.

Deke had only a split second to react. He lifted his rifle and fired. At this range he didn't have to aim—just point.

The soldier fell to the ground and lay still, apparently dead before he hit the forest floor. The sharp crack of Deke's rifle had almost immediately been swallowed by the surrounding leaves and branches, leaving the forest as silent as ever.

He kept the rifle pointed at the dead Japanese, but the body didn't stir. The soldier's mistake had been trying to skewer Deke with his bayonet. If he'd taken a shot at Deke, the outcome might have been very different.

It turned out that the soldier who had attacked Deke wasn't the only Japanese in hiding.

A shot rang out, and Deke froze. He heard the crack of a bullet passing overhead. Had the bullet been intended for him? It seemed likely—he was the man closest to the forest.

"Sniper!" Philly shouted, almost by reflex.

"No shit," Deke grumbled. "Tell me something I don't know."

Ever so slowly, he backpedaled through the weeds and brush. Sweat trickled down his back. An ant crept over his face, but Deke ignored it, not even bothering to flick it away.

Even in the middle of a war, with the sky filled with planes and the beaches crawling with troops, sometimes everything came down to a single bullet, especially if you were either the one trying to dodge that bullet or the one trying to deliver it.

Another shot was fired, the bullet singing through the air, close enough this time that Deke heard it whip through the brush nearby. The crack of the bullet made his skin crawl.

Dammit. Where the hell is that sniper?

Working his way backward like a retreating crab, Deke eased first his legs and then the rest of his body into a patch of kunai grass and shrubs. He kept working his way into the greenery until not even the muzzle of his rifle was visible. But it was there all the same, pointed in the direction of the enemy. All that Deke could see ahead was a wall of green.

His oasis of greenery provided cover, but like the rest of the patrol, Deke was basically pinned down. He still had no idea where the sniper was hiding, knowing only that the enemy marksman was out there somewhere close and seemed determined to put Deke in his rifle sights.

Now seemed as good a time as ever to try one of the tricks that he had up his sleeve. He remembered the metal shaving mirror in his pack.

Deke had bought it from a vendor selling all sorts of baubles in the ruins of Ormoc. Sure, he could use it for shaving, but he'd also had another idea in the back of his mind. It was just what he would need now to distract the enemy sniper.

The flat metal mirror was polished to a bright shine, much like a military-issue signal mirror. It was similar in its dimensions to the cover of one of Yoshio's paperback Western novels. There was a hole in one end so that he could hang it from a nail and shave or maybe comb his hair. That took care of the grooming needs of your average GI, including Deke.

The wind rippled the jungle every which way, causing the foliage to flow in a dull green blur that masked any movement by the enemy. Keeping out of sight and working quickly, Deke tied the mirror into the brush nearby so that the breeze made the dangling mirror flash occasionally, a shiny bauble in the jungle to fake out and distract the enemy sniper.

The light caught the mirrored surface and flashed, surely as irresistible to the enemy sniper as a shiny lure was to a bass in Old Man Thompson's fishing hole back home.

The enemy sniper was good, but he wasn't good enough to escape the trap that Deke had set for him.

Sure enough, the Japanese sniper fired at the mirror.

Deke had been sure to keep well clear of the mirror, but he

immediately planted his face in the dirt, wishing he had more cover. He could hear the others shouting and cursing as they took up positions and began scanning their surroundings.

"Where is he?" Steele whispered urgently.

Deke scanned the trees and foliage, his heart still hammering. He couldn't see anything. The sniper was too well hidden.

Another shot rang out, the crack of the bullet once again passing dangerously close to Deke's head.

Had he actually seen the muzzle flash that time, or had it been his imagination?

"He's up in the trees," Deke yelled, pointing at the canopy overhead.

Without another word, the rest of the patrol began firing volley after volley into the trees. Branches were ripped apart, leaves scattered in the wind, but there was no sign they had taken out the sniper.

Deke scanned the trees, searching for any sign of movement. His eyes were fixed on a patch of dense foliage high above, and he caught a glimpse of something moving.

He brought his rifle up, firing at the movement.

There was a scream, and then silence.

"I think I got him," Deke announced, relaxing somewhat.

The silence was deafening, with only the sound of his own heartbeats filling the void, and the tension was palpable. If the sniper hadn't been eliminated, the slightest noise could give away Deke's position.

As he crawled across the jungle floor toward the sniper's position, Deke couldn't shake the feeling that the sniper was still watching him, waiting for the perfect opportunity to take him out. His whole body itched with anticipation of the bullet that didn't arrive.

He parted the foliage and looked up at the nearby trees, relieved to see the sagging corpse of the enemy sniper. The man had wedged himself into the fork of a small tree, several feet above the ground, offering a vantage point. The sniper's rifle had fallen to the jungle floor, and Deke retrieved it, popped out the bolt, and hurled the rifle deep into the jungle. He threw the bolt in a different direction. Others would have kept the rifle as a souvenir, but he wasn't interested in collecting trophies.

He walked back out and signaled to the rest of the patrol that the coast was clear.

"Just another day at the factory," Philly said.

"I don't know what the hell kind of factory you worked in, but remind me not to put in for a job there."

Moving along the forest perimeter, they sought out any other Japanese presence. For the moment, the enemy seemed to have retreated.

They drifted back to what might be called the suburbs of Ormoc, glad to be free of the immediate threat of the Japanese.

Bone weary, they returned to the city streets that had been so hotly contested just a few days before. It was getting so that they recognized a few of the city's landmarks. While many of the houses had been destroyed or damaged in the fighting, a few buildings remained largely intact.

"I've been thinking that I might buy a house here as an investment," Philly said. "You know, get in early on some of this waterfront property. I'll bet I could buy one of these houses cheap."

"You may want to hold off on that, Philly," Lieutenant Steele reminded them. "There are still a few Japanese soldiers hiding out in these houses."

"Well, now, there goes the neighborhood," Deke said.

CHAPTER TWO

LIKE A STRAY CAT on the prowl, Deke moved through the ruins of the port city, studying the streetscape with more than casual interest. He didn't need Lieutenant Steele to remind him that each window, each pile of rubble remaining from an artillery strike, even the wreck of a battered jalopy, might very well be the hiding place for a Japanese sniper.

Danger lurked everywhere. They had learned that lesson the hard way, losing a surprising number of soldiers to sneak attacks and enemy snipers.

While it was true that Ormoc had been captured, there were still a few stubborn enemy holdouts. They remained a thorn in the division's side, but one by one the stray snipers and saboteurs were being rubbed out.

The sniper that Deke had encountered in the forest just beyond where the city streets ended was a case in point.

Like a fighter on the ropes, a few enemy soldiers still awaited their chance to pop up and take one last swing at the enemy.

None of that managed to suppress Philly's need to yak about nothing.

"I heard of a guy in the 306th who walked ten miles dead asleep," Philly said. "He would've kept right on walking all the way to Tokyo if somebody hadn't woken him up."

"It's kind of hard to walk to Tokyo from an island," Deke pointed out absently, his eyes on the surroundings.

"That's not the point of the story."

"You know what's funny? I'm actually asleep right now," Deke said. "It just looks like I'm listening to you."

"Very funny, Corn Pone."

"Keep it up."

The banter helped keep them awake. Deke's legs dragged wearily with each step, but his eyes never stopped moving, flitting from one spot to the next. To give in to fatigue made you vulnerable to attack.

Some of the others had slung their weapons now that they were back in the city, but he kept his rifle in his hands, just in case.

Despite the dangers, commerce was returning rapidly to Ormoc. It was a reminder of the population's resilience. After all, the city had survived more than its share of raids and pirate attacks over the centuries.

Over the police department hung a makeshift sign in English: "The Chief of Police of Ormoc wishes all People to know that the Police Station is not a Morgue. Cadavers are not to be deposited here."

Someone had hung a smaller sign beneath that one, setting the going rate for washing the GIs' clothes:

PANTALONES, 25 centavos
   Shirts, 15 centavos
   Socks, 5 centavos
   Violators will be punished

. . .

PHILLY SAW the sign and shook his head. "I don't know, fellas. Anyone brave enough to wash my socks deserves hazardous-duty pay. Hey, somebody give me a nickel, and I'll see if I can get my socks washed."

They all laughed at that. "I reckon when the time comes, we'll just hold a funeral for your socks and bury them," Deke said.

"With full honors, I hope."

"Of course."

Shops had sprung up, selling a colorful variety of fruits and vegetables to the other hardy civilians who had returned. Not all the civilians had money, though. Swarms of children had appeared like mayflies after a rain, begging candy off the soldiers. A few of the children looked so painfully thin that the GIs didn't think twice about giving them all their chocolate bars or even full cans of rations.

Even adults weren't shy about begging for cigarettes.

Fruits and vegetables weren't the only goods on display. A few working girls in bright skirts lingered on the corners, trying to entice the GIs. Just a week ago, it was likely that these same girls had been providing their services to the Japanese.

Philly saw them and groaned. "Just give me five minutes, boys. That's all I'd need. I swear to God—"

"Hell, I'd only need three minutes," Radio said. "I haven't had any lovin' since Hawaii. How about you, Deke? You want a piece of that?"

Deke grunted. "Hell, who wouldn't?"

The response had sounded a little forced, even to Deke's own ears. Rodeo hadn't seemed to notice, but Philly gave him a look.

The truth was that Deke had precious little experience with women—the kind you paid or otherwise. He had steered clear of them as a general rule because he had feared that the scars on his face left by the bear would scare them off. Even the ones who said it didn't matter—he had caught them studying the angry red furrows with a mixture of fascination and horror when they thought he wasn't looking.

An MP unit arrived to shoo the girls away, resulting in disappointed jeers from the passing soldiers.

But every now and then shots rang out.

The enemy just didn't know when to quit. A few remained hidden within the city, but they weren't about to surrender and allow themselves to be taken prisoner. Most would rather die fighting.

"It seems so futile," Yoshio lamented. They had long since grown used to Yoshio tossing out words that a normal guy wouldn't use. They chalked it up to the fact that he was always reading a book whatever chance he could get—even if it was the same book, over and over again. "One man against so many."

"The Japanese are stubborn bastards—you have to give them that," Philly said.

"Such a waste."

"Don't go getting a soft spot for your dead cousin there," Philly advised, jerking his chin at the body of an enemy soldier in the street. The motion caused his helmet to bobble loosely. "If that Nip was still breathing, he'd be more than happy to stick a bayonet between your ribs, given half a chance."

They were passing the corpse of the lone saboteur who, under cover of darkness, had apparently lobbed several grenades at a group of supply trucks parked for the night before making another run to the beachhead.

The dead Japanese had short legs but a long torso and what appeared to be powerful shoulders. His face was dark and contorted in death, lips curled in what might have been a snarl or a final hateful shout.

"That's the ugliest Nip I've seen yet," Philly remarked with a whistle.

"That's saying something, all right."

"I sure am glad that I didn't run into him. Looks like he was a mean son of a bitch."

From the fact that the corpse was riddled with bullet holes, it was easy enough to guess the enemy soldier's fate. He must have thrown his grenades and then been cut down by rifle fire. He didn't even seem to have been carrying a rifle of his own, unless someone had nabbed it as a souvenir. Given the average GI's propensity for souvenirs, that was entirely possible. Deke judged that the soldier was in his late twenties or early thirties. *What had he been in civilian life?* Deke wondered. Maybe a factory worker, a teacher, or a farmer like Deke had once been.

He pushed any further speculation from his mind. It was better not to think of the enemy as anything but the enemy.

The dead man's lone attack had successfully burned two trucks, vehicles that the division couldn't spare. There simply weren't any extras to be had.

They had even pressed a few captured Japanese vehicles into service, covering them with hastily painted white stars to avoid confusion. Even a truck driver who had proudly driven an American-made Chrysler had to admit that the Japanese vehicles were sturdy and even more reliable than the US vehicles.

The blackened hulks of the trucks were still smoking, filling the air with the stench of burned rubber and charred automotive paint. Their steel frames had blistered with heat, burning down to the bare metal, as if the fires of hell had exploded on its surface. Oddly enough, the only markings that had survived were the white stars painted on the doors, although these were smudged with soot and ash.

The reek of the burned trucks wasn't the only offensive smell.

Nearby, the body of the Japanese soldier was also starting to stink in the growing heat, but nobody made any effort to move it.

Dead Japanese were not a priority, although the living ones certainly were.

Lieutenant Steele soon explained that they wouldn't be staying in Ormoc for long. He had received new marching orders for Patrol Easy.

"Take a good look," said the lieutenant, who went by the nickname Honcho around his men. It came from a Japanese word that meant something like "boss." Anyhow, it was better than being addressed as "lieutenant" and drawing enemy sniper fire as a result. "This may be our last glimpse of what passes for civilization for a while. We're heading back out."

"Gee, I was hoping to maybe catch a movie and get a haircut," Philly said.

"Yeah, yeah," Steele said. "What you really might want to do is find some hip waders. We're about to slog through some rice paddies."

Philly groaned, summing up how they all felt. Nobody enjoyed rice paddies. They were muddy, crawling with snakes and occasionally land mines, and there were few places where a man was so completely exposed as a target. But it didn't sound as if they were going to get much choice.

Gathering them around, the lieutenant spelled out the situation. Now that Ormoc had been taken, the next target for the division would be Palompon. Although smaller than Ormoc, the coastal town provided the Japanese with their last operational port on Leyte. A few Japanese supply vessels and troop transports still managed to come and go, dodging American planes by operating under cover of darkness.

"It's a straight shot right up Highway 2 from Ormoc to Palompon," Steele explained.

"Straight shot? I like the sound of that, Honcho. Sounds like there's nothing to it," Philly said. "It's about time we got an easy job."

"If only it was that simple," the lieutenant said. "The Japanese have every mile of that road locked up tighter than a farmer's daughter."

"I knew there was a catch."

"There always is, or what would they need us for? Not only is the road well defended, but the Japanese have wired the bridges for demolition. The ones that aren't ready to fall down, anyhow. Rumor has it that they've set up ambushes whenever there is a sharp bend in the road."

The designation of Highway 2 was overly optimistic, considering that in places it wasn't much more than a wide dirt road through the rice paddies and forests. Steele added that intelligence reports indicated there were at least forty-two bridges to cross, though most spanned relatively small rivers or streams. Unfortunately for the advancing American troops, each bridge might prove to be a substantial obstacle.

You had to hand it to the Japanese, Deke thought. Having lost Ormoc, they had simply pulled back and planned to defend every inch of the path that US forces would have to take to reach the next objective. By demolishing bridges, and perhaps by planting land mines, they could certainly roll up the carpet behind them.

But the GIs weren't going to cooperate by marching right into the enemy guns. Instead, Lieutenant Steele went on to explain that the plan was to cut across the highway and come at the Japanese farther up the road, where they might not expect an attack.

"Our job will be to reconnoiter that route for the rest of the division," he explained. "That's where the rice paddies come in."

"Dammit," Philly swore. "I guess I won't bother getting my socks washed, after all."

"That's the spirit," Steele said.

On the outskirts of Ormoc were sprawling rice fields that bordered both sides of the so-called highway. Where the rice paddies ended, there were sometimes a few dry, open acres of pastureland used for cattle. Of course, the cattle were long gone, having been taken to feed the enemy. Beyond the rice paddies and pastureland was where the jungle tended to begin, rolling all the way up into the hills deep in the interior.

A few low-hanging rain clouds chased each other around those low, distant hills. From time to time they could hear booming noises that were either thunder or artillery, or maybe a little of both.

Rice was an important commodity in the region, another reason the Japanese were so eager to keep and hold Ormoc. Not only did rice feed their troops, but the hope was that some of the abundant crop might even find its way back to Japan.

However, a drought that corresponded with the war, along with a labor shortage, had dashed those hopes. Still, the Japanese had made tending the rice paddies a wartime priority in terms of how the Filipino laborers were used. Rice was a crop that required water, meaning that these large open fields were flooded.

It wasn't long before the soldiers headed out. It was tough going once they left the dry land behind and struck out across the rice paddies. The water only amplified the heat, reflecting the tropical sun like a vast mirror. The proximity to so much water added to the humidity, and they were all soon dripping with sweat. Bad as the jungle could be, Deke felt the sun flogging his back and missed the shade that the forest trees provided. At least his nonregulation broad-brimmed hat offered some relief.

Their slow progress across the vast flooded field was emphasized by the occasional fighter plane that zipped overhead with a roar—and then was gone.

The rice was planted in haphazard fashion so that it grew in scattered clumps rather than neat rows. Having grown up on a farm, Deke had more than a passing interest in the crop. The lack of order bothered him, and he thought it would have been more efficient to plant the rice in rows. He grinned to himself and hefted his rifle, realizing that the farming life was far behind him now. Although he missed the land, he doubted that he'd ever want to go back to the plow.

Due to the unevenness of the underlying ground, the depth of the water varied. In some places, they sank up to their knees in the muck and mire. Mud sucked at their boots.

"One thing for damn sure, if someone starts shooting at us, we won't be able to get out of the way in a hurry," Deke remarked.

"Keep your eyes open," the lieutenant said.

"What the hell is that?" Philly demanded, pointing to something cutting a slithering path through the water.

"Snake," Deke said. "Big fella too."

Philly pointed his rifle, as if intending to shoot the snake.

"Knock it off, Philly!" Steele shouted. "We're out here in the middle of a big shooting gallery. Let's not call any more attention to ourselves than we need to, or we'll sure as hell have bigger problems than snakes."

"I think what Honcho means is that snakes don't shoot machine guns."

"Yeah, yeah," Philly said, nervously watching the surrounding water. Now and then they spotted smaller snakes weaving among the rice shoots. Danilo gave them a wide berth, muttering something that sounded like a curse. This was not reassuring, considering that they had seen their Filipino guide face down everything from giant spiders to Japanese warriors without so much as batting an eye.

"Those appear to be poisonous," Yoshio pointed out.

"Good to know," Philly replied through gritted teeth.

Deke mostly kept his eyes on their surroundings. He shared the school of thought that machine guns were a whole lot worse than the local reptiles. He kept both hands on his rifle, just in case. Unfortunately, a Nambu machine gun could reach out from quite a distance, being an effective long-range weapon.

At this point, they began to leave the American lines behind and were moving into Japanese territory. Their mission, in part, was to determine where the Japanese were and the best path to bisect Highway 2.

They walked for another half hour, covering precious little ground and fully exposed all the while.

"This isn't going to work," Lieutenant Steele announced, pausing to take off his helmet and wipe his dripping brow. "The Japanese are up ahead somewhere, and they'll see a group of us coming from a mile off. You boys stay here and I'll go ahead. One person has a better chance of getting through unseen."

Deke spoke up. It didn't seem right that the lieutenant was proposing to strike out on his own toward enemy territory. "Hold on, Honcho. Why not let me go?"

"You know me, Deke. I wouldn't ask someone to do something that I wasn't willing to do myself."

"Deke is right, Honcho. For once. If the Japanese pick him off, that's better than losing an officer," Philly said.

"I wasn't planning on debating it," Steele said, but his voice had lost some of its certainty. The lieutenant could be as stubborn as any of them, but even he had to realize that it was true that it would be far worse for the patrol, even their small one, to lose their leadership.

"Aw, Honcho, you know us better than that. We're just saying we can't afford to lose you."

Finally, Steele cracked a grin. "And we can afford to lose Deke."

Deke said, "You ain't gonna lose me, you dumb sons of bitches. Honcho excepted, him being an officer and all. Now somebody come over here and take my shit. The only thing I want to drag through these paddies is my rifle and my ass."

Deke got Philly to carry his haversack, since he might as well be useful for something. In addition to his rifle, Deke hung on to his canteen and his bowie knife. A rifle might get clogged with mud, but with a sharp knife, a man was never defenseless.

Danilo stepped forward as if to go with him, but Deke waved him back. "I appreciate it, but if I get killed, then somebody has to make sure the rest of these boys get their sorry asses back to Ormoc."

It was always an open question as to how much English Danilo understood, but he gave Deke a nod.

"Yeah, yeah," Philly said. "I think the rest of us can find a whole goddamn town if we need to. Anyhow, get back here as soon as you can, all right?"

"What, you miss me already?"

"Nah," Philly said, hefting Deke's haversack. "I just don't want to be hauling your crap around for you."

"You know what, I have one more thing for you to carry."

Using Yoshio's shoulder for balance, Deke took off his boots. As a boy, he had often worked the fields barefoot. He knew that the muddy combat boots would be only a hindrance. He tied the laces together and hung them around Philly's neck.

"Are you shittin' me?"

"I reckon it will be easier to walk barefoot. My boots will just get stuck in this mud."

"I know where I'd like to stick these boots."

"That's just gonna have to wait until I get back."

CHAPTER THREE

DEKE HEADED OUT, leaving the rest of the patrol behind. They were still sitting ducks out in the rice paddy, but at least there didn't seem to be any Japanese in the immediate vicinity. The closer that they got to Highway 2, that was unlikely to be the case.

He moved ahead, feeling as exposed as he ever had. The open rice paddy stretched around him in all directions. But he was headed straight ahead, where there were certainly enemy lookouts. Deke just hoped to hell that he would see them first.

Sunlight glittered off the muddy brown water. It was a tough slog. Even without the boots, mud sucked at his feet. He would take a few steps and hardly be in water that was more than ankle deep. At the next step, he would suddenly plunge up to his calves or even to his knees in mud.

As for snakes, he ignored any that he did see—that was the least of his worries.

The heat beat down and he moved on. If what they had been moving through previously was no-man's-land, then Deke supposed that he was behind enemy lines by now—even if he hadn't seen any actual enemies.

It wasn't long before that changed. There was a collection of huts in the distance, surrounded by a handful of scrawny trees. To be sure, it was one of the few places that offered any shade. It would have been home to the rice paddy workers if they hadn't wisely fled due to the fears of war. He watched the oasis warily, keeping a steady grip on his rifle.

Sure enough, he spotted movement among the huts.

Enemy soldiers. At least a half dozen of them.

If he could see *them*, then they could sure as hell see *him*, exposed as he was in the middle of this flooded field.

As he watched, the soldiers emerged from the scattered huts and started moving along a slightly elevated road in the direction of the highway. There was no longer any doubt that he was behind enemy lines.

There was also no doubt that the soldiers had seen him. They stopped and looked in his direction. One man shaded his eyes against the glare and stared at Deke.

There was nowhere to run and nowhere to hide, short of diving down into the water. But it was too late for that. Any effort to hide would only raise their suspicions.

He didn't like his chances trying to shoot them all. There were six of them, and it was beyond the range of an easy shot. They would be shooting back. If there were more Japanese in the vicinity, the sound of gunfire would alert them. The enemy would already be on edge, expecting the American advance. It was the last thing Deke needed.

Instead of opening fire, he lowered his rifle and waved. Two or three of the Japanese waved back; then the whole group moved on, not even giving Deke a second look.

I'll be damned.

They must have thought he was just another Japanese soldier. Or maybe they even mistook him for a rice farmer. He was more or less covered in mud, and the glare off the water had provided the rest of the camouflage.

He continued on toward the collection of huts, hoping that there weren't any more Japanese lurking about. But a quick look around revealed that the huts were empty. A few trappings indicated the huts were normally occupied by farmers—tools and other implements were leaning against the walls. Whoever lived there must had fled in a hurry. In addition to the tools, they had left behind everything from blankets to cookware. The Japanese must have been making use of the huts to escape the sun and weather.

Looking at the tools, Deke got an idea. He picked up a hoe, thought about it, then tied his rifle to the handle, using cordage he found. On top of that, he wound an old piece of blanket. Satisfied, he put the hoe over one shoulder. From a distance, he might look like a farmer out tending his crop, carrying some tools over his shoulder. If push came to shove, he could easily bring his rifle into play. It was what you might call a shooting hoe.

Reluctantly, he left the shade and headed out again, this time following the narrow road through the rice paddies that the half-dozen Japanese troops had taken. Fortunately the enemy soldiers had enough of a head start that they were no longer in sight. Although the road meandered, it provided a high-and-dry route through the rice paddies that seemed to lead directly toward Highway 2. It was exactly the route that Patrol Easy had been sent to find.

But Deke knew they couldn't send an entire regiment down the road on his hunch. He would have to follow it a bit longer just to make sure that the road through the rice paddies went somewhere.

He looked around uneasily. Each step carried him deeper into Japanese-held territory. Up ahead along the road, he could see another collection of huts. Were there more Japanese sheltering there?

He couldn't take that chance. He left the dry road behind and moved back into the rice paddies. By now he had left the vast flooded field behind, and there were smaller fields filled with the green shoots of rice, bordered by ditches and levees to help manage the flooding of the fields. He kept the hoe over one shoulder, maintaining his disguise. He swung out into the fields, giving the huts a wide berth and keeping to the western side so that the sun would be more directly in the eyes of anyone watching him.

As he came even with the huts, he saw more Japanese soldiers—a lot more, this time. They appeared to be more organized and better armed. In addition to the helmet-clad soldiers, there was a noncommissioned officer wearing the telltale campaign hat with its sun cape down the back of the neck.

In his experience, it was the sergeants you had to watch out for. They were mean, suspicious bastards.

Deke's belly clenched. He fought the urge to unbundle his rifle. Once again he had been spotted, and it was too late to hide, so he walked as nonchalantly as possible along a berm, keeping his feet dry. His ruse was helped by the fact that he was barefoot and had rolled up his trousers almost to his knees.

He waved at the enemy soldiers, and again a few waved back. The Japanese sergeant gave Deke a long look, and he forced himself to keep his eyes on the ground, then stopped to swing the hoe at an errant clump of mud, chopping it up. He moved on and hoed another clump.

When he looked up again, he half expected to see a contingent of soldiers rushing toward him or a dozen rifles leveled in his direction. But there were no gunshots. The sergeant was no longer paying any attention to him.

Deke kept going, pausing now and then to hoe at the ground just like a rice farmer might.

He decided that this was one of the few times in the history of war that it was best to be armed with a hoe.

Once he was sure that he was little more than a distant figure and of no more interest to the Japanese, he put the hoe over his shoulder and walked parallel to the road through the rice paddies.

After another fifteen minutes of walking, keeping to the paths between the flooded fields, where the going was easier, he spotted just what he was looking for. It was a larger road winding through the countryside. As he watched, a Japanese truck moved along it. It was the same model that they had captured in the fight near Camp Downes and redirected to bring supplies from the beach. He had reached Highway 2.

He kept moving until he got to higher ground that offered the cover of bushes and trees, then bedded down like a deer to wait out the rest of the day.

His next task would be to return to Patrol Easy and relay word about the route he had found through the rice paddies to Highway 2. Aside from the small contingent of soldiers in the larger collection of huts, there promised to be little standing in the Americans' way. It was exactly what he had hoped to find out.

Deke didn't return right away, because he didn't like his chances in broad daylight. He had gotten lucky with the ruse of waving at the Japanese soldiers, or pretending to be a farmer. He didn't want to press his luck and count too much on the enemy being oblivious. The Japanese were many things, but they sure as hell weren't fools. Instead, he would return under cover of darkness.

He was so close to the highway now that he could hear the rumble of passing supply trucks and the occasional shouts of a few soldiers, even laughter. The Japanese sure as hell didn't sound like they'd been beaten. Maybe nobody had told them yet.

It was hot among the trees, but at least the foliage offered cover and shade. He hadn't brought anything to eat, which was too bad. His belly growled. Just like the good old days growin' up, he reckoned. There had been more than a few hungry times on the farm. Back then he hadn't known any better and just figured it was part of life. He had never complained about C rations the way some men did.

Being hungry for a few hours wouldn't kill him, he knew from hard experience. A bigger concern was exhaustion. He realized how tired he was and even managed to nod off.

He woke with a start, having fallen into a deep sleep. It was the best sleep that he had gotten in a while. He chalked it up to knowing that the enemy was on the highway nearby, oblivious to his presence, so different from being in a foxhole awaiting an attack. He was also alone—which meant not having to listen to Philly's bitching or his snoring.

It was starting to get dark. The day's heat had faded, but not the humidity. It was as steamy as ever, like the hottest August night you could imagine back home. The flooded rice paddies were no strangers to mosquitoes, and now great flocks of them emerged, filling the spaces in Deke's grassy refuge with their whining. He grinned at the humor in the fact that it wouldn't be the Japanese who drove him out of his hiding place, but the mosquitoes.

Time to get moving.

He figured that Patrol Easy had covered maybe five miles after leaving the outskirts of Ormoc. Moving alone, Deke had gone another three miles or so. All told, that meant covering

seven miles in the dark, with the added challenge of the presence of Japanese troops.

His disguised rifle would no longer be of any use in the dark,
so he unwrapped it and left the trappings behind in the tall
grass. There was still plenty of movement on the road, especially
because American planes would leave the Japanese alone at
night. The rumble of trucks filled the night, with vehicles busy
ferrying men and supplies away from the coastal areas and
deeper into Leyte and the port the enemy still held at Palompon.

He returned along the dirt road he had found, so the first
couple of miles were fairly easy. Once he had to dodge off the
road and into a ditch after he heard enemy troops coming his
way. Even in the dark, he was able to count a half-dozen soldiers.
He supposed that they were on patrol, keeping a lookout for any
Americans or Filipino guerrillas. Deke held his breath until they
walked on.

He gave the larger collection of huts a wide berth, just in
case there were more Japanese spending the night there. He
stuck to the fields instead. The mud squishing between his bare
toes actually felt good, and he didn't even mind the water on this
hot night.

Splash.

Deke froze at the sound. There was something else out here
in the rice paddy. Something at least as big as a man, from the
sounds of it.

He kept his rifle ready and waited.

There it was again. *Splash*. A pause. *Splash, splash*.

The splashes were unevenly spaced, very much like a man
trying to move with stealth through a very watery environment.

He strained to see in the gloom.

The darkness seemed to shift and gather at a point just to his
left, exactly where the sounds were coming from. He kept his
finger on the trigger and waited.

If it was a false alarm, then the last thing that he wanted was to alert any Japanese in the vicinity with a rifle shot.

Then the night coalesced around a lone cow, making its way across the rice paddy, pausing every now and then to dip its head and graze at the rice shoots.

"Son of a bitch," he muttered.

Shaking his head, he moved on. Normally he might have covered that distance in a couple of hours if walking at a swift pace. But in the muck and water, it took him closer to three hours.

By the time someone challenged him with the password, it was close to midnight.

"I wasn't sure if that was you or the swamp thing," Philly said. "Then again, I wasn't sure if we'd ever see you again."

"What, just because I had to walk about three miles by myself behind enemy lines, waving at the goddamn Japanese the whole way? Shame on ye of little faith."

"Waving at the Japanese?"

"For some reason, they kept thinking I was a rice farmer."

Lieutenant Steele approached. "Glad you're back, Deke. What did you find out?"

"I came across a good road we can use," he said. "We can pick it up about a mile from here. Leads right to the highway—which is crawling with Japanese, by the way."

"Headquarters said it might be," Steele said. "That's why they want the 307th to cut across the road and stop the enemy from using it."

"Then what are we waiting for?"

"It's going to take more than us to win and hold that road. We'll have to go back to division and lead another unit out here. Put your boots back on. We have some walking to do."

They recrossed the territory they had covered the previous day. Although they were close to enemy lines, they didn't worry as much about stealth. It was almost impossible not to cross the flooded rice fields without making at least some noise. Soon enough, the lights of Ormoc came back into sight. The country-side behind them had been pitch black. There wasn't any elec-tricity out here, just the starlight and hazy tropical moonlight.

They gave the password and crossed through American lines.

"I thought you guys were Japs," the sentry said. "They told us there were some patrols out, but I didn't believe it. There's nothin' out there but rice paddies and Nips."

"Believe it," Lieutenant Steele said.

The sentry looked them all up and down. "You're muddy enough." He wrinkled his nose. "You all kind of stink like those rice paddies too."

"You don't smell so good yourself, buddy," Philly growled.

"Never mind that," Steele said. He jerked his chin at a battered Jeep parked nearby. "We're commandeering that thing."

"Sir?"

"Son, we just walked through miles of mud. We have impor-tant information for the division, and I'll be damned if I'm going to walk all the way back to HQ."

"Yes, sir." They could tell the sentry didn't like it, but he couldn't argue with a lieutenant. Besides that, the soldiers who had just waded in from patrol looked like a rough bunch.

"Get on, boys. Rodeo, you drive. We're riding in style," Steele said. The passengers on the sturdy Jeep were soon a jigsaw puzzle of arms, legs, and weaponry. The lieutenant looked around at his muddy, tangled patrol and laughed. "Just don't get used to all the luxury."

Nobody minded. They had just traversed miles and miles of desolate enemy territory. It wasn't exactly comfortable, but a ride in the Jeep sure beat walking. Despite Steele's wisecrack, it really did seem like luxury at that moment. There was nothing in the world that made a man appreciate a ride so much as taking a load off his own two exhausted legs.

The engine cranked, and the Jeep sped off into the night, carrying the soggy GIs and their information on the backdoor route that would be used to hammer the Japanese the next day.

CHAPTER FOUR

It wasn't all glory being a soldier. On this steamy morning, as the 306th Infantry Regiment slogged across the flooded rice paddies surrounding the newly captured port city of Ormoc, it was even less glorious than usual.

Thanks to Patrol Easy, the unit had its route toward Highway 2, a major supply road for the Japanese. The mission was to bisect the road, essentially creating a roadblock to cut off the enemy supply lines. Other units would attack the Japanese position separately. Once a section of the road was in American hands, the plan was to start rolling up it toward Palompon. To be sure, the Japanese wouldn't like this plan and would fight them the whole way.

After the roadway moved north from the rice paddies, the territory became more rugged. The highway was lined with low hills and jungle-filled ravines. There were dozens of bridges to cross. The situation favored the Japanese defenders, who could ambush the Americans at every bend in the road if they chose to do so. It promised to be an ugly business.

But for the fun and games to begin, they first had to get to

Highway 2 by striking across country. Hopefully, more or less, they would catch the Japanese by surprise and seize the road without too much of a fight.

"Mud, mud, and more mud," Philly muttered, slogging through the flooded field. "Let me just point out that this is our third time crossing these damn rice paddies. I've got to say, I'm sick and tired of it."

"Nobody gives a damn if you're sick and tired of it," Deke pointed out. He was reminded of being a boy on the farm and putting up endless rows of hay on a hot July day. "You ain't got no choice but to do it."

"You'd think I'd get better at it by now," Philly said, "considering all the practice I've had with it."

If it was possible, the flooded fields felt even hotter than they had the previous day. The intent had been to start out at dawn, but any large military operation never got off to a smooth start. Consequently, the tropical sun was already well on its way to its zenith, and the heat beat down upon them. Once again, the humidity was amplified by the surrounding water.

This was a major operation, but due to the impossible terrain, there would be no mechanized support. This meant that everything the regiment needed for what was planned to be a three-day operation to seize and establish a presence on Highway 2 would have to be carried across the empty miles of the rice paddies.

Under the circumstances, it would have been hard enough for each soldier to carry his rifle, ammunition, pack, canteen, and rations—all topped off by a steel helmet that was doing its best to boil his brain under the tropical sun.

For the operation, soldiers were loaded down with all sorts of additional equipment. They carried machine guns and mortars, plus ammo for both—and lots of it. The last thing you ever wanted was to run out of ammunition.

That was just for starters. There were also boxes of hand grenades, extra radio batteries, even cases of blood plasma. Finally, there were litters for the wounded that would surely result from the operation.

A Catholic priest was quietly helping with the burden of medical supplies, a litter carried sideways across his shoulders. One couldn't help but think of Christ at Calvary, silently bearing his cross.

The burden was amplified by the soft ground, the mud sucking at boots, even the damp air itself. The rice paddies were fertile with organic matter, meaning that with each step, men sank to their ankles. In some places, they sank to their knees in mud and water. A few unlucky men stepped into holes and were nearly swallowed up, so that they had to be pulled out by their comrades.

To make matters worse, they had to be ready to fight—or flee. At any moment, a contingent of Japanese might appear on the horizon. At least they would see them coming. A far more worrisome threat was that one of the stray Japanese warplanes would appear out of nowhere and strafe them. There were still enemy fighters in the air.

For now their luck held.

However, the heat and the exertion took their toll. Every few minutes, a soldier would succumb and collapse into the muddy water. They had passed out and had to be saved from drowning due to being loaded down with all that gear. A few had given their all and literally dropped dead from the heat. Those who could be saved were given water and put onto the stretchers, adding yet more to the soldiers' burdens.

Walking at the head of the column, Patrol Easy was mostly spared from carrying any of the extra load. Their role on point was to guide the men behind them and keep an eye out for any sign of the Japanese. Still, they did not have an easy task, considering that they were expected to be the advance eyes and ears. In the distance, heat shimmered off the flooded fields, making it difficult to see who—or what—was out there.

"There could be a whole division of Japanese out there and we can hardly seem them," Philly said.

Deke wasn't as concerned. He was thinking about those huts he had seen on his earlier reconnaissance. "All the Japs need to do is set up some machine guns in those villages. There's no cover at all out here. Let's just hope they don't know we're coming."

Walking nearby, Lieutenant Steele had overheard. Deke could guess from the frown of concern etched on the lieutenant's face that he might have been thinking the same thing about the machine guns. "Just keep your eyes open," he said.

With their added burdens, it took the regiment most of the day to cover the same amount of territory that Patrol Easy had crossed in much less time. Even so, by late afternoon, they reached the dirt road that Deke had found, making the going that much easier.

Seeing the men moving along the road behind him, Deke felt a sense of pride. Deke wasn't one to inflate his own value. There was nothing like growing up poor on a mountain farm to make you realize how insubstantial you were. Nonetheless, he felt rewarded for the risks he had taken now that the advance was able to follow the route that he had scouted. Now, if he could just help keep them all from being ambushed. There was no telling what tricks the Japanese might have in store for them.

As nightfall approached, they came to the second, larger collection of huts. Deke and Danilo crept forward, investigating to make certain that there were no Japanese in residence. Satisfied, he signaled for the rest of the advance to move up. Orders were given to dig in on the dry ground nearby.

"Whatever you do, no lights, not even a cigarette," an officer said, making sure that each man heard the order. "So far the Japanese don't seem to know we're here. Let's keep it that way, unless you want a bunch of mortars or maybe artillery coming down on your head."

Nobody could argue with that, so they settled down to eat their rations cold. Some men were so desperate for tobacco that they simply sucked on an unlit cigarette. Not for the first time, Deke was glad that he hadn't gotten in the habit of smoking. Some men couldn't go more than an hour without their nicotine fix. Deke didn't like the idea of being beholden to anything in that way. Also, he was convinced that too many cigarettes made you get winded too easily.

Despite all their precautions, it had probably been too much to expect that they would get through the night without any encounters with the Japanese. But when trouble did arrive, it came in a surprising way.

Toward midnight, a truck came rumbling up the road. The night was just bright enough with moonlight reflected off the surrounding flooded fields that they could see the dim outline of the vehicle and a few details. It clearly wasn't American. The markings were Japanese, and the truck lacked the familiar silhouette of the GMC trucks, although it had a canvas cover across the back. Finally, the engine sounded different, pitched higher than the US truck motors.

"Who the hell is that?" Lieutenant Steele wondered.

"Not one of our guys, that's for damn sure. But what the hell is he up to?"

The truck lumbered into the village, came to a stop, then reversed as if looking for a good spot to turn around. It didn't seem like an attack, and the truck wasn't in any particular hurry. Instead, the truck driver seemed to be expecting to find other Japanese in the village. You could almost hear the driver thinking, *Where the hell is everybody?*

Ominously, they could hear a few shouts from within the canvas covering. The truck must be carrying Japanese troops.

Nobody was interested in taking prisoners.

Several rifles were already trained on the truck. A machine gun was also brought up.

Lieutenant Steele raised his shotgun. "Pour it into 'em, boys!"

As the first shots rang out, the driver must have realized his mistake. The truck hurtled forward, returning the way it had come, but it didn't get far. The windshield shattered in a shower of glass. The machine gun stitched holes down the canvas. A single enemy soldier managed to tumble out the back, but he was immediately riddled with bullets. Driverless, the truck came to a stop only when it crashed into a hut and lost its forward momentum. Smoke and steam leaked from the engine, but the motor was still running. Finally, a sergeant approached, reached through the shattered window, and shut down the engine.

Despite the sobering sight of the wrecked truck, a few soldiers cheered. It had been deeply satisfying to pour out their frustrations on the truck.

"Everybody shut the hell up!" Steele shouted. The cheering died away.

Deke and Philly had been among those firing at the truck.

"If the Japanese didn't know we were here, they sure as hell do now," Philly said.

"You got that right," Deke agreed.

Steele headed off in the direction of the sentries posted on the road.

"I wouldn't want to be those fellas," Philly said. "I believe Honcho is about to tear them a new asshole."

"What the hell were they thinking?" Deke wondered.

The truck should have been stopped by sentries who had been posted on the road, but the explanation that they stammered out to an angry Lieutenant Steele was that the driver had waved at them, and they had momentarily thought that the truck might actually have been commandeered by American forces, similar to trucks that had been captured earlier near Camp Downes. In the confusion of nighttime, the Japanese driver must have mistaken the sentries for troops from his own side. It was just another one of those wartime incidents that defied explanation.

The rest of the night passed uneasily. Nobody slept well, expecting an attack in force from the Japanese. Deke and the others moved far up the road, closer to Highway 2, which was surely the direction that an attack would come from.

However, nothing materialized. As the sky brightened on the horizon to reveal another tropical dawn, the GIs were relieved to see that the road ahead and the surrounding rice paddies were empty. Either the truck hadn't been missed all that much, or the noise of the attack on the truck had been swallowed up in the night.

The sun was barely up when they reached the supply highway. Although this section of the highway was well traveled, it was not defended. This meant that the soldiers quickly moved across it and set up a defensive position. They had created a roadblock, cutting the enemy's ability to move supplies and men to and from the last open port that the Japanese held.

Up and down the highway, other units from the division were also moving into position. Judging by the sound of distant gunfire, those other units were not having such an easy time of it.

Although their arrival had not been contested, the plan was not to stay put. A company was left behind to dig in and stop any approaching vehicles. The remainder of the unit was to move north up the highway, securing the road and sweeping any Japanese defenses out of their path. The last phase of wresting control of Leyte from the Japanese had begun.

"Let's move out!" shouted an officer.

The 306th headed up the road, with Deke and the rest of Patrol Easy once again at the front of the column. Step by step, they moved deeper into enemy territory.

"What I'd like to know is, where the hell are all of the Japanese?" Philly wondered out loud.

Deke nodded at the road ahead. "I reckon we'll find out soon enough."

The column continued its advance northward on Highway 2. The open fields fell away and were replaced by a wall of vegetation that marched right to the edge of the mostly dirt highway. The ground began to rise as well, the road winding through small hills that would eventually become the distant mountains, where it was rumored that entire Japanese divisions lay hidden, waiting for the right moment to attack. Looking at the dark hills, it seemed to Deke that anything was possible.

This was territory that favored defense.

It didn't take long to prove that point, as if anyone had doubts. They rounded a bend in the road and were greeted with a flurry of gunfire.

Deke hit the ground, Danilo beside him, as bullets stitched the dirt road.

"Son of a bitch!" Philly swore, but managed to pop off a few shots from directly behind them. Much farther behind the men on the point, the larger column came to a halt.

Deke didn't see a target but realized that it didn't matter. What they needed now was suppressing fire. He put shot after shot into the greenery. The shooting subsided, which meant that he had either gotten the bastards, or that they had slunk away, probably to prepare for another ambush.

Cautiously, he raised himself to one knee, then finally stood and dusted himself off. He was so covered in dried, caked mud from his journeys through the rice paddies that a little more dirt hardly mattered.

"Everybody all right?" Lieutenant Steele asked. By some miracle, they'd all come through the Japanese ambush unscathed. "Keep an eye out. We can expect more of the same up ahead."

"Then I reckon it's gonna be a long walk to Palompon," Deke said.

CHAPTER FIVE

THE COLUMN CREPT along the road, burdened by their gear and watching the surrounding vegetation warily. They had begun to pass refugees streaming in the opposite direction, running away from the Japanese and the fighting that was sure to come. Men hurried by with children or the elderly clinging to their backs. What few possessions they could carry were stuffed into baskets and battered suitcases. Cows and dogs were led on ropes.

Fear was etched into the faces of the civilians, although a few gave the Americans encouraging smiles and nods. But for most of the Filipinos fleeing war, getting their families to safety was their only priority.

Although Deke's attention was drawn to the refugees, for the most part he kept his eyes focused on the road ahead, his senses sharp and alert. The sounds of shuffling feet and protesting animals created a constant background noise, but he kept his ears open for the first crack of an enemy rifle that would indicate an ambush.

He could feel the weight of the humid air and the oppressive heat that permeated the crowded road. Sweat beaded across his forehead, but he made no attempt to wipe it off, his hands steady on his rifle.

The soldiers had not only the Japanese and the tropical heat to worry about, but also the terrain. Their first real obstacle turned out to be the bridge over the Tagbog River. This was just one of the many rivers and streams that drained the lush jungle highlands and flowed toward the sea.

The muddy brown river ran between high banks, swollen by recent rains to the point where it resembled an overflowing rain gutter. Though not more than ninety feet wide, the river appeared deep, with a strong current. It would be impossible for the troops to cross the river without the benefit of the bridge.

The Japanese had known this all too well. Realizing that the Americans were coming, the Japanese had made an effort to close off the road behind them by wrecking the bridge. Earlier, Patrol Easy had heard the boom of a large explosion up ahead. The wreckage of the bridge made it clear what all the ruckus had been about.

They arrived at the scene to find some of the timbers still smoldering. In all honesty, the bridge probably hadn't been all that substantial to begin with. Here in the countryside, bridge construction relied on whatever materials were on hand, which meant wood and stone and sometimes even rope lashing rather than steel girders.

The smashed and broken lumber resembled oversize Popsicle sticks rather than properly sized bridge timbers. Halfway across the river, the single stone pillar that anchored the span remained upright.

While a few stringers were still intact, the bridge appeared to be rickety at best and a death trap at worst. In its current condition, there was no way that what was left of the structure could handle the number of men and the weight of the supplies that needed to cross.

"I was afraid of that," the lieutenant said. "The Japanese are trying to pull up the drawbridge behind them."

"From the looks of things, they won't have to try too hard," Deke said. "Now what?"

Steele replied, "We need to rebuild the bridge, that's what."

Deke looked doubtfully at the brown water and the structure that remained. "I was afraid you were going to say that."

At that moment, a single bullet sang through the air near their heads.

"Sniper!" someone shouted.

They sprinted for cover. The wreckage of the bridge on this side of the river provided just what they needed.

Another shot split the air overhead. Then there was a long stretch of silence.

"Anybody see him?" Philly asked.

"Nah, he's gone for now," Deke said.

"Well, boys, I have to say that it looks like our job won't involve construction," Steele said. "Our job will be keeping the men rebuilding the bridge from getting shot."

Steele was correct in that regard. An officer arrived and started directing the reconstruction of the bridge. It was no easy task, considering that the building would need to be done mostly with salvaged materials.

Meanwhile, the scouts and snipers of Patrol Easy fanned out, keeping out of sight, and trying to get a glimpse of the enemy sniper or snipers.

It was a familiar game of cat and mouse, with the Japanese attempting to pick off the Americans trying to get the bridge into working order, while Deke and the others tried to stop them.

Like any good hunter, Deke relied on movement to spot his target. The enemy wasn't visible behind the wall of green, but the occasional motion of the brush betrayed them.

Deke saw something stirring in the greenery on the far side of the river and fired. Seconds later he was rewarded with the sight of a Japanese soldier tumbling down the bank into the water. The enemy sniper landed face down and slowly floated away.

"One down," Philly noted. "Who knows how many more to go."

"Then why don't you help me out and shoot some Japs?"

"Hey, I'm trying!"

Philly was right—it was challenging to line up the sights on an actual target on the other side. The enemy kept to cover and took potshots at them from the trees.

Meanwhile, the team of bridge builders worked valiantly, knowing that this structure was holding up the entire advance. Part of the problem was that anchoring the bridge would require someone to not only get in the water, but also to go *under* the water and secure supports to the stone piling that stood upright in the middle of the river.

A raft was made by lashing together logs and empty fuel barrels that the Japanese had helpfully, if unwittingly, left by the side of the road. However, that didn't solve the problem of going underwater.

A resourceful soldier had an idea. Using a gas mask and tubing, he was able to rig a diving mask. It wasn't much, but the idea was that it would be sufficient for him to stay under long enough to secure a rope around the stray timbers so that they could be lifted into place and lashed securely to the pillar.

Watching the diver's preparations from the riverbank, Philly shook his head in awe. "That is one brave bastard," he said. "I wouldn't trust that contraption in a bathtub, much less that river."

Deke tended to agree. He had never much cared for the water himself, that was for damn sure, especially muddy brown rivers. He thought the diving mask looked flimsy at best. But he knew that in combat situations, men took chances to do what needed to be done.

To complicate things, the enemy snipers on the far bank redoubled their fire when they saw what the dive team had planned. Bullets began to splash on the muddy surface like rain-drops from a summer downpour. Troops on shore returned fire until shredded green leaves flew like confetti. This gave a tempo-rary reprieve from the enemy, but they soon returned, forcing the dive team back to shore.

There was also the problem of time. If the Japanese brought up mortars or machine guns to add to their firepower, this would turn into a full-scale battle. Crossing the river at this exact loca-tion would become that much harder, if not downright impossi-ble. Valuable time might be lost if the troops were forced to try another route.

Against his better judgment, Deke had an idea. It wasn't necessarily a good one, considering his dislike for anything that had to do with water. But they were stuck sure as a fat cow in a cattle chute and needed to get something going. To that end, a plan began to take shape in Deke's mind.

The dive team had reached shore and taken shelter behind the stone bridge pillar on the riverbank held by the GIs. Deke went down and found them.

"Show me how that mask works," he said.

"It's easy," said the soldier, who was obviously proud of his invention. "Honestly, it's more like a snorkel. You slip it on and make it as tight as possible with the straps. The breathing tube goes in through this slit here. As long as you keep the other end of the tube above water, you can breathe."

"Can you put together another one of these masks?" Deke asked the inventor. "I want to pay those Nips on the other side of the river a visit."

"Sure I can."

Deke had dragged Yoshio along, mainly because he knew that he was a good swimmer. He looked at him now. "What do you think? Are you ready to help me give these bastards some hell?"

Yoshio grinned. "Let's do it."

While the soldier made another mask, Deke and Yoshio got organized. Deke decided to leave his rifle behind. Instead, he gathered several hand grenades. Yoshio did the same. If the grenades didn't do the trick, he always had his bowie knife.

When the rest of Patrol Easy saw what he was planning, they made it clear that they thought he was crazy.

"The Japs will see you coming," Philly said.

"In this water? You can't see your hand more than six inches down," Deke replied. "Besides, you are going to be shooting up a storm to distract them. The last place they're going to look is the river."

"If you say so," Philly said. "You sure you want to do this?"

"Have you got a better idea?"

Philly didn't.

Lieutenant Steele put it more bluntly. "You are a crazy bastard. If I thought there was another way, I'd tell you to forget it."

A few minutes later, Deke and Yoshio slipped into the river. On shore, several GIs opened fire along with Patrol Easy. As expected, the Japanese shot back from the cover of the vegetation on the other side.

The two swimmers started out at a point somewhat above where they wanted to end up on the far shore, hoping that the current would carry them in that direction. From shore the distance hadn't seemed that great, but once Deke was actually in the water, the muddy waterway looked as wide across as the Pacific.

Deke slipped beneath the surface, and Yoshio followed suit. Despite the weight of the grenades, the swimming was fairly easy. Deke used a scissor kick and a sort of breaststroke to carry him across. He swam awkwardly at best, but it was good enough to keep him moving.

Once or twice his legs bumped against something solid that bounced away. He hoped to hell that had been a submerged log and not a fish—or worse yet, a crocodile.

I've already been chewed on by a bear, so I reckon it can't get much worse, he thought.

What he hadn't counted on was how difficult it was to see anything underwater. From time to time, he had to lift out his head to get his bearings.

The snorkel itself worked well, as long as Deke didn't dip too far below the surface. He made that mistake once or twice and nearly got a lungful of water as a result.

It also didn't help that the gas mask was not watertight. Deke had cinched the straps until they nearly cut into his face, but water still leaked in. Before long, it was sloshing around his nose and eyes, but he kept going. He was already more than halfway across, too close to the opposite shore to surface undetected. Dealing with a little water was far better than getting a bullet in the head.

After what seemed like an hour, but what he knew couldn't have been more than the five minutes needed to swim ninety feet, he reached the opposite bank and hunkered down at the waterline. He felt confident that he couldn't be seen by the Japanese higher up on the bank. He was more worried about the gunfire coming from the American side of the river. Someone must have spotted him and had the same thought, because the fire slackened.

Now where the hell was Yoshio?

He got his answer a few seconds later when Yoshio surfaced,

looking very much like some kind of frogman. They both removed their masks, glad to be breathing freely again.

"Ready?" Deke asked.

Yoshio nodded.

They crawled stealthily up the bank. At a nod from Deke, they pulled the pins. Deke's hand curled around the cold metal of a grenade, palming it; then his fingers tightened for fear of losing his grip, what with the sweat and the river water still clinging to the grenades. He hoped to hell this worked—he didn't much like the idea of having to fight the Japanese with nothing more than his bowie knife once the grenades ran out.

He threw the grenade as far as he could up the bank.

There was a sharp blast, then another. A tornado of grass, mud, and debris swirled across the riverbank. Deke kept his head down. Shrapnel sang overhead, punctuated by the dying enemy's screams. By the time that the last grenade had been thrown, the shooting from the Japanese side had stopped.

For the bridge repair crew, it was now or never.

Out on the river, the GIs launched their small boat again and got to work repairing the bridge. Deke and Yoshio had bought the repair team the time they needed. It turned out that there was at least one more mask that could be rigged for going under-water, so Deke and Yoshio didn't need to swim back to return their masks.

That was just fine with Deke, who preferred not to brave the muddy water again. They stayed under cover on the far bank, hoping that the regiment managed to cross before any Japanese returned.

It was a difficult process. First, one of the soldiers lengthened the tubing and used the mask to work underwater, securing ropes to the submerged beams.

They watched as the soldiers rigged a tackle system for the rope and, teetering in the unsteady boat, managed to raise the stubborn beams into place. As soon as the beams were in position, more soldiers raced out and lashed them into place.

The entire operation took no more than half an hour. The river had been bridged once again. The repaired bridge wouldn't hold a tank, but it was solid enough for men on foot to cross. Once the area was secure, a team of engineers would be able to build a proper bridge or even a pontoon crossing. For now, this was enough.

Patrol Easy was among the first to cross.

"What took you so long?" Deke asked as Philly gave him back his rifle.

Philly just shook his head. "I tell you what, Corn Pone. You are one crazy son of a bitch. You and Yoshio both. I've never seen anyone pull a stunt like that."

Deke was glad to feel his rifle back in his hands. "Stick around, City Slicker," he said. "You ain't seen nothin' yet."

Deke returned the masks to their grinning inventor. "Thanks for that," he said.

"You've got guts," the GI said. "I had no idea if that mask would keep out the water long enough to get to the other side of the river."

"I'm glad you didn't tell me that beforehand," Deke said. "Anyhow, I won't be in any hurry to do that again. But you better keep those masks handy. I understand that there are several more rivers to cross between here and Palompon."

As it turned out, Patrol Easy was never going to see Palompon, the destination at the end of Highway 2.

"We just got a message by radio," Lieutenant Steele said. "We're being recalled to division HQ."

"All the way back at the beach? That's an awfully long walk."

"Then we'd better get started."

CHAPTER SIX

IT HAD BEEN A LONG WALK, after all. Thankfully they hadn't run into any enemy patrols. It was still a mystery why they had been pulled back to the beachhead in the midst of the operation to seize Palompon. More than likely their orders would involve heading back out into the jungle and hills to deal with the Japanese who remained entrenched elsewhere.

For now the war could wait. Judging by the appearance of the tired men lounging on the sand, they weren't in any hurry to get back to the fighting. The push across the rice paddies and then Highway 2 toward Palompon had left them exhausted.

"The Nips are beat, all right," Philly announced to no one in particular. "The trouble is that they don't know they're beat."

"They don't seem like they're beat to me," Deke responded. "But they will be."

"You wait and see. They'll send us right back out again. No rest for the weary."

"I reckon *somebody* has to actually fight the Japanese instead of unloading more gear on the beach. Maybe the plan is to bury them alive with packing crates. Do you think there's even anything left back in the States? If nothing else, we'll have to take back some ground from the Japs just so we have somewhere to put all this stuff."

"You might just be right about that."

Deke spent a moment watching the laboring men, then said, "I hate to say it, but I'd rather be on patrol than humping crates up the beach."

Philly shook his head. "Honestly, I might not mind if the Japanese weren't so damn determined to kill us—or kill themselves in the process. A normal enemy ought to know when to give up."

It was a familiar refrain among many soldiers. Truth be told, Deke couldn't have agreed more with Philly. The Japanese soldiers were bent on destruction—preferably the destruction of American forces, but self-destruction also seemed fine with them. They would fight until their last breath. Time and again they had proved that determination to the bitter end, taking more than a few GIs with them in the process. It was a mindset that Americans still struggled to understand. When faced with defeat, the enemy seemed to think that the only option was death.

Yoshio, the Nisei soldier who also served as an interpreter, had rarely been called upon to translate, because there were seldom any prisoners. Then again, Japanese prisoners did not always survive being captured by troops who had seen too many of their buddies killed.

Deke shook his head to clear it. He knew that he had to stay focused if he wanted to make it out of this war alive. If your thoughts wandered too far, they might not come back, lost as a stray coonhound on a midnight hunt in the mountains.

Philly was right about another thing, although Deke refused to admit this out loud for fear it would swell the other man's head any bigger than it already was. They all knew that they wouldn't be on this beach for long. Snipers were in high demand —too high to be allowed to sit around for long. Part of the problem was that the Japanese themselves had so many snipers, which proved to be a highly effective technique in the jungle terrain. A single enemy sniper could easily hold up an advancing platoon or company. Patrol Easy was kept busy dealing with the enemy snipers who waited in the jungle beyond. They had become specialists in the kind of up-close-and-personal jungle warfare that the enemy preferred.

Deke looked around at the men on the beach, studying the determined faces of the other members of Patrol Easy. They had already been through a lot, and there were sure to be more tough times ahead. For the moment they looked content to take it easy.

The question was, What was next for them?

Deke's eyes scanned the area, taking in the other scouts and snipers strewn out across the sand nearby. The tension was palpable, everyone wondering what their next mission would be, but nobody griped about it except for Philly.

They lay sprawled in the sand, glad to be off their feet, making use of whatever shade they could find. To keep out of the sun, he and Philly had rigged a ragged blanket supported by sticks. It was a rickety contraption that threatened to blow away whenever the wind did more than puff at them, but their goal had been to create the maximum amount of shade with the minimum of effort. If there was one thing a soldier knew, it was that he'd soon be moving on.

The others were taking what rest they could. Yoshio had his nose in a book again. Deke was certain that he'd seen that cover portraying an Old West gunslinger many times, but it didn't seem to matter to Yoshio if he was reading the same book over and over again.

Deke never had been much of one for reading, but he

couldn't help but envy Yoshio's ability to transport himself out of this time and place with the help of those pages.

Their Filipino guide, Danilo, squatted on his haunches and watched the activity on the beach with his typical impassive gaze. It looked uncomfortable to Deke, but it was how most Filipinos sat. Danilo never wasted energy when he could avoid it. The only movement he made was to wave off the flies that occasionally buzzed into his face whenever the sea breeze slackened.

Rodeo appeared to be napping. Out of everyone in the patrol, Deke had decided that Rodeo was the least skilled in terms of being a scout or sniper. However, his talents lay elsewhere. It was always Rodeo who carried their walkie-talkie handset or extra supplies. He ran errands for Lieutenant Steele. In a sense he had become the patrol's gopher, but he was useful all the same.

If it came down to who was the best shot in Patrol Easy, that was simple. Deke grinned. All he had to do was look in the mirror—or the nearest mud puddle.

Egan and Thor sat nearby. The war dog's tongue lolled out as he panted in the heat. Thor had saved their bacon more than once when he had sniffed out a hidden Japanese soldier or warned them of an infiltrator's approach at night. It was a wonder that the war dog and his handler were still assigned to the patrol, but they had all become so attached to Thor that they wouldn't have it any other way.

Two of the original patrol were missing. Most recently, Alphabet had been wounded in the fighting at Ormoc and had eventually been evacuated off the beach to the relative safety of a hospital ship. Back on Guam, they had lost one of their patrol members, Ingram, to a Japanese sniper. The memory of Ingram's death at the hands of that sniper still nagged at them all, along with the eternal question every soldier asked himself, *Why him and not me?*

Lieutenant Steele had been called away for a powwow with the other officers, leaving Patrol Easy on its own. No matter—they were too tired to get into any sort of trouble. They had also picked an area beyond the prying eyes of officers or the attentions of the beach masters who were attempting to manage the chaos of the landing zone. A beach master would shanghai any stray soldiers he could and put them to work.

Deke looked around, astonished by the activity on the beach. Even over the course of a few days, the beachhead had been transformed since the initial landing under hostile fire. Since then, the enemy had been pushed back, and the nearby port city of Ormoc had been captured, along with its all-important airfield. After a slow start, due to the threat of enemy ships and planes, more and more cargo was being brought ashore.

Other support areas had been established on the beach. In addition to a command post, there were tarps set up to keep the sun off a group of clerks who labored at typewriters, keeping up with the division's recordkeeping. This included typing up the lists of the dead and wounded, which grew ever longer thanks to the enemy. Deke was sure that one of those clerks would be Corporal Rafferty, who had been thrown into combat with other rear-echelon troops when the Japanese had threatened to overwhelm the tentative grip on the beachhead. Rafferty had shown that he could handle a rifle as well as a typewriter. When it came down to it, sometimes even a clerk or a cook had to be a fighting infantryman. They had done a damn fine job of fighting on the road to Ormoc.

There was also a tent where Doc Harmon and other medical staff were busy treating the wounded. Some were patched up and sent back out. Wounded who needed more serious treatment were ferried out to the navy vessels for treatment. There was still the threat posed by the Japanese Navy and aircraft, but that had diminished considerably since the capture of Ormoc.

A few enemy air bases still operated, but these scattered planes had been pressed farther from the coast, and the US planes were constantly hunting for them.

Despite these efforts, a Japanese Zero or two still appeared to threaten the beach from time to time, sending the soldiers scurrying like ants.

For other men wounded in the fighting around Ormoc, it was too late. They were buried in a cemetery that expanded by the day. The fresh graves were a reminder to the living that there were no guarantees in a war zone. Almost every man on that beach knew someone whose grave was now marked with a simple cross. These were husbands, fathers, sons, brothers, buddies—none of whom would ever be going home again. As the losses mounted, the best that you could do was put the memories of the dead out of your mind.

Hundreds more had been hurt in the fighting. It was easy to pick out the wounded with their white bandages. The air around the medical tent was pungent with the acrid smell of iodine—and blood. Most of the men bore their wounds silently, and those in pain were dealt with using a dose of morphine.

But there were some men whose wounds were less visible. Deke and the other members of Patrol Easy had passed them coming in. These men simply sat and stared into the distance. The infamous one-thousand-yard stare. It was called combat fatigue. These men weren't cowards—they had simply seen and done more than they could take. Every man was different. Some would be fine after a decent meal, a kind word, and the time to sit for a while with a blanket over their shoulders. Others would need additional time to come around. For a few tragic cases, their minds were permanently broken by the horrors of war. They were simply a different sort of casualty of war.

He could see the breakers foaming on the coral shelf beyond the beach. However, there was no hope of hearing the soft sound of waves crashing on the shore or the distant squawking of seabirds. This was not a restful beach.

Instead, the breeze off the sea carried the sound of roaring engines from landing craft, Jeeps, a bulldozer or two, and even a few planes overhead. All that engine noise was punctuated by irate shouts. It was easy to pick out the source, because the beach masters were notoriously short tempered and foul-mouthed.

Transports ran right up on the beach, and soldiers had stripped to their waists, laboring under the tropical sun to unload the vessels. The toiling troops glistened with sweat, their arms and shoulders and torsos long since tanned nut brown by the tropical sun. You could always tell the replacement troops, because they were either fish-belly white or sunburned as red as a boiled lobster.

They didn't have an easy task, because the soft sand at the tidal line sucked at their feet with every step. Some men had to work in the actual surf, getting soaked in addition to sunburned.

Watching them work, Deke was reminded of growing up on the farm and all the endless chores, from taking to the fields to hoe weeds to putting up hay. Like these men, he had often stripped off his shirt in the heat, exposing his scars from the bear attack he had survived as a boy. The skin across the scars sometimes felt tight as a drum in the morning. The sun always felt good on them, like it was somehow healing them, but maybe that had been only his imagination.

His sister, Sadie, had worked right alongside him. Even now, Deke rarely took his shirt off, because he was self-conscious about the angry red scars that raked down his side. People asked too many questions. Sadie never commented—she knew well enough how he'd gotten them. She'd been there that awful night.

Watching the laboring soldiers, some of whom bitched and complained the whole time, Deke was sure that Sadie could have worked most of them right into the sand. He grinned at the thought. He and Sadie had come through a lot together. Life on a hardscrabble mountain farm had been hard, but it had gotten a lot worse when the farm had been lost to a greedy banker when the Coles could no longer pay the mortgage.

He missed her and hoped that she was doing all right as a police officer in Washington, DC. It had been a while since he had received a letter from her.

"I could get used to this," Philly murmured. "Doing nothing and answering to nobody."

Deke looked over. He had thought that Philly was asleep. Like most soldiers, he could drop off in seconds. Deke always seemed to have a hard time, his thoughts rambling, his senses uneasy about what was out there.

"No, you couldn't," Deke said. "After a day of this, you'd be volunteering to head back out on patrol. Worse yet, nobody would let you lay around. You'd find yourself unloading crates."

"There you go, busting my bubble again. A guy can dream, can't he?"

"Sure, why not. Dream all you want, Philly. But it just makes it worse when you wake up."

"Aw, stuff a sock in it, Corn Pone."

Even after just a few hours on the beach, Deke felt a restlessness settle over him. He cleaned his rifle and sharpened his knife. From time to time, he heard the dull thud of artillery in the distance. It was the sound of unfinished business.

Deke finally allowed himself to doze, but his prediction that they would not be left alone for long was soon proved true. Nobody was going to let them sleep the day away, blissfully forgotten. A shadow soon fell across the lounging men. Deke raised one eyelid to see a young, sweaty private standing over them. He had the nervous look about him that staff clerks tended to get when coming face-to-face with grizzled combat veterans.

"You lost?" Deke drawled.

The private turned out to be a runner from division HQ. He managed to stammer out a message that they were being summoned there.

"Right away," the runner emphasized, when he saw that the soldiers were making no effort to raise themselves off the sand.

"Yeah, yeah," Philly said, finally stirring to the point where he managed to lift himself up on one elbow. "Run along now. We're coming."

Message delivered, the private appeared glad to retreat. He lost no time trotting away.

"Now what?" Rodeo wondered.

"I'll bet we've done such a crackerjack job that we're being sent back to Honolulu for some R & R and then on to the States for a Liberty Bond tour. Nothing but steak, booze, and broads."

"Like hell we are," Deke said. "It's never a good thing when somebody comes looking for us. It means there's a job to do that they can't find anybody else to do."

"Or dumb enough to take it," Philly added.

"Well, there is that," Deke agreed.

CHAPTER SEVEN

HAVING BEEN SUMMONED TO HQ, Deke and the others quickly dismantled their makeshift sun shelter, knowing it was unlikely they'd return. Then the six of them—plus Thor—made their way to the command tent.

They took their time crossing the beach, similar to men on the way to the executioner. Nonetheless, Deke felt a stubborn pride in the fact that when there was a hard job to do, it was usually Patrol Easy that was called to do it.

At this point it was still anybody's guess why they had been called to HQ, but recent experience indicated that it wouldn't be to take part in a division cookout and baseball game.

Headquarters was a hubbub of activity, with a steady stream of men and messengers going in all directions. Weary officers and sergeants trudged in and out of the tent that had been set up on the beach. The tent's canvas flanks were buffeted by the tropical sea breeze. The constant flapping made a sound like a tethered sail. Two guards were posted outside the tent, just in case some diehard Japanese suddenly appeared. Their uniforms had the ragged and filthy appearance that could only be the result of several days spent fighting across the interior following the landing that had taken place on the beach.

"Maybe we'll get guard duty," Rodeo said.

"Fat chance of that," Philly muttered. "Look around. Almost every poor bastard on guard duty is walking wounded. No, they've got something else in mind for us."

One of the guards, a soldier with a thick bandage on his shoulder, reached out to scratch Thor's ears, but the war dog was having none of that. His warning growl was a low rumble.

"I wouldn't do that unless you want to lose a hand," Egan advised.

The soldier quickly withdrew his hand, as if he had just touched a hot stove.

"We're supposed to meet our lieutenant here," Deke told him.

"Go on in," the soldier said, keeping a wary eye on Thor. "But if I were you, I'd leave that dog out here. The Filipino too."

Egan obliged by taking a cigarette break, Thor sitting beside him. "Fill me in later, fellas."

But Deke wasn't going to leave Danilo behind. He turned to the guard. "He's one of us. He goes where we go."

The guard squared his shoulders as if he might make an issue of it, but looked away from Deke's hard glare. "Suit yourself," the guard replied. He stepped to one side so that they could pass.

The tent was full of tired-looking men in uniform, most of them with a few days' worth of stubble on their faces. It was quite dark compared to the relentless brightness of the beach. The tent flaps had been left rolled down to keep all the paperwork from blowing around, which meant that the interior felt stifling.

A haze of tobacco smoke added to the murkiness within. The atmosphere was not improved by the proximity of soldiers who had not had the luxury of showering for several days. On the plus side, everyone stank about the same.

Deke looked around for someone in charge, but it seemed like every officer there was too busy to pay attention to them. Where the hell was Lieutenant Steele?

Finally, after a few moments, an older man in a major's uniform stepped out from the gloom at the back of the tent and greeted them keenly. "You boys must be Patrol Easy?" he said with a smile.

"Yes, sir," Deke replied. Although he didn't outrank anyone in the patrol, he always seemed to become their point man by default. After all, headquarters was just another jungle of sorts.

The officer introduced himself as Major Henry Flanders, an intelligence officer from General MacArthur's staff. Hearing that, all sorts of alarm bells began to go off in Deke's mind, as he recalled their earlier mission to take out the guns on Hill 522 near Palo ahead of the first landing on Leyte. Those orders had come right from the top. Now what?

"You boys are doing one hell of a job out there, and I want to thank you for that," Major Flanders said quietly. Deke couldn't help but notice that the major's combat uniform was sweat stained, but clean in the sense that it wasn't covered in grime, gun oil, and flecks of dried blood.

Deke's first impression was that Major Flanders was a no-nonsense sort of man, right down to the .45 on his hip. The worn leather of the holster hinted that the sidearm had seen some use. The major was in his late forties and heavyset but not fat—it looked as if he could still throw a punch or two that would get someone's attention, and probably had done just that from time to time.

Coming from most officers, Deke would have dismissed the major's words of thanks as only so much biscuit gravy, but Flanders appeared nothing but sincere. He offered them cigarettes from a fresh pack. Rodeo and Philly accepted, and when Philly tried to hand back the pack, the major waved him off. "Keep it," he said.

"Thank you, sir," said Philly, sounding like he meant it for once. Then again, when a man said he was from MacArthur's staff, that tended to prompt respect.

"Let's grab ourselves a corner of this circus tent and let me explain what this is all about."

The major led the way to an unclaimed corner of the tent and told them to grab a knee, while he remained standing. Once again, Deke looked around for Honcho. To his relief, he saw him come through the tent flaps, spot his men, and make a beeline for the corner. He was carrying several bottles of Coca-Cola, which explained his absence from the tent.

"I see you boys have met Major Flanders," Lieutenant Steele said. He handed the bottles around, and the men accepted them eagerly. To Deke's surprise, the soda pop was even somewhat chilled. It had been weeks since they'd had anything to drink other than canteen water and coffee that was just this side of rusty water. "I thought you all could use something cold to drink while you heard his proposition for us."

"Proposition?" Philly snorted, then took a long drink from the bottle and wiped his mouth with the back of his hand. He smacked his lips in satisfaction. "That makes it sound like we have any choice in the matter."

"Just shut up and drink your soda," Steele said. "Major, they're all yours to brief."

"Thank you, Lieutenant."

Major Flanders once again praised the men for what they had done up to this point, saying that MacArthur was pleased with the progress on Leyte.

The major filled them in on what they had accomplished so far—they had located several Japanese positions scattered throughout the jungle and hills and were actively rooting out any remaining resistance they came across. It wasn't anything that the men didn't already know, but the major's words made it official.

Then Major Flanders got down to business, revealing why Patrol Easy had been summoned to HQ. Lieutenant Steele had framed it as a proposition, but it soon became clear that the men were being presented with something that they couldn't turn down—it just wasn't in their nature.

"You men know that General MacArthur is especially concerned with the status of prisoners of war held by the Japanese. The Japanese have several POW camps, some that we know about and some that are just coming to light. He has warned the enemy in no uncertain terms about the dire consequences of harming any of these POWs. However, the fear is that the enemy will use these prisoners as pawns or bargaining chips."

"That's against the Geneva Convention," Philly complained.

"When has that ever stopped the Japanese?" Deke responded, some heat in his voice as he remembered how the Japanese had killed his buddy within minutes of the beach landing on Guam. He had witnessed nothing but cruelty from the Japanese. More incidents came to mind. "For starters, you saw how they killed all those civilians back in Palo."

Flanders jumped back in. "Speaking of which, there's a fear that the Japanese may kill the prisoners outright rather than release them. The prisoners are mostly Americans, airmen who've been shot down, sailors picked up at sea, maybe even a few infantrymen captured back in forty-one. There are a few Australians mixed into the bunch."

"I like those Aussies," Philly said. "They sure know how to fight."

Flanders continued, "Unfortunately, we have evidence that

there has already been some killing of prisoners, although these are isolated incidents, thank God." The major paused, looked around to make sure no one else in the tent was eavesdropping, then lowered his voice. "There was a situation recently where the enemy forced our men to dig what they said was an air-raid trench, but it turns out our boys were digging their own grave. They doused our men with gasoline and set them on fire. Burned alive."

"Those slant-eyed sons of bitches," Philly muttered.

Deke felt a white-hot surge of anger go through him. He was sure that the others felt the same way.

"If General MacArthur is so damned concerned about the POWs, then why the hell doesn't he send in some paratroopers or a bunch of tanks to go liberate them? Seems to me that this is all a lot of hot air."

"Deke," Lieutenant Steele said, growling a warning. "That's enough of that, soldier."

A look of irritation passed over Major Flanders's face at Deke's outburst. He opened his mouth to say something, then reconsidered when he met Deke's angry gaze.

Deke knew better, but he couldn't help it. His anger bubbled over sometimes when it came to the hot air spouted by the likes of officers, businessmen, and bankers. There were those who talked about it and those who acted. Deke didn't have much patience with the first group.

Sadie had once compared him to a chicken pot pie that was all hard crust on the outside and bubbling hot on the inside.

"You're nothin' but a mouthful of hot gravy waiting to burn somebody," she'd said.

He felt Yoshio touch his arm in an attempt to calm him down.

"Look, son, we're all on the same side here," Flanders eventually said with something that sounded like empathy. "I'm getting to the part where we do something about it."

"Yes, sir."

"Conditions at these camps are pretty rough," Major Flanders continued. "It's doubtful that the Japanese have enough food to feed their own troops at this point, let alone any prisoners. Our boys are kept on starvation rations at best."

"We ain't exactly livin' high off the hog ourselves," Deke said. "But it's a whole lot different when you're a prisoner."

"You said it, soldier," Flanders said, warming to the topic. "But it gets worse. The conditions are filthy—no showers, no clean clothes. Medical attention is almost nonexistent. Finally, our boys are badly mistreated, everything from slave labor to beatings just because it amuses some Jap prison guard."

None of them liked the thought of fellow Americans being held captive by the Japanese. One thing for sure was that Major Flanders did not paint a pretty picture of the American POWs' fates. He went on in gruesome detail, describing everything from starvation to beheadings.

"Bastards," Philly muttered. "I'd really like to get my hands on those Japs."

"That's the spirit," Flanders said. "General MacArthur does not want any more of our men to be abused or murdered by the Japanese, nor does he want our boys to be used as hostages or cannon fodder. As we become aware of these camps, he wants our men liberated by any means necessary. Some of the larger camps near Manila are still beyond our reach."

"The Japanese still hold Manila," Lieutenant Steele pointed out.

Flanders nodded, then looked pointedly at Deke. "Here's the part where we do something about it. There's at least one POW camp here on Leyte that's cause for concern. Some of our sources with the Filipino resistance say that the commandant is a real hard case. The Filipinos have given us a location, and we've verified it through aerial photographs. We want our men freed from that camp. That's where you boys come in."

If the major had intended to whip them up into a righteous frenzy, he had succeeded.

It had been one hell of a sales pitch.

It was all Deke could do not to grab his rifle and set off there and then to liberate the camp—and he didn't even know where it was yet.

Flanders continued, "We didn't want to send just anyone on this job. We need just the right men. Your lieutenant here says that you are the best jungle warriors in the division."

"Damn straight we are," Philly said.

"Good. That's just what we need," Flanders said. "You know as well as I do that we're shorthanded here—we're tied up fighting all these damn holdouts—so we can't spare a lot of men. General Bruce has agreed to free you up for this mission. I can tell you that General Bruce takes this very personally. He cares as much about freeing the POWs as anyone."

"I've only got a handful of men," Steele pointed out. Lieutenant Steele had surprised them by speaking up. Since he had handed off the show to Major Flanders, they had almost forgotten he was there.

"Don't you worry, Lieutenant. You'll have some help from the Filipino guerrillas. There's a local guerrilla leader named Father Francisco, a Catholic priest, and he's agreed to help."

Several of the men nodded. They had fought alongside Father Francisco and his men near Palo. Deke remembered the priest as being tough and smart, a natural-born leader of the fight against the Japanese occupation. It sounded as if the priest had expanded his area of operations since then. Of course, the fight for control of Leyte had also widened considerably since the initial beach landing.

"We can use all the help we can get," Steele said.

Major Flanders nodded thoughtfully as Steele spoke, then said, "I'd send a whole company if we could, but a patrol will move faster."

"That's why they call us Patrol Easy."

The major seemed amused. "You're probably not wrong about that."

"Don't we have anything else to go on, sir?" Deke asked. "Can you tell us anything else about this POW compound."

"I'm glad you asked, soldier." Major Flanders had been hanging onto a folder, which he opened now. Inside were a half-dozen black-and-white photographs. "We do have some aerial reconnaissance. Unfortunately, our boys were dodging a couple of Japanese fighters at the time and had to skedaddle in a hurry. They did get these pictures."

He had handed the photos off to Deke, who passed them around. The photographs showed the compound from various overhead angles. However, none of the photographs were particularly close or showed much detail.

The overall impression was of a gloomy, forbidding hellhole carved into a jungle clearing. Looking closely, it was evident that there were two separate clusters of rough buildings—one cluster likely housing the Japanese guards and the other cluster for prisoners.

There was a guard tower and a tall fence evident in the photographs. Outside the fence there appeared to be newly turned soil, as if someone was trying to grow something—or more ominously, trying to bury something.

"Do you reckon that's a garden or a graveyard outside the fence?" Deke asked.

"I don't know about the garden," the major said. "Under a magnifying glass, you can see that the disturbed ground is consistent with several graves."

Philly was squinting hard at the photo in his hand, but without the benefit of a magnifying glass it was hard to see the details. "I'll be damned," he said to no one in particular.

"Those photographs don't tell us much," Steele said. "Is that all we have to go on?"

"We have a rough approximation of the prison camp's location," Flanders said. "The Filipino guerrillas that you'll be working with do have some local knowledge of the area, although the camp isn't located near any towns or villages. That information and the photographs are pretty much all the intelligence that we have."

"The commandant's shoe size might be nice to know," Steele said, characteristically tongue in cheek. "Short of that, it would be good to know how many guards we might be facing."

"Look, this won't be an easy mission," the major admitted. "You'll have to cross through the interior, which you know is mostly jungle and hills, sprinkled with more than a few Japanese patrols. Once you get there, you may be facing overwhelming odds. In all honestly, we really don't know what you'll be up against or how many Japanese are garrisoned at this POW compound."

Philly spoke up. "So we're going into this more or less blind, huh? In other words, business as usual."

The major's smile faded as he said, "I'm glad that you feel that way, soldier. But just to be clear, only volunteers will be going on this mission. This isn't going to be a cakewalk. If anyone doesn't want to be part of this mission, now is the time to speak up. No questions asked, right, Lieutenant?"

Now it was Steele's turn to smile. "I guess you don't know my men very well, Major. But since you brought it up, I suppose I have to ask. Does anybody want to sit this one out?"

One by one, the men stood and stepped forward, coming to attention in front of the intelligence officer.

"That settles it, then," Major Flanders said. "I can't thank you men enough."

"You can thank us when we bring those POWs home," Steele said.

Now that they had all agreed to go on the mission, the major revealed a few more details. As much as possible, they were to avoid any Japanese forces that they might encounter in the jungle terrain, although they were welcome to relay any information about the strength and whereabouts of the enemy back to headquarters, using their radio or one of the Filipino guerrillas as a runner.

"I wouldn't normally say this, but avoid taking any prisoners. They'll only slow you down. This is a rescue mission, not a combat mission," he pointed out. "As much as possible, avoid engaging the enemy. There might be plenty of fighting to do, anyhow, once you get to that POW camp."

He thanked them again for all that they had done thus far—and wished them luck as they went off into the unknown dangers of the Filipino jungle once more. In fact, the major seemed genuinely moved. He shook their hands, one by one.

"Do whatever it takes," he said. "And bring our boys home."

Lieutenant Steele looked around at them with satisfaction, as if he hadn't expected anything less. There was also a glint in his eye that seemed to indicate that he was as affected by the major's description of the mission as much as any of the men. "It's decided, then. Let's saddle up. We'll be traveling light, so leave the tea service at home."

"Dammit," Philly muttered. "I just got that new teapot and everything."

"If you're going to carry anything extra, bring ammo," Steele said. "From the sounds of things, we're going to need it. One more thing, Major. How soon do we leave?"

"I hate to say it, but this is one of those situations where each day counts. The Japanese are getting desperate enough to do something stupid."

The major hadn't come right out and said it, but no interpretation was needed. The POWs might not have much time.

Steele grinned again, the eye that wasn't covered by the patch glittering intensely in the dim gloom inside the tent, bright as a lighthouse on a stormy night. "In other words, sooner is always better than later," he said. "We can resupply and head out before dark."

Major Flanders nodded. He knew better than to wish them good luck. Some soldiers had a superstition that wishing someone good luck was sure to bring the opposite result. "Give 'em hell," he said.

CHAPTER EIGHT

REX FARADAY WOKE up in a sweat, tossing and turning on the hard boards of his bunk in the POW barracks. In his dream, he'd been on the plane again, a bomber that the crew had dubbed *Blind Date*. In the disorienting dark, it took him a few moments to get his bearings.

It's all right, he soothed himself. *You're on the ground.*

He still had nightmares about the plane going down. They had taken fire during a long-range bombing run to the shores of Japan.

"We're hit!" cried the pilot, a laconic Oklahoman named Tommy "Okie" Clarkson who was a couple of years older than Faraday.

"Dammit, must have been that last burst of flak," Faraday said. "How bad?"

"We're still in the air, aren't we?" Okie replied through gritted teeth.

The pilot's calm reassured Faraday. The age difference made Okie feel like an older brother not only to Faraday but to the rest of the crew.

They were all young enough that a difference of a few years in their ages mattered. After all, the average age of the aircrew was twenty-two. Back home, they would barely have been trusted with the keys to the family car, yet here they were, operating a bomber carrying nearly eight thousand pounds of ordnance.

The plane shuddered once, twice, the controls lurching as if gravity itself was making a grab for them.

"Give me a damage report," Faraday said over the intercom while the pilot struggled with the controls.

"We've got a hole back here the size of a beer keg," said the rear gunner. "In fact, I wouldn't be surprised if that's what hit us. How the hell are we still in the air?"

"Hey, this is the good ol' *Blind Date* we're talking about," Faraday replied. "We're lucky. Everybody OK?"

"Yeah, yeah."

In the seat next to Faraday, the pilot remained calm. "Steady, steady," he said, as if soothing a spooked horse back in Oklahoma instead of a damaged bomber. "You still have three engines, gal. Bring us on home. You can do it."

At first, the coaxing seemed to work. The Japanese shrapnel might have knocked out an engine, but it was true that they could remain airborne as long as they did not have additional problems.

They had been fortunate in that while the Japanese shell had knocked out an engine, the white-hot flak had not started any fires or severed any fuel lines. He had witnessed more than one plane explode into a fireball over Tokyo, the crew never having a chance to bail out.

Faraday looked out the window at the blue expanse of the sea below, reminded of the fact that the Pacific was a very wide ocean, and they were a very small plane in comparison. It was a long way back to base.

In the sunlight, the ocean was the color of emerald with just a hint of sapphire, exactly the shade of the tumbled bits of glass that beachcombers often found. There were times to admire the dazzling enormity of the Pacific, but this wasn't one of them. Their aircraft was in trouble.

Not for the first time, Faraday was struck by the fact that the Pacific was also an empty ocean, the surface below them stretching uninterrupted by ships or land. They had lost air speed so that the rest of the squadron had faded from sight. Out here it was just sea and sky. Their plane was merely a speck limping along through that sky.

"Dammit, we're low on fuel," the pilot said. He flicked a finger at the glass face of the gauge, as if it might be stuck. The reading did not change. "We must have a leak, after all."

"Enough to make it home?" Faraday asked.

Okie didn't reply, which was all the answer that Faraday needed.

Faraday knew their situation wasn't helped by the fact that bombing runs were made over incredibly long distances, which was why it was vital for American forces to take back the Philippines and reestablish their air bases. This would make missions to the Japanese home islands that much easier—if not exactly a milk run. There were still vast distances involved, crossing nothing but water, but at least the chances would be better of making it home when there was damage or mechanical failure.

Their plane was a B-24 Liberator, a class of plane semi-affectionately known as a "Flying Boxcar." The plane had been manufactured at a Ford plant in Michigan, where the planes were built at the rate of one every hour. It was a rate of production that the enemy could never hope to match.

Although the B-24 had been the foundation for much of the initial bombing campaign against Japan, it was rapidly being replaced by the more advanced B-29 Superfortress, capable of high-altitude bombing runs beyond the reach of Japanese defenses. Even if a Japanese fighter managed to climb up to meet a squadron of the new bombers, it could not hope to keep up with them.

Blind Date couldn't have kept up either. Though sturdy and nimble enough when not fully loaded, she was not fast. In all honesty, the B-24 never had been an ideal aircraft and was already showing its age when compared to the B-29.

The controls were so heavy that the plane was difficult to fly, especially at lower airspeeds when fully loaded. Even Okie had been known to bitch about that.

The systems leaked fuel constantly, to the point where they had to open the bomb bay doors periodically just to air out the fumes. It was a problem common to the Liberator. Smoking was out of the question, considering that lighting up might have turned them into a fireball.

Their B-24 had flown several missions and had all the dings to prove it. Faraday liked to joke that she was held together with bubblegum and good luck. He hoped that *Blind Date* held up one more time.

"C'mon, baby. You can do this," he whispered, as if the plane could hear him.

Faraday knew that he could hope all that he wanted, but that didn't change the fact that their current situation remained grim.

Then again, even with the hole in their plane, they were still alive. That was something, at least. Their Flying Boxcar was built to take a lot of punishment.

Faraday felt his nerves quiet as he looked over at the pilot. They were in capable hands. Maybe Okie could pull off yet another miracle. It wouldn't have been the first time. It helped to have a pilot who was both skilled and lucky—and who had an ample supply of bubblegum.

His thoughts were cut short as an explosion rocked the plane. They had lost another engine.

"That's not good," Faraday muttered into the quiet. He could hear the wind beating at the metal skin of the plane, a noise that was usually hidden by the roar of the engines.

"Hold on tight, boys," announced the pilot, the shrill tone of his voice showing that he was trying to hide his own fear. What scared Faraday even more than the shudder of the plane was the alarmed tone of the pilot's voice. Normally there wasn't much that rattled the pilot. "We're going down!"

"Brace for crash landing!" Faraday shouted into the intercom as the pilot struggled with the controls. He grabbed at his seat belt and made sure it was as tight as possible, then braced himself. They had practiced crash procedures what seemed like a million times, so he did this automatically. But somehow it still didn't feel real.

Their only bit of luck was that Okie had spotted land. Without a chart in front of them, it was hard to say where the land was, but any version of terra firma was better than the ocean, where they might drift for days in a tiny rubber life raft. While the plane still had some power, Okie got *Blind Date* pointed toward the mottled green and brown far below.

Faraday felt his heart racing as the plane began to descend rapidly. His ears ached painfully with the sudden change in pressure, and he swallowed to "pop" them, but he could barely keep up, because the plane was losing huge amounts of altitude by the second.

He looked out of the window and could see the ground approaching fast. He closed his eyes, bracing for impact. This was it. Faraday figured that he was about to die, but there wasn't a damn thing he could do about it. He would just have to ride it down.

Next to him, he could hear Okie coaxing the plane. "C'mon, now, you can do it. That's it, here we go—"

Each final second of his life dragged out like an eternity. What did a man think of when he was about to die? He thought of home and family. For a moment he saw his mother's smiling face. Behind her his brothers and sisters were gathered around the kitchen table, eating pancakes.

Next came a fragment of a happy memory with his father, just the two of them fishing for bluegills in a farm pond, using bits of hot dog for bait. The memory was so strong that Faraday wrinkled his nose as he caught a whiff of those hot dogs mixed with the odor of fish.

Now why the hell couldn't I smell those pancakes instead?

He glimpsed the fresh-washed face of his high school girl-friend, smiling up at him as they kissed after a dance. He still carried a letter from her in his pocket, a little piece of home that had kept him company as *Blind Date* crisscrossed the vast skies.

Faraday was snapped out of his reverie as treetops swatted at the plane, tearing chunks from the fuselage. First one wing was ripped away, then another. The nose of the plane dipped lower and cracked off a tree trunk whose jagged point ripped down the length of the plane like a butcher's knife gutting a pig. Through the intercom, he heard screaming.

Roiling greenery filled the view out the cockpit windows. It was a sensation not unlike sinking into the sea. All that Faraday could do was close his eyes and hang on.

After what felt like an eternity, the plane gave one final jolt and then came to a stop.

He opened his eyes and looked around. The plane had crashed into a forest. The trees had simultaneously broken their fall and also made it worse by battering the plane to bits.

The sudden stillness of the plane after their bumpy ride down felt strange. Miraculously, he had survived. He quickly checked his arms, legs, and torso. Not so much as a scrape, although he was sure there would be some bruises.

His next worry was fire. It was hard to say how much fuel they still had on board. But again, Liberators were infamous for their fumes. He glanced behind him and saw the shower of sparks from the fried electrical system. Not good. He tried the intercom, but it was dead.

"We need to get out of here," he said for Okie's benefit. Faraday started unbuckling his harness.

When there was no response from Okie, he looked over at the pilot. Okie sat slumped in his seat, eyes wide, hands still gripping the controls. But it was a true death grip. The eyes stared sightlessly.

"Okie?"

But there was never going to be a response, not anymore. A broken tree limb had speared Okie in the chest, piercing his body and even running clear through the back of the pilot's seat. The gory, jagged point of the spear was clearly visible.

The shock of the last few minutes meant that Faraday didn't even know how to react. He only registered that Okie Clarkson, his big brother, was dead. He finished unbuckling himself from the seat as more sparks popped behind him and filled the cockpit with their ozone stink. He could also smell fumes.

Dear God, don't let me burn to death.

But before he could abandon the aircraft, he had to check on the rest of the crew. Leaning into the dark fuselage behind him, he called, "Hello? Can anybody hear me?" There was no answer. He thought about entering the fuselage to search for any survivors, but the creaking and groaning of the airplane made him decide against it. He fled out a hole in the plane and climbed down.

Safely on the ground, looking directly above him, he could see that the plane remained suspended in the trees. Overhead, the groaning and shifting of the plane grew louder. Faraday quickly got out from underneath the wreckage—not a moment too soon. What was left of the bomber hit the jungle floor with a resounding boom.

"Hello?" he called. "Anybody?"

Nothing but silence. It was beginning to look as if he might have been the only one who made it out. Much of the fuselage—in fact, most of the rest of the plane—had been pulled apart and scattered through the trees, the crew along with it. Nonetheless, he probed through the wreckage, calling out as he did so.

Much to his surprise and relief, he heard an answering shout. Moments later, he saw a figure limping toward him through the trees and brush. It was Ron "Lucky" Mason, who had also somehow survived the crash landing.

"You're a sight for sore eyes," Faraday said, hurrying toward his fellow survivor. He could hear the emotion in his own voice, relief mixed with sadness for all the rest who apparently hadn't made it, although he still held out hope that some of the others might have survived.

"Hey, they don't call me Lucky for nothing."

"You OK?"

"I'll live."

Faraday looked Lucky up and down. The young man had a bad gash in his forehead, but otherwise seemed intact. He was swaying a little, however.

"Let's get you to sit down before you fall down," Faraday said.

"I won't argue. Got any water?"

"I'm afraid not. Maybe we can find some in the plane later."

Lucky looked back at the wreckage. It was none too promising. "Maybe."

They camped nearby that night, even lighting a small fire, hoping against hope that if there had been any other survivors scattered through the jungle, they would find their way back to the plane's wreckage.

He wasn't sure what to do about Okie's body, still pinned in the pilot's seat. He doubted that he could face the sight of his dead "big brother" once again. At some point, he and Lucky would have to try to find supplies in the wreckage. He'd also lost his sidearm somewhere, but he wasn't about to go back to the cockpit to look for it just yet.

Blind Date had carried a crew of eight young men. As the night wore on, it became increasingly evident that he and Lucky were the only survivors. As for their location, he could only guess that they were somewhere in the Philippines, but all that he really knew for certain was that they hadn't crashed into the sea. As bad as the landing had been, he knew that the bomber would have fared even worse had they taken a swim in the Pacific.

With his back against a tree, Faraday hadn't realized just how exhausted he really was until he fell into a dreamless sleep. Lucky was already asleep. As it turned out, it would be the only blissful sleep he would have for months to come.

When he opened his eyes, it was morning. Sunlight streamed down through the trees, illuminating the patches of dawn mist. The morning chatter of birds and insects filled the air. The fire had gone out. Lucky was still sleeping. No other survivors had appeared.

But they weren't alone.

He found himself peering up into the face of a Japanese soldier who was pointing a rifle at him. The dark muzzle of the rifle looked as big as a cannon. Oddly enough, nearby stood another Japanese, holding a bow and arrow.

Faraday realized that he had survived the plane crash, only to become a prisoner of war.

CHAPTER NINE

FARADAY WAS AN OPTIMIST AT HEART, but after a few months as a POW, even he had to admit at times that maybe being killed in the plane crash might have been a blessing. Life as a prisoner of war was filled with hard labor, starvation rations, and constant fear.

They were a ragtag bunch, numbering forty-seven prisoners. There had been forty-nine when Faraday arrived. A year before his arrival, he learned, there had been sixty-seven POWs, and even more before that. It was a situation of constant attrition, with the men who had been at the camp the longest being most likely to succumb next. Those who hadn't made it were now buried in a grubby-looking dirt boneyard beyond the perimeter fence. The Japanese had not allowed any grave markers, so that each heavy rain diminished any signs of a burial.

Faraday and Lucky had arrived at the camp in good health, but the conditions slowly wore them down. He could see and feel himself growing thinner, having to punch new holes in his belt to hold up his pants. Nobody was going to gain any weight eating the slop that the Japs fed them once a day.

The days passed slowly, with them rising before dawn to work at some task that was usually sweaty and futile. The harder it was, the more the Japanese seemed to like watching the prisoners do it. For the last several weeks, they had been working up to twelve hours each day, hauling stones from a nearby creek bed. Using buckets, they carried the stones up a steep hill and then spread them on the road leading from the prison gate.

Faraday didn't know how far the road went, only that it stretched off into the forest and disappeared. The stones stopped well short of where the trees began. All the rest was dust or mud, depending on the weather. It seemed pointless, considering that at this rate the prisoners would have to work for all eternity to pave the road for even the length of a mile.

Then again, perhaps that was exactly what the Japanese had in mind.

It was a dreary, hot, cruel place to be.

"I promise you one thing," Lucky whispered in his ear almost daily. "I'm getting out of this place, one way or another."

"Just don't do anything crazy," he warned.

Faraday had become something of a leader among the prisoners. The Japanese did not distinguish between officers and enlisted, so they all lived and suffered together.

For the most part, the guards went about their duties, treating the prisoners with all the indifference that they would have shown sheep or goats. He had learned which Japanese to watch out for, especially the nasty sergeant they had nicknamed Mr. Suey, which was as close as they could come to pronouncing his real name.

Another Japanese of note was Lieutenant Osako, who spoke English and thus did most of the day-to-day communicating with the prisoners. Osako ran hot and cold, showing glimmers of humanity one day when the other Japanese weren't around, then looking the other way the next day when Mr. Suey decided to beat a prisoner for spilling a bucket of rocks. The lieutenant was Dr. Jekyll and Mr. Hyde all rolled into one, so that you never really knew who you were going to be dealing with. More than most of their captors, it was clear that Lieutenant Osako was at war with himself.

The Japanese commandant cast the longest shadow of all. From time to time, he came out to watch the prisoners working. Faraday couldn't have known how close to the truth he'd been when he had told Lucky that the commandant must have really messed up to get assigned command of this remote prison camp.

The commandant sometimes had them assemble in the prison yard and then gave long political speeches in Japanese, which Lieutenant Osako translated whenever his commanding officer paused to catch his breath. It was such an odd contrast to see the enemy soldiers and officers standing at attention in their neat uniforms, facing the ragged prisoners. Faraday could have sworn that the commandant was drunk during these speeches.

The other odd thing about the commandant was that he was never without his bow and arrow, making him something of a strange sight or even an eccentric character.

But as Faraday soon discovered, the bow and arrow were for more than show.

* * *

FARADAY WAS NOT FAR off the mark in thinking that the prison camp commandant, Colonel Kaito Yamagata, must have done something wrong to wind up in charge of this remote, mosquito-infested camp. In Yamagata's case, it had really been a series of mistakes and career blunders, some purely bad luck or bad timing, the chief one being a disastrous skirmish that he had led against the Chinese early in the war, resulting in an embarrassing defeat of his unit.

However, even that might have been overlooked. But the Japanese military was quite political, and Yamagata had never learned to play the game. He was now what was known as a "permanent colonel," without any hope of advancement to general. The truth was that the Japanese army could not care less if a POW camp was badly run, but they didn't want to lose any battles due to poor leadership.

Yamagata had determined that he would run his camp efficiently, and he had. Unfortunately for the POWs, his definition of efficiency meant feeding the prisoners as little as possible and working them to the bone.

* * *

COLONEL YAMAGATA HAD DECIDED that it was time to teach the prisoners a lesson. He had tired of their lazy ways and constant disrespect. To that end, he summoned to his office the two subordinates most responsible for operating the camp.

Lieutenant Ryota Osako was his second-in-command, although he found the young officer too idealistic for his own good. He had made it clear that he did not always agree with Yamagata's methods, although he knew better than to protest. He carried out his orders, but without much enthusiasm.

The commandant relied more heavily on Sergeant Hiromu Matsueda. The sergeant was a man of simple tastes who appreciated a full belly, a drink of sake, and a cigarette. Yamagata saw to it that the sergeant never wanted for any of these things. As a result, the man never questioned Yamagata, from whom all good things flowed.

Matsueda had been a farmer before the war, and the prisoners seemed to occupy the same place in his mind that had once been reserved for his pigs and goats. They were just shuffling, troublesome animals. When they didn't do what you wanted, it was best to beat them with a stick. Sergeant Matsueda had a brutal mean streak that served Yamagata well in keeping order.

The commandant's office was a neat but sparse space, the wooden floorboards recently swept, overseen by a portrait of the Emperor that was the only decoration on the walls. The office felt crowded, however, due to an ornate desk that would have looked more at home in a plantation office.

Two plain wooden chairs stood before the desk like servants in the presence of their master. The only other nods to luxury were a wood-encased Yamanaka electric radio and a bottle of expensive liquor on a side table. Notably, Yamagata did not offer the men a drink, although he had a small glass of amber-colored liquor on his desk.

Yamagata had not asked his subordinates to sit, which was an indication of his seriousness and the formality of this meeting. They both stood at attention, awaiting what the commandant had to say.

"I have concerns about the prisoners. They are lazy," he explained to Lieutenant Osako and Sergeant Matsueda. "They do not work hard enough. What they lack is motivation."

Both of the other men shifted uncomfortably, the one mentally blaming the other. Osako would have said that Matsueda was too cruel and broke the spirit of the prisoners, and Matsueda would have said that the namby-pamby lieutenant was too weak and allowed the lazy Americans to do whatever they wished. Had they been questioned, they would have been more than happy to throw the other man under the bus. No love was lost between them.

However, both men knew better than to say anything in the presence of the commandant other than "Hai!"

"Tomorrow morning, we shall prepare a demonstration for

them," the commandant said, glancing meaningfully at his bow in the corner.

Most officers carried a sword as a badge of office, but Yamagata preferred his bow. He practiced with it constantly, firing endless arrows at a target at the far end of the prison yard. He had rediscovered his love of the bow and arrow that he had hunted with as a youth, and he found archery to be a good way to alleviate the boredom of this remote posting.

Both men standing before him in his office knew that he rarely missed, although a bow and arrow was not a very useful weapon in the war they were fighting.

Neither man was sure what the commandant had in mind, which was why it was so surprising the next day when the prisoners were assembled in the yard, and instead of another political speech, the commandant had ordered that the gate be opened.

"Sir?" Lieutenant Osako made the mistake of hesitating.

Glaring at him for questioning the command, Yamagata barked, "Open the gate!"

"Hai!"

The lieutenant hurried to carry out the commandant's order, although he didn't see the sense of it. He glanced over at Matsueda. If the sergeant had guessed the commandant's intent, his face remained inscrutable.

Although the commandant spoke English passably well, he usually spoke Japanese and had Lieutenant Osako translate for the POWs. This seemed to indicate the commandant's authority and avoided any embarrassment about his shortcomings in speaking English.

Today was different, however. Carrying his bow, he approached the assembled prisoners and spoke directly to them in English.

"Some of you do not seem happy here," he said. "So I am

giving you an opportunity to leave. All that you must do is reach the gate and escape my arrow. Is this not fair? Who would like to try first?"

The prisoners stared at Yamagata as if not sure they had heard him correctly. Over his shoulder, the open prison gates beckoned.

"What's the catch?" a prisoner called.

"No catch. Those who do not like it here may try to leave."

Yamagata offered no further explanation, letting his offer sink in. The sun beat down, and the day seemed to grow hotter, or maybe it was only the tension of the moment.

After what seemed like an eternity, Yamagata pointed at one of the Filipino prisoners. There were a handful held here, and they were not well liked by the Japanese.

"You," Yamagata said. "You will go."

When the stunned prisoner made no effort to go anywhere, Sergeant Matsueda walked over and shoved him forward.

That was when one of the Americans took a half step out of the formation and said, "Hold on, I'll go."

* * *

FARADAY SWIVELED his head and stared in consternation at Lucky, who had stepped forward to announce to the bow-wielding commandant that he would be willing to make a run for it.

"Lucky, what the hell are you doing?" Faraday whispered. "Get back in formation!"

"I can't stand this place anymore," Lucky replied. "If this is a chance to get out of here, I'll take it."

"Even if you make it through that gate, there's nothing but jungle out there!"

"Doesn't matter. I won't be in here."

Faraday wasn't ready to give up. "We've all seen the commandant practice with that bow. He's a good shot."

Lucky winked. "All I've got to do is outrun that Filipino fella."

"That only works when you're being chased by a bear. It doesn't work with arrows."

Lucky just shook his head. "Listen, Rex. We all know the Japs plan on killing us, one way or another. They're working us to death in this place. Maybe it's better to die quick." He grinned at Faraday, and for a moment he was the same old carefree Lucky. In his mind, maybe he had already escaped. He then added, "Besides, they don't call me *Lucky* for nothing."

Faraday might have argued further, trying to convince his buddy not to risk it, but Mr. Suey approached and poked Faraday sharply in the ribs with a swagger stick. He shouted something in Japanese that Faraday took to mean, "Shut the hell up!"

Lucky stepped up beside the Filipino prisoner whom the commandant had singled out. The Filipino turned as if to go back into formation, but Mr. Suey was there to take his arm and stop him.

"You both go," the commandant said. He stepped off to one side and nocked an arrow. The metal tip gleamed wickedly in the sun.

Lucky crouched like a sprinter, awaiting the signal. The Filipino still looked as if there was anything else that he would prefer doing. Finally, he made the sign of the cross and followed Lucky's lead by getting into a sprinter's crouch.

Among the prisoners, it was so quiet that you could have heard a pin drop. Faraday realized that he was holding his breath. He was sure that the thickness of the tropical air would weigh Lucky down.

The distance to the open gates was no more than three

hundred feet, all of it across dusty, open ground. Essentially, Lucky was making a one-hundred-yard dash like they had done in training. Fifteen seconds had been considered a good time when they had been fit and well fed. How long would it take Lucky now? And how many arrows could the commandant let loose in that same time frame?

Lucky didn't bother waiting for a signal, but took off running. He seemed to explode from the spot, racing away across the prison yard and quickly outpacing the other man trailing him. For the first time, Faraday actually felt hopeful. Maybe Lucky could pull it off.

Unable to help themselves, some of the prisoners began shouting encouragement. "Go! Go, Lucky!"

The Japanese soldiers got in on the act, shouting what sounded like jeers.

The two runners had taken different strategies. Lucky zigzagged from side to side, suddenly changing direction. It would take him longer to cross the open ground, but it made him a more difficult target. The other prisoner ran flat out in a straight line. In seconds, both men had covered half the distance to the open gates. The shouting from both sides grew more intense.

Colonel Yamagata drew his bow, held the string briefly by his ear, then released. The arrow sang through the air and just missed Lucky, who dodged out of the way at the last instant. Faraday had the thought that Yamagata was discovering that moving targets were much harder to hit than a stationary bull's-eye.

"Run!" Faraday shouted.

The commandant drew back again, this time having to elevate his aim as the distance between him and the runners increased. When he released, the arrow had so much energy that

Faraday could clearly hear the hiss it made leaving Yamagata's bow.

This time, Yamagata had been aiming at the Filipino. The arrow arced up, then sank back down in a blur of motion, somehow seeming to gain speed as it did so. In the next instant, the arrowhead buried itself in the Filipino's back. The man fell to his knees and managed to crawl a few feet before collapsing and lying still in the dirt.

Lucky was still running, his feet churning toward the gates that now seemed so close, almost within reach.

Faraday couldn't believe it. *He's going to make it. He's actually going to escape.* Around him, the other prisoners shouted wildly.

Off to the side, Colonel Yamagata nocked another arrow and drew back his bow. He pulled the string back well past his ear and held it there. The tip of the arrow pointed high into the air. Though powerful, his arms shook slightly with the strain, but he took his time aiming. Then the bow string was released with a sharp twang, and the arrow hissed skyward.

At first assessment, the arc appeared too high, as if Yamagata had overshot his mark. Beneath the falling arrow, Lucky juked and dodged. He had almost reached the gates. In seconds, he would be home free.

The arrow struck, piercing Lucky just below his left shoulder blade. He kept running at first, then went down to his knees. The gate was right there.

"C'mon, c'mon," Faraday urged under his breath, hoping against hope that his buddy would still be able to make it through the gate.

Lucky had gone to his hands and knees, leaving a trail of blood in the dirt. Then he collapsed to his belly but kept going, dragging himself toward the gate, unwilling to give up.

Mr. Suey was crossing the prison yard now. He paused long enough to check the still body of the Filipino prisoner, then kept going. Lucky was barely moving now, spread eagle in the dirt, almost like a swimmer trying to tread water but going nowhere.

The Japanese sergeant unsnapped the flap of the pistol on his hip, drew the weapon, and pointed it down at Lucky. Faraday turned away but winced at the sharp report of the pistol.

Colonel Yamagata handed his bow to Lieutenant Osako, who looked almost as stunned as the prisoners. The commandant raised his voice to address the POWs.

"The rest of you will be happy here. You will do as you are told. You will work hard. There will be no complaints."

Yamagata turned toward his own men and shouted something. Just beyond the grisly scene of Lucky's body, the prison gates were slowly closed again.

CHAPTER TEN

WITH NO TIME TO spare before dark, Patrol Easy headed back into the interior of Leyte, leaving the beach behind. The tropical sea breeze was soon replaced by the stifling heat and humidity of the island interior. The breeze had kept the worst of the insects at bay, but the flies and midges now returned in hungry, biting clouds.

"Here we go again," Philly grumbled. "I thought the front lines were dangerous, but what do you know, hanging around too close to HQ turns out to be just as hazardous when someone decides to volunteer you for a mission deep into enemy territory."

"Out of the frying pan and into the fire," Deke agreed. "It's gotten so that I can't tell which one is hotter."

"But if it means getting those poor bastards out of the POW camp, then it's worth it," Philly pointed out.

"Let's just make sure we don't end up in the boneyard in the process, or ambushed. We won't be much use to anybody if we're dead."

After that brief exchange, no one seemed inclined to say

more. As the vegetation deepened around them, a silence settled over the group.

Even just a stone's throw from the sea, the jungle grew lush and thick right up to the edge of the dirt road. The jungle was a riot of green, with trees of all kinds and sizes. Deke was more than familiar with the mountain forests where he'd grown up and could identify oaks, maples, and hickory trees. He didn't even know where to begin here, these being far different from the species back home, but the trees were just as impressive.

Overgrown vines hung from the trees, the creepers adding to the lush vegetation that snaked down from the canopy.

The scary part was that Deke realized he was starting to feel right at home. There were hidden dangers lurking in the jungle, to be sure, but it also provided cover. The protection offered by the forest was a lot better than feeling exposed on the beach.

In any case, it felt good to be on the move. A few hours of rest in the relative security of the beach area had felt good, but now it was time to get back into the action.

It would have made sense to head out the next morning, but even the few hours they had before darkness arrived suddenly seemed essential.

Nobody had come out and said it, but by unspoken mutual agreement they were all double-timing it. The area was securely in American hands—more or less, aside from a few infiltrators and small bands of enemy soldiers—so there wasn't much worry yet about encountering any stray enemy units. That would come later. For now they could hurry it up.

Major Flanders's description of the fate that might await the American POWs added to their sense of urgency. They all knew only too well what the Japanese were capable of doing. They had witnessed the enemy's cruelty too many times to count.

Maybe Americans weren't always saints, and the frustrations of the battlefield resulted in a few captured Japanese not making it to the rear. However, wholesale slaughter of defenseless Japanese POWs was unthinkable. Once the captured enemy troops were safely corralled in the POW compound, they were treated with respect and well fed. The men of Patrol Easy would find out soon enough that the treatment of American POWs held by the Japanese fell far short of what anyone might expect.

"Hey, Deke, do you think the Japanese will really murder those POWs?" Philly asked.

"You heard what that major had to say, same as I did," Deke replied. "Also, you know the Japanese as well as I do. What do you think they're capable of doing?"

Philly clammed up for once, thinking it over. He didn't respond directly, but turned to shout with annoyance at Rodeo, who was lagging behind. "Pick up the pace, why don't you? It would be nice to get where we're going before Christmas."

If Lieutenant Steele had overheard, he chose not to comment. Deke figured that the lieutenant had other things on his mind—such as how they were all going to survive this mission and bring home those POWs to boot.

The plan to liberate the POWs had sounded well and good back in the relative safety of the tent at HQ. It hadn't taken much to get them fired up about rescuing the POWs. The plan had unhatched in the shadowy corner of the tent. But now in the harsh light of day, they were headed back in what Deke thought of as Indian country.

The last that they had seen of Major Flanders was him piling into a transport to ferry him back to General MacArthur's HQ aboard USS *Nashville*, taking his reconnaissance photographs with him. Deke supposed that you couldn't really blame the major for not heading into the field with them. That wasn't the man's job.

One thing for sure—they were on their own.

There were just a handful of them on this patrol: Lieutenant

Steele, Deke, Philly, Yoshio, and Rodeo. Philly was already grumbling about having to walk who knew how many hours before they reached that POW camp.

Their Filipino guerrilla guide, Danilo, was on point. There hadn't been any discussion about him joining this dangerous mission. He had simply attached himself to their patrol, ready to go—and silent as always.

Deke felt reassured by his presence. The deeply tanned Filipino was wise in the ways of the jungle—plus, he was a tough nut to crack. Danilo appeared to have a select knowledge of English, understanding only as much as he wanted to. Nonetheless, they would welcome even his limited communication skills once they linked up with the Filipino guerrillas somewhere up ahead.

At least that was the plan. Deke knew well enough that trying to locate another friendly force in the hills and jungles would be a bit like trying to hit a tin can from one hundred yards while wearing a blindfold and swatting at bees. It was only the enemy that nobody ever had trouble running into.

Glancing up ahead at their guide, Deke realized that he still couldn't determine just how old Danilo was. He was certainly older than the GIs or possibly even Lieutenant Steele, which put his age somewhere between forty and Methuselah territory. Yet the man's wiry arms and legs seemed tireless.

Egan and Thor were sitting this one out. Instead, they would be carrying out guard duties at the beachhead. Thor's powerful nose would be needed to sniff out any Japanese infiltrators bent on sabotage during the night.

It was true that a mission such as this, which involved traveling fast and light through rough terrain, was no place for the war dog. Still, Thor had become their mascot of sorts. Egan did not encourage them to show too much affection toward the dog, fearful that Thor might lose his aggressive edge, but the war dog wasn't averse to allowing Deke to scratch his ears from time to time.

Deke had grown up with dogs and felt a soft spot toward Thor—he also felt like a war zone was no place for a dog. It was bad enough for the two-legged soldiers.

Steele had ordered them to travel as light as possible, carrying nothing more than a few rations, canteens, their weapons, and plenty of ammo. Nobody bothered with blankets in the tropical heat. They didn't bother with ponchos, either— hell, they were already soaked through with sweat, so what would a little rain matter? Spare clothes were a luxury they couldn't afford. The only real extra they were bringing along were two sets of wire cutters to deal with any fence or barbed wire that the Japanese were using to contain their prisoners.

Rodeo lugged along a handheld radio to keep in touch with HQ, although it was doubtful that the device would have much range once they got back into the hills. Rodeo also carried their scant medical supplies, which included a few bandages, some morphine, and aspirin. Any wounds or injuries that required more serious treatment likely meant that you were a dead man, anyhow.

Deke was grateful that he had finally shaken his jungle fever, an illness that had plagued him for most of the fight to seize Ormoc. The fever had left him feeling weak and hollowed out, but he had mostly regained his strength in the last couple of days. He just hoped and prayed that the fever didn't return. The last thing he wanted was to be a burden to anyone on this mission. They trudged along, weapons at the ready, eyes scanning the jungle terrain for any sign of danger. There was no time to set up camp, no time to rest. They had to keep moving if they wanted to reach the POW camp before it was too late.

They soon reached the vicinity of Camp Downes, which had been the scene of a sharp fight only recently. The old outpost had been turned into a supply base, with material being moved up from the beachhead. They also passed the concrete bunkers that had given them so much trouble when passing through initially on their road to Ormoc.

The Japanese within those bunkers had proved to be a tough nut to crack. It had only been the arrival of the flame-thrower tanks known as Satans that had enabled them to burn out the enemy. In some cases, the tanks had fired point-blank into the bunkers.

Deke recalled how a few soldiers had insisted on collecting souvenirs in the midst of that chaos. It hadn't ended well for them. An officer's sword or pistol was hardly worth getting shot over.

As they approached the bunkers, they could see the blasted and blackened ruins. The area was too quiet, too still. The air was thick with an overwhelming stench of death and decay. The team approached with caution, weapons at the ready, unnerved by the quiet, and soon found themselves in the middle of what was essentially a graveyard. Any American dead had been treated with respect and buried, but the enemy dead had been left out in the open.

Scorched enemy bodies were strewn everywhere, some still in uniform, others stripped down to their underwear. In the oppressive heat inside the bunkers, some of the enemy soldiers had evidently fought wearing as little as possible.

Some had simply been shot as they fled the bunkers, but many of the bodies were burned beyond recognition, looking like something that had been left on the barbecue too long. This had once been a battleground filled with the earsplitting sounds of combat. Now the only sound was the buzzing of flies.

Deke couldn't help but feel a sense of horror and disgust at the gruesome scene before him. He clenched his jaw, his hand tightening around the grip of his rifle.

"This place gives me the creeps," Philly muttered, his voice barely above a whisper.

Steele motioned them forward. "Let's keep moving," he said. "There's nothing for us here."

They were glad to leave the battleground behind. The jungle canopy overhead thickened, and the air became harder to breathe. Sweat poured down their faces and soaked through their clothes. Mosquitoes and the ubiquitous gnats buzzed incessantly around their faces, but swatting them away was a futile effort. After a while, it was easier just to let them be. The breeze on the beach kept the worst of the bugs away, but here in the jungle the insects were relentless.

As they trekked deeper into the forest, the trees grew taller, and the underbrush became denser. It was like stepping into another world, one where danger lurked around every corner. Every rustle of leaves, every twig snapping underfoot, only managed to set their nerves even more on edge.

Up ahead, a tree branch cracked somewhere to their left, and they all froze in their tracks. They all ducked down, expecting a volley of gunfire.

"Hold your fire," Steele whispered in a voice that was barely audible over the sound of the wind stirring the branches and palm fronds.

Seconds later, a pig and piglet wandered across the road, gave the soldiers a disinterested glance, and then disappeared into the foliage on the other side.

"We could've had bacon for dinner," Philly said.

"Yeah, and we would have let every Japanese soldier in the vicinity know that we were here," Steele replied. "Stick to the pork and beans in your ration cans."

"You got it, Honcho."

After a while, Steele traded places with Danilo and took point. It was rare for him to do that, but the lieutenant seemed unhappy with the pace. Somehow the sense of urgency was lost in translation when he had tried to explain it earlier to the Filipino.

They couldn't afford to waste any more time. Every minute that passed was another minute the POWs were being held captive, and who knew what kind of torture they were being subjected to. Major Flanders had painted a dire picture of Japanese savagery, igniting their sense of outrage. They had to get there fast, before it was too late. They all felt the fact keenly that there were many miles to go between their current position and the POW camp.

The jungle grew darker as they wove their way through it. The only sounds aside from their footsteps were the occasional rustling of leaves and the chirping of insects. It was eerily quiet, as if the jungle were holding its breath in anticipation of their next step.

Steele led the way, his one good eye scanning the path ahead. He moved with a silent confidence that even Danilo lacked. Deke found himself following Steele's lead without even thinking about it. It was faster than he was comfortable moving, but he trusted the lieutenant with his life.

Steele held up his hand, signaling for them to stop. He pointed ahead, where they could just make out a crumpled form on the dirt road. The figure wore a uniform—and it wasn't an American one.

"I'll be damned," Philly whispered. "If that's not a dead Jap, then I'm the president of the United States."

Nobody was going to call Philly the president anytime soon, because there was no doubt that this was a dead enemy soldier. They approached the body cautiously, wary of tricks.

"Watch out for booby traps," Lieutenant Steele warned. "Whatever you do, don't touch the son of a bitch."

"You got it, Honcho."

The Japanese soldier had been shot in the back, with a pool of blood mixing with the dirt of the road. Flies buzzed in and out of the pool, which gave the appearance of only recently coagulating. The enemy soldier had not been dead for long.

There was always a strange "otherness" to dead Japanese. It was rare to catch an actual glimpse of the enemy, even a dead one. He looked small and compact. There was no weapon in sight.

"What the hell was he up to?" Philly wondered.

"Nothing good, I'd expect," Deke replied.

Lieutenant Steele inspected the area surrounding the dead soldier carefully for any trip wires, then leaned over the corpse and poked at the body with the muzzle of his shotgun. The man's hand opened, and a small object fell into the dirt. It appeared to be a small stone carving.

"What the hell is that?" Steele asked, bending down to take a closer look.

Yoshio spoke up. "I believe that it is a lucky stone for a warrior. It is called a *maneki-neko*."

"Are you kidding me?" Philly asked. "A good-luck charm? It sure as hell didn't do him much good."

"No, I don't suppose that it did," Steele agreed. "The only luck this poor bastard had was that it looks as if he died quickly."

Deke was busy scanning the nearby forest, the road ahead, and a few isolated treetops, his eyes focused as far out as he could see. He was looking for any flicker of movement.

"What I want to know is, Does he have any friends?"

His question was answered in the next instant, when a rifle shot cracked. They all heard the round zing overhead, barely missing them.

They all scattered off the road. Deke threw himself into

some thorny weeds at the road's edge. Instantly he slid the Springfield to his shoulder and put his eye to the scope.

"Anybody see where that came from?" he shouted.

"Hell no!"

Another shot cracked. This time Philly fired off a couple of rounds.

"Do you see the bastard?"

"No, but I'm giving him something to think about!"

Deke had the sneaking suspicion that the enemy sniper had been using his dead comrade's body as bait, waiting for some curious GIs to happen upon it. The dead soldier was being used as a booby trap of sorts.

Silently he cursed their own stupidity. Like a bunch of idiots, they had walked right into the sniper's trap.

CHAPTER ELEVEN

DEKE SCANNED the forest for some clue as to where the enemy sniper was hiding.

But he wasn't quick enough. Meanwhile, there was another sharp crack as the sniper tried to pick them off. The bullet whined uncomfortably close, snipping off the tip of a nearby bush. The sprig of greenery spun away and slapped Deke in the face.

Each shot will get closer, Deke thought grimly, and meanwhile they were pinned down.

"All right, we'll have to go around him if we can," Steele spoke quietly. "The son of a bitch has got the road covered, so we'll have to slip off into the trees before he sends us all to hell. Deke, you stay here and cover us. Better yet, shoot that bastard if you can. We don't have time for this."

It was yet another proof of the effectiveness of a sniper. A single enemy sniper could pin down an entire company, let alone a patrol. It was a defensive tactic that the Japanese had put to good use throughout the Pacific islands. Snipers remained a better defensive weapon than an offensive one, which usually

meant that American tactics favored anti-sniper countermea-
sures—Patrol Easy itself being a case in point.

Everyone gave Steele a quick word of assent before rushing
to gather up their gear. They prepared to scurry away from their
current position.

The jungle seemed darker now as evening slowly descended
on them. Each second felt like an eternity as they carefully made
their way through the thick undergrowth, silently praying for no
one to stumble or make any sudden noise that would betray
their position and offer the sniper a target. Worse yet, there was
no telling if the enemy sniper had friends. Japanese troops might
be trying to flank them. At any moment, from any direction,
they might run into enemy soldiers.

They advanced until they came upon a small clearing that
looked as if it was a bedding place for a family of wild pigs. It
certainly smelled like it, rank and musky. They quickly settled
into their cover in what little shelter was provided by nearby
foliage while simultaneously setting up some basic defenses
against potential assaults from enemies who might be moving
through the surrounding trees. Their efforts were hindered by
the fact that nobody could see more than a few yards into the
gloom of the forest.

All in all, it wasn't the best position to be in, but it was better
than being exposed to sniper fire on the road.

"Stay put," Steele ordered. "I'm going to check on Deke."

Deke was keeping watch over where he thought the shots
had come from, hoping for some hint of the sniper's location.

The best possibility for the sniper's hiding place was a clump
of trees near a bend in the road. The higher trees would offer an
excellent vantage point. He studied the tree canopy through the
scope and, sure enough, spotted the silhouette of a man among
the branches.

His target was just beyond the range of an easy shot. This

helped explain why the enemy sniper hadn't managed to hit any of them. Maybe the Japanese wasn't a crack shot. If his sniper's lair had been set up a little closer, events may have had a different outcome.

But the distances involved were no problem for Deke.

Got you now, Deke thought.

He lined up the crosshairs on the enemy soldier's silhouette.

Before he could fire, another shot split the tropical air like an angry hornet. Dirt flew up just inches from Deke's face, but he ignored it, focused on the target.

Crawling up beside Deke, the lieutenant crooked a finger at the tree that Deke was watching through his scope.

Steele had also spotted the sniper.

"Deke, do you see him?" he asked gently.

"Yeah," Deke replied, and squeezed the trigger.

The gun kicked into his shoulder none too gently. The recoil of the Springfield was impressive, considering that the rifle delivered a wallop. Even at one hundred yards, each bullet still packed more than two thousand foot-pounds of energy.

Deke's round hit with a solid *whunk*. Even at this distance, he could almost feel the breath getting knocked out of the Japanese.

The figure in the tree slumped but did not fall. It was a common practice for Japanese snipers to tie themselves into the tree branches. While it gave them stability, it also meant that there was no quick escape from the tree. To Deke, that just seemed like a one-way ticket to hell.

Nobody shot back.

"I think you got the son of a bitch," Philly said.

"Yeah," Deke replied.

He worked the bolt, feeding a fresh round into the chamber, the spent brass spinning away. Maybe someone would find it years from now and wonder about it.

They picked themselves out of the mud and dirt and weeds, brushing themselves off in the process. Nobody felt sheepish about it. When somebody was shooting at you, the deeper that you pressed into the dirt, the better your chances were of staying alive.

"I think he was using his dead buddy here like a staked goat, trying to lure us in," Deke announced. "He knew we'd stop to take a look."

"I don't think you'd be wrong about that," Steele said. "The question is, Did he shoot his buddy for that purpose, or was the man already dead?"

"I hadn't thought about that," Deke said. As usual, Honcho was one step ahead of him. "Then again, you had to admit that would be kind of messed up to use someone on his own side for bait."

Steele looked pointedly at Philly. "Maybe it was somebody who talked too much. Kind of got on his nerves. Glad to get rid of him."

"Geez, Honcho." Philly snorted indignantly. "Don't go getting any ideas."

It was all familiar banter, and it felt good slipping into their old roles. They all felt a sense of relief that the sniper had been eliminated. Might as well enjoy a few wisecracks while they still could.

They moved on. The shadows stretched longer as the sun dropped lower in the sky. The decreasing heat was welcome, but not the thought of the coming darkness itself. The enemy always seemed to have an advantage at night and even preferred operating under cover of darkness.

"We have to get off this trail and make camp before nightfall," Steele said. "The last thing we need is to go wandering right into a Japanese patrol once it gets dark."

At the same time, they were trying to squeeze every bit of

daylight out of the air. Every foot they covered would be one less step to take in the morning.

Steele's fears about running into an enemy patrol soon seemed justified. The lieutenant froze and raised his shotgun. There was no need for orders. Everyone knew what Steele's reaction meant.

Trouble.

Up ahead, the branches of the trees stirred, moving in a way that was out of proportion to the snatches of breeze that reached down among the trees.

Deke squinted into the shadows, trying to make out what he had seen. After a moment, he saw it again—movement among the trees—something or someone moving with enough force that it shook the branches.

"It's got to be an enemy patrol!" Philly whispered loudly. "Everyone get down!"

Steele motioned for him to be quiet. For the next several seconds, they all held their breath to see what was next.

Deke listened intently, but there was no sound. He leveled his rifle at the greenery and waited, finger on the trigger, as the branches slowly parted.

Each one of their muzzles was pointed at that patch of brush, ready to open fire.

"Come on out, you bastards," Philly muttered, rifle at the ready.

The branches parted like the curtains of a stage being opened to reveal the next act.

But the man who stepped onto the trail was not Japanese. First, he was too tall and broad. Second, he wore a simple dark-brown cassock, to which a few leaves and twigs clung.

"Hello, my friends," said Father Francisco, stepping into the jungle road. "God bless."

"I'll be damned," Steele said, then added, "No offense, Father."

"None taken. Those rifles of yours are a welcome sight, believe me." He smiled. "However, I would prefer that they not be pointed at me."

"Sorry, Padre." Steele lowered his weapon, and the rest of the patrol followed suit.

Although the priest was not armed, he was not alone. The gap in the brush widened as several men pushed the branches aside. Deke counted a dozen Filipino guerrillas. They were a hard-looking bunch, wearing tattered civilian clothes rather than uniforms and broad-brimmed hats as protection against the tropical sun and whatever creepy crawlies might be inclined to drop down the back of one's neck from the vegetation above. Deke understood, considering that he had long since abandoned his steel helmet in favor of the Aussie-style outback hat with the brim pinned up on his shooting side.

However, there was no mistaking the deadly intent of these guerrillas. Most carried captured Japanese rifles, although some had recently upgraded to American M-1 rifles. In some cases, a length of rope served as a rifle sling. Deke noted with approval that the battered rifles looked clean and well oiled. The damp tropical environment was not kind to weaponry.

Even more menacing than their rifles, many of the Filipinos wore their customary bolo knives hanging at their sides like small swords or even slung across their backs. The bolo knife was essentially a machete, honed razor sharp to hack through jungle vegetation—a useful tool on Leyte. In some cases bolo knives were passed down from father to son, one of the more treasured possessions of a family that did not own many material things.

In the hands of Filipino guerrillas who had an especial hatred for the Japanese occupiers, it also made a terrifying weapon.

Danilo stepped forward and greeted the other guerrillas. It was one of the rare times that a genuinely warm smile crossed his normally expressionless face. Usually he bore the hardships of war like a true jungle stoic.

No wonder he was smiling for a change. Patrol Easy had just found its reinforcements.

* * *

THEY WERE ACQUAINTED with Father Francisco and his band of guerrillas from their earlier mission to take out the massive artillery battery on Hill 522 outside Palo, ahead of the initial beach landing on Leyte. The removal of the gun had been critical to success, because with its twenty-mile range and devastating shells, the invasion fleet might have suffered heavy losses. The gun had been manufactured for the huge Japanese battleship *Yamato* and its twin, the *Musashi*, sunk in the sea battle of Leyte Gulf. Considering that the battleships already had their full complement of weapons, the guns had not been needed on the ships. Rather than let the impressive guns gather rust, the Japanese had installed them in shore defenses.

Technically Patrol Easy had undertaken a mission behind enemy lines—although that line was actually an island in this case. The only reason they had been successful was because of Father Francisco and his guerrillas, who had provided the support and local knowledge to make the mission possible.

The guerrillas had paid a heavy price. As part of a diversionary tactic, some of those guerrillas had attacked Hill 522 and been captured. Deke and the others had watched in horror as the captured Filipinos were beheaded. The brutality of the enemy was difficult to believe, even when witnessed firsthand.

By turns kind and fierce, Father Francisco might have made a good stand-in for Friar Tuck. Growing up, Deke's encounters

with religion had mainly been of preachers of the fire-and-brim-
stone variety, whose God seemed to resemble a mean old county
sheriff intent on punishing humans for every transgression.
Father Francisco spread the word with a quiet kindness and his
own example. Deke found the priest's presence reassuring.

The priest had the appearance of being mostly of Spanish
descent, being taller and broader than any of the guerrillas. If he
hadn't been garbed as a priest, he would have resembled a
bouncer at an off-base dive bar. Even with actual Spanish
heritage, his Filipino roots would have limited his career as a
priest just a few years before. The Jesuit priests who tightly
controlled the church had all been trained and educated in
Spain, of which the Philippines was a colony. The Spanish had
preserved a system in which the ruling class did not include
actual Filipinos.

The capture of the Philippines during the Spanish-American
War had brought changes in that the new US government had
ordered all the Spanish priests to be sent home. These priests
were seen as representing the old Spanish empire, and the
church was closely aligned with the Spanish government.

There had been little animosity toward Spain or the Spanish
compared to what would come with American feelings toward
Germany and even German immigrants in WWI. In fact,
popular books of the day published positive accounts of Spanish
life and culture, with Spain typically portrayed as a "quaint"
European "old country" whose glory days were behind it. The
war had certainly resulted in bloodshed, but ultimately it was
more of a passing of the torch from an old, tired empire to the
up-and-coming American empire.

The old Spanish administration was sent on its way, Spanish
Jesuits included, and control of the churches had then fallen to
actual Filipino priests.

As part of that new generation, Father Francisco had shepherded the flock in Palo, overseeing the centuries-old church there. The Japanese invasion had caused more upheaval. He had been forced to go on the run by the Japanese. From the jungles, Father Francisco had ministered to the spiritual needs of his flock and played a leadership role in the Filipino resistance.

As it turned out, Father Francisco and the guerrillas had only an inkling of the details of the mission, so Lieutenant Steele quickly filled them in.

When he had finished, Steele asked the priest, "What do you think?"

"Some of my men know this camp. They can certainly guide us there." Concern clouded the priest's face. "I am afraid that it won't be easy. The garrison there is organized, and by all accounts the POW camp is well defended. I think you would say, 'It won't be a walk in the park.'"

"That's why we're glad to have your help."

"Perhaps the Japanese will do us all a favor and surrender," the priest said, a wry twist to his mouth. "Everywhere, the Japanese are being pushed back on Leyte."

Steele shared the concerns Major Flanders had expressed, that the enemy might simply kill the American POWs outright rather than see them released. "It would be a sharp stick in the eye," he said. "But you know the Japanese as well as I do. They can be vindictive bastards."

"Sadly, I have some experience with that," the priest agreed.

It was true that the occupiers had mistreated the locals, sweeping through the towns and countryside in the last few months to round up any able-bodied men to put them to work building defenses. Essentially, the Filipino population had been used as slave labor.

There had been no recourse or any avenue for appeal. The Philippines was commanded by the military rather than a civilian administration. The local officials allowed to remain in

place were often puppets of the Japanese, seeking any crumbs
that the occupiers offered them. In Ormoc and Palo, many of
the local leaders were skilled at appearing loyal to the occupiers
while actually working against them.

"We need to reach that POW camp and free those prisoners
before the Japanese get desperate," Steele said. "They won't stop
short of murder if it means not having to release those men.
They'll do anything to cover their tracks now that MacArthur
has made it known that he considers mistreatment of POWs a
war crime."

"In that case, we have no time to lose," Father Francisco
replied.

CHAPTER TWELVE

Now that Patrol Easy was reunited with Father Francisco and his tough band of guerrillas, all of whom hated the Japanese fervently, they began to move through the jungle.

The ad hoc task force was not without some tensions. First and foremost was the language barrier. The guerrillas spoke either Spanish or the Filipino dialect known as Tagalog. As usual, Danilo remained cagey about how much English he knew. This left Father Francisco as the only interpreter due to his ability to move seamlessly from one language to the next.

At the same time, this kept Lieutenant Steele dependent on the priest to relay any and all orders to the guerrillas. While the lieutenant was nominally in charge of the operation, it was clear that nothing was going to happen without the priest's cooperation, and the guerrilla force outnumbered Patrol Easy. Deke noticed that Lieutenant Steele was diplomatic enough to confer with the priest rather than issuing direct orders. However, the added step took time.

When push came to shove and the bullets started to fly, there might not be an opportunity for discussion. Who was going to be in charge? Deke hoped they didn't find out the hard way that the lieutenant and the priest had different ideas regarding strategy.

Deke had almost forgotten how impressed he had been with the Filipino guerrillas during their mission behind enemy lines against the massive gun battery on Hill 522. He was reminded of their ability now, watching the dozen guerrillas move silently along the jungle path. They moved with a relaxed gait that challenged the Americans to keep up.

There was no talking, and each man appeared alert to the jungle surroundings, almost as if he were moving entirely on his own even though he was part of the patrol.

The Filipinos wore an odd assortment of clothing that included uniform parts scavenged from the Japanese, along with captured Japanese weapons. Most wore sandals rather than boots, enabling them to move quickly and silently down the trail.

Whenever an offending tree limb hung over the path, one of their long bolo knives flashed, its sharp blade clearing the trail. The guerrillas knew their business, that was for damn sure.

Not for the first time, Deke was glad that the guerrillas were on their side, fighting against a common enemy.

Walking near Deke, Philly expressed the same thought aloud. "I've got to say that I'd rather fight the Japanese than these guys," he said. "Tough bastards, aren't they?"

"I suppose you'd be tough, too, if you'd been living in the jungle for years," Deke replied.

"I wouldn't be tough," Philly admitted. "Hell, I'd be dead!"

Deke chuckled. Philly might be on to something. Once again, it spoke to the guerrillas' innate toughness and determination to oust the Japanese that they had endured so much.

Then again, he understood that it hadn't always been the case that the Americans and Filipino guerrillas had been on the same side. Many years ago, the fathers or grandfathers of these same guerrillas had fought against the American "occupiers" who had taken control of the islands following victory in the Spanish-American War. Some determined Filipinos had wanted autonomy and had been willing to fight for it.

There had been a series of running battles that stretched across two decades in the early part of the century. Several thousand US troops had died—most from disease rather than combat. Interestingly, General Douglas MacArthur had been one of those combatants. However, that conflict had long ago settled into an easy peace, and the people of the Philippines were now considered to be US nationals.

The Japanese had turned out to be far more high-handed in ruling the islands, and no Filipino was ever going to be a Japanese "citizen." They were simply chattel of the Emperor.

Some of the guerrillas' skill had even seemed to rub off on Father Francisco, who easily kept pace with the members of his band. Unlike them, he did not carry a weapon, not even a bolo knife, but he did have a large pack that he had explained was filled with extra food, medical supplies, and even a chalice for celebrating mass.

He had brought the chalice with him when the Japanese occupiers had forced the priest to vacate the church at Palo, fleeing for his life into the forest. Since then, he had provided leadership to the guerrillas—and kept them in touch with their spiritual side as well.

Deke learned that the Filipinos had even given Father Francisco a nickname earned because the priest visited the camps where the guerrillas' families lived to tend to basic medical care and to celebrate mass as well. He'd become known as *Padre del Bosque*—Priest of the Forest. Deke reckoned it was an apt name.

The going was not easy due to the oppressive heat and

humidity that clung to everything. Here in the Pacific, it was constantly like the most oppressive late-summer day back home.

Deke wiped the sweat from his brow with the back of his hand and took a deep breath, but he couldn't seem to get any real air. He couldn't help but find himself longing for the clear skies and crisp air of an autumn mountain morning back home. Here the sun always seemed to burn down through a tropical haze.

The comparison to his memories of home made the present conditions seem only worse. He could see the fatigue in the faces of the other GIs, perspiration dripping from their faces, their hair matted to their foreheads under the lips of their steel helmets that grew heavier with each step. Once again, he was glad that he had abandoned his helmet in favor of a broad-brimmed bush hat.

Moisture draped like a wet blanket over everything, heavy and viscous. The air was so loaded with humidity that it made it hard to breathe. Wherever you were, you were enveloped in that blanket of humidity that seemed to weigh down your motions. When a man walked through it, the humidity clung to him like a giant spiderweb.

Speaking of spiderwebs, there were plenty of those across the trail that the guerrillas on point had to break through. Some looked large enough, and the webbing looked thick enough to capture birds, let alone insects. The presence of the spiderwebs was reassuring, however, meaning that no one—in this case the Japanese—had used the trail since the spiders had busily spun their webs the night before.

The jungle seemed as thick as the air, with tangled under-brush and trees creating a latticework of greenery. The jungle canopy of leaves and branches proved so dense almost no sunlight reached the forest floor, creating ominous shadows. This canopy obscured the sky from view, although from time to time they heard aircraft passing overhead. Once or twice a plane flew so low that he could see it clearly through the trees.

To his surprise, both times he had spotted the unmistakable bright-red Japanese meatball on the underside of the wings. Clearly the enemy was still managing to put a few planes in the air. They still had plenty of fight left in them.

Philly had seen the planes too. "Japs," he muttered as if afraid the pilots could somehow hear him. "You don't suppose they can see us?"

Deke grunted. "If they could, you'd probably be getting some Japanese lead up your tailpipe right about now."

Although they had spoken quietly, the exchange appeared to annoy the nearest guerrilla, who looked back over his shoulder to glare at them with the dark, accusing eyes of a jungle cat.

Deke returned the glare, but not for long. He knew that the guerrilla was just interested in staying alive, which meant moving quietly. The terrain forced Deke to watch where he was going, so he mainly kept his eyes on where he was putting his feet next. The trail cut across a jungle floor that was a tangle of vines, roots, and branches that sometimes blocked their passage. His feet felt clunky in his army boots, and he envied the light-soled shoes and sandals the guerrillas wore.

Around them the jungle was thick with the smells of damp earth, decomposing vegetation, moldering wood, and the musk of hidden forest animals—smells not so different from the deep mountain forests back home, Deke realized.

Father Francisco moved up and down the line, saying a word or two of encouragement to each man, both the guerrillas and the GIs. When he stopped by Lieutenant Steele, the two leaders even exchanged a laugh. The guerrilla gave them another stink eye.

To Deke's surprise, when the priest fell into step beside him, he greeted Deke by name.

"Hola, Deke. I remember you from last time," the priest said, keeping his voice low. "That business back on Hill 522. You are quite the shot."

"I reckon that I get lucky now and then. Like my daddy used to say, you can't hit any of the targets you don't shoot at. In other words, you have to take your chances now and then."

"He sounds like a wise man."

"He wasn't a fool," Deke quickly agreed, surprising himself by expressing a thought aloud that he didn't realize he'd even had. "But my pa sure did have a knack for turning a dollar into dust."

The priest chuckled. "Wealth is not everything in the Lord's eyes," he said.

"Tell that to the bankers when they want their money for the mortgage," Deke muttered. "They ain't much interested in prayers and promises."

For a long time he had held a grudge against his father for losing the family farm by taking out a loan from the bank that he couldn't repay. Slowly he had been changing that view. Pa had just been doing his best, trying to keep the farm going with that loan, and the Depression hadn't helped. Almost everyone in the mountains had suffered hard times.

His appreciation of his father had grown deeper in other ways. Pa had fought in the Great War, and now as a soldier himself, Deke understood that his father may have been broken in some way by that war. He certainly never talked about it. He'd just wanted to be left alone on his farm.

But he had not gotten that chance. The Great Depression had taken a toll of a different kind.

"You know that God says it is easier for a camel to pass through the eye of a needle than it is for a rich man to get into heaven," the priest said.

"That sounds about right," Deke agreed. "There's nothing

so close to a devil on earth as a rich man. Anyhow, you are always asking after everybody else. How have you been, Padre?"

The priest took a long moment to consider Deke's question. "Do you have faith, Private Cole?"

"I never was much of a churchgoer growing up," Deke replied, just as thoughtfully. "But I believe in the Lord above. You need to give the Lord his due. If there's nobody up there, and there's no heaven and no hell, no right and wrong, no Golden Rule, then what's it all for?"

"You still believe that, even with the war?"

"Padre, I believe it even *more* because of the war."

For the first time, the priest nodded and gave Deke a wistful smile. "I must admit that the war has made me doubt my faith at times. The things I have seen . . . the things we have done. I have asked myself, How can God allow that?"

"I'm no expert, Padre, but I'd say God is like the big boss man. He doesn't get his hands dirty much. I think he leaves the right and wrong of it up to us, to make our own choices. You know how when you work for the big boss man, you have to line up with everybody to collect your pay at the end of the week? Just like that, we'll have to answer one way or another on Judgment Day."

The priest nodded. "Thank you, Deacon Cole. I think you have an eye that sees more than targets. You have given me much to consider."

* * *

FOR THE NEXT TWO DAYS, the patrol moved deeper into the interior of Leyte. They could still hear artillery in the distance, one side giving the other a pounding, but the sound grew fainter. The sheer oppressive density of the jungle closed in around them and seemed to swallow up any attempt at conversation, devouring words and sound like a great green anaconda.

On that second afternoon, the sky darkened and the wind picked up, churning the trees overhead. While showers and downpours were a frequent occurrence, the wind indicated that this was a stronger storm. They could hear the gale build force and head for them, howling through the lower depths of the forest. The roar of the approaching wind and thunder was more than a little unnerving. A few heavy droplets began to fall, creating mini explosions as they pummeled the bare soil of the trail.

"Here it comes, boys," Lieutenant Steele said glumly. "Batten down the hatches."

When the wind struck, it was like a bowling ball rolling through a forest of tenpins. Around them, branches cracked and trees fell. It was the worst kind of tropical storm, almost like a tornado. Deke worried that the storm was leaving them blind and deaf, vulnerable to attack, but then realized that the Japanese would not have been faring any better in these conditions.

They had been traveling too light to bother bringing ponchos. The soldiers had no choice but to tuck in their chins and bear it as the rain swept in, plastering their clothing to their bodies, leaving them soaked through. The sheer force of the water drummed on their helmets, rain sluicing off them. The guerrillas didn't fare any better, but they didn't complain.

Forward motion through the storm became impossible. In the blowing wind and rain, it would be too easy to simply lose the track and wander off into the jungle.

Without any hope of shelter, they hunkered down right there on the narrow trail. All around them, leaves and branches danced in the storm's hurricane winds. Off to the right, a tree suddenly gave way and crashed to the jungle floor with such force that it shook the ground. If it had fallen a few feet closer to the trail, the massive trunk might have wiped out half of the patrol.

Through the fresh gap in the canopy, they could see lightning stitch the darkened sky in a blazing quilt. Nearby, a bolt struck with all the sound and fury of an artillery round. Deke and the others hit the ground just in case there was another electrical blast in store for them.

There was nowhere to go, nowhere to run. Or so it seemed.

Up ahead, Danilo was shouting something and pointing. Then he was beckoning them forward.

Deke got to his feet. Although he trusted Danilo implicitly, he couldn't help wondering, *Where the hell does he think he's going?*

Blindly, they followed the Filipino guide, squinting through the rain and even losing sight of him for several seconds at a time. The trail climbed upward, which was disconcerting, considering that each step seemed to carry them infinitesimally closer to the lightning-laced sky. But then Danilo reappeared, motioning them toward a structure that rose out of the forest.

In the flickering light, Deke could see that it was a bunker of some kind, apparently abandoned by the Japanese—or so he hoped. How Danilo had known it was here was anybody's guess, but the man seemed to have a sixth sense when it came to navigating the forest.

This deep into the interior, the Japanese had been unable to use concrete. Instead, the walls were built of rammed earth, stone, and heavy timbers. Deke was sure that like many of the enemy fortifications, it had been built using slave labor. One weak point was the roof, which seemed to be constructed of the same heavy material to defend against shrapnel and mortar bursts, but which leaked water like a rusty bucket.

For whatever reason, the Japanese must have decided to

abandon this position. If nothing else, it would provide some shelter against the storm.

The patrol piled inside. The space was cramped yet able to accommodate everyone, although some of Father Francisco's guerrillas preferred seeking shelter in the forest nearby.

As the soldiers crowded inside, the space immediately felt claustrophobic, and the roof was too low—perhaps it was adequate for Japanese soldiers, but the taller Americans, especially Lieutenant Steele, were barely able to stand up. Still, it was a relief to be out of the thrashing wind and rain.

Flashlights provided some light. A couple of bunks had been built against one wall, and there was a rough table lashed together out of sticks and branches. Otherwise, the interior was rudimentary at best. Deke wrinkled his nose against the smell of musty earth and that fishy odor he had come to associate with the Japanese, although he was half-convinced that smell was only in his imagination.

Deke looked through the firing slits. In a flash of lightning, he got a glimpse of wet leaves and driving rain as the storm continued unabated. However, they were now sheltered from the wind and relatively dry. His opinion of the Japanese bunker suddenly improved considerably.

"Make yourselves at home," Lieutenant Steele said. "We'll wait out the storm here. Good work, Danilo."

Danilo nodded at the mention of his name, but his face remained impassive. As always, it remained a mystery as to just how much English he understood.

"I hope to hell the Nips don't suddenly decide to come back," Philly said. He looked wet as a drowned rat and was starting to shiver. "I'm not sure this place is worth fighting over."

"Nobody has been here in a while," Deke pointed out.

The lieutenant had noticed that Philly was shivering, and he wasn't the only one. Their cotton uniforms did nothing to retain body heat. It was hard to believe, considering that they usually suffered in the heat, but the rain and the sudden drop in temperature brought by the storm had left them all chilled to the bone.

"Everybody, get out of those wet clothes," he said. "Your body heat isn't enough to dry them. You'll only get colder."

The men shed their clothes and hung them from the rafters to drip dry. For simple ease of movement and function, they all went commando in the field rather than deal with an added layer of baggy and soggy boxer shorts. Consequently, the interior of the bunker soon resembled a locker room, and the soldiers were more like young men after the big game than warriors.

Philly looked Deke up and down, then laughed. Deke reddened at first, feeling his temper flare, thinking that Philly was ridiculing the deep scars that raked his torso.

As it turned out, that wasn't what Philly found funny. "You know what, Corn Pone? If the flashlights go out, that lily-white cracker ass of yours will be enough to light this whole place up."

"You're one to talk, Philly. The last full moon wasn't as bright as your backside."

Philly laughed again. The truth was, they all had serious farmer's tans, with hands, necks, and faces burnished to a deep brown by the tropical sun. The rest of their bodies typically remained a pale white. There were only rare occasions when they had shed their shirts to sun themselves on a beach or on a ship. Notably, none of the soldiers had tattoos—that was a tradition for the boys in the navy and marines, usually acquired during a drunken shore leave.

Despite the damp conditions, Deke quickly built a fire—he always had been good at that. The smoke gathered around the rafters, but it was a small price to pay for the warmth of the flames. Naked as jaybirds, the lieutenant included, they gathered around and heated up their rations. Gradually the raging storm

began to subside. Night was coming on, so they posted a guard
and got ready to sleep.

They had escaped the storm. They had dodged the Japanese
who had built this place. However, the men of Patrol Easy might
not have slept so soundly if they'd known that those enemy
soldiers were waiting just around the corner.

CHAPTER THIRTEEN

AT FIRST LIGHT, the soldiers shrugged back into their clothes, which were not entirely dry, but better than the sopping-wet rags they had been. Considering the constant damp and humidity, they would likely be soaked again in no time.

All around them could be heard the constant patter of water droplets shedding from the foliage following last night's rain. Morning mist lingered among the tree trunks. The forest bore the scars of the storm, with a few broken tree limbs scattered around. Nearby, a large tree had split cleanly in two, the new wood bright and running with sap. No doubt the tree had been struck by lightning. They had certainly heard a few lightning bolts strike near their shelter.

Above them, through the canopy of trees, a blue sky shimmered. It was the calm after the storm, the rain having cleansed the air and thinned the forest of weak trees. Deke thought that the day looked promising.

Philly seemed to be the only one compelled to talk and interrupt the silence. "Hey, somebody call room service and order up some breakfast. I'll take some coffee for starters, then some bacon and eggs."

"Pancakes for me," Yoshio said.

Of course there wasn't any pot of fresh coffee, and certainly no pancakes, so they had to settle for a few swigs of canteen water that tasted stale and metallic. Deke sighed. He never had stayed in a fancy hotel, but his mouth watered at the thought of some biscuits and gravy. The closest thing a soldier in the field could get to breakfast was the "Chopped Ham, Egg, and Potato" C-ration. It came in a sixteen-ounce can and was wildly unpopular. Deke munched on a few crackers instead.

Their small task force reunited. A few of the guerrillas had taken their chances sheltering in the forest, none too eager to spend the night in the confines of the abandoned Japanese fortifications. They emerged dripping wet from the forest, but evidently ready to face whatever the day presented. Many of the guerrillas had lived rough like this for weeks, if not months. They were a hardy bunch.

"How did you sleep?" Father Francisco inquired pleasantly, as if they had all just passed the night at a roadside inn rather than in a jungle potentially crawling with enemy troops.

"Just fine, Father," Lieutenant Steele said, looking amused. "The maid even left a mint on the pillow."

The priest shook out his damp cassock, and a centipede the size of a pinkie finger fell out and crawled away. "Look at that little fellow," he said. "I have to say, I would have preferred a mint."

The guerrillas ate a quick breakfast, sharing a loaf of home-baked bread that was only somewhat damp from the rain. Father Francisco said a brief prayer over it first. Religion seemed to thrive in these bitter conditions.

Then the group moved out, Danilo and Deke once more in

the lead. In the wake of the storm, the air among the trees felt more oppressive than ever. They moved through a humid funk.

It was not easy going. The storm made it necessary to constantly stop and clear fallen trees and brush blocking the jungle trail. The guerrillas' bolo knives made quick work of the obstacles, while Deke used his bowie knife to hack at the coils of vines that had fallen across the trail.

Mosquitoes pestered the men, clouds of them so thick that they buzzed constantly in their ears. Spiders hadn't wasted any time weaving new webs across the path, taking advantage of the swarms of insects that had hatched in the wet conditions left by the storm. Out at the front of the column, Deke broke through the webs and tangled with a few spiders that would have given a tarantula a run for its money.

Along with the humidity, the tension of this mission seemed to have grown more palpable. A cloud passed over the morning sun, plunging the path into gloom once again. The day suddenly felt less promising.

"According to the map, we still have a ways to go," Lieutenant Steele said. "The storm cost us a lot of time, and the mess it left isn't helping any."

"At least there haven't been any Japanese through here," muttered Philly, who was following a few feet behind Deke, more than happy to let him clear the way.

"I wouldn't be so sure about that," Deke responded. "The closer that we get to that POW camp, there's bound to be some Japanese around."

Deke had a sixth sense about these things, and his instincts had never let him down before. He knew for a fact that he wouldn't still be here if he hadn't learned to trust those instincts. It was like some sort of internal weather vane that you ignored to your peril.

He wasn't the only one attuned to the surroundings. Up

ahead he saw that Danilo had also adjusted his pace and grown more cautious. Instead of bulling through the debris across the path, Danilo was going under it or around it, moving quietly. Deke followed his lead and did the same.

He could sense that they were being watched, although it seemed impossible that anyone else could be out here in this dense forest or see any distance through it. He raised his rifle and peered through the scope, scanning the trees ahead for any sign of movement.

Except for a few birds flitting through the trees, there was nothing.

Slowly, Deke lowered his rifle. Something about this section of forest they were moving through just didn't feel right.

As they rounded a bend, they came across a small clearing. In the center of the clearing were several small huts made from tree saplings and thatch. Deke counted at least a half-dozen huts— not enough to count as a village, perhaps not even big enough to be a hamlet, but an outpost of some kind.

A thin wisp of smoke curled up from one of the huts, as if from a small cooking fire. Clearly this village had been occupied recently, but no one appeared to greet them. The place was empty as a ghost town.

Deke had a bad feeling about this.

The column came to a halt. Both the lieutenant and the priest crept forward to confer with Deke and Danilo.

Deacon scanned the area for any signs of movement, rifle at the ready.

"This can't be the compound," Steele whispered, nodding at the huts while he kept both hands wrapped around his shotgun. "There's sure as hell no fence around it, for starters. This is something else altogether."

"No, we are not nearly close enough to where the POWs are being held," Father Francisco agreed. "My men who have seen it say that the compound is much larger and well defended."

"Then what is this place?" Philly wondered. "I don't see any Japanese."

"Philly, just who the hell else would be out here?" Deke asked.

"I don't like it," Philly said, pointing at the chimney smoke rising from the hut. If somebody wasn't still in there, then they were nearby. "It's spooky."

"Yoshio, give them a howdy," Steele said. "Let's just see if anybody is around."

Yoshio crept forward cautiously and shouted a greeting in Japanese.

"Ohayou!"

The only response was silence.

They would soon have their answer as to who occupied the huts.

Steele issued his orders. "Deke, you and Philly work your way around the back. I'll cover the front with Father Francisco and his men. Keep your eyes open, everybody. Let's figure out just what the hell is going on here."

The team split up, moving silently through the jungle toward their assigned positions. Deke and Philly circled the huts cautiously, their rifles at the ready. The damp ground enabled them to move silently.

Deke felt that, just maybe, they were going to get lucky for once and get the drop on whoever was in these huts. It would be even luckier, he supposed, if whoever was here had simply fled.

As they moved around to the rear, the rest of the group slowly advanced into the village itself.

The silence was broken when a shot was fired from the hut that had the smoke trailing out of it. Apparently it had been occupied, after all. One of the guerrillas went down.

In that moment Deke realized it was a trap.

"Get down," he shouted, shoving at Philly's shoulder.

No sooner had they hit the ground than rifle fire began pouring from the trees beyond the clearing. Bullets ripped the air overhead.

Deke gritted his teeth and took a deep breath, feeling a rush of adrenaline course through his veins. He didn't feel any fear, but only an eagerness for action. He raised his rifle and started firing at the edge of the forest, where the enemy was hidden.

Philly followed his lead, firing back at the enemy. The firefight was intense, with bullets whizzing past them and clipping the leaves and branches at the edges of the jungle.

Deke could feel the sweat pouring down his face, his heart racing. He knew that his life was on the line, that he was exposed out here in the clearing, but he also knew that he had a job to do. He kept firing, although none of the enemy had shown themselves. He did hear a few of the unseen enemy shouting at one another in voices that were distinctly Japanese.

Fortunately there were no machine guns in the mix, or they would have all been goners, caught as they were in the open. The intense rifle fire was punishing enough. The crackle of rifles on both sides punctuated the air.

The enemy had known they were coming and had been ready for them. Perhaps the Japanese had heard the patrol hacking its way up the trail, or maybe they had even glimpsed the lights and activity in the abandoned bunkers the night before. In any case, the trap had been set, and they had waited for the Americans to blunder right into it.

Desperately, Deke looked around for a target. He couldn't see any of the enemy, so the best that he could do was fire at the muzzle flashes visible in the shadows. He fired, once, twice, three times, until there were no more shots from that section of the forest. More shots came from the hut, but Rodeo tossed in a grenade, and that was that.

Meanwhile, the Filipinos weren't about to stay pinned down. They made a dash for the forest, closing the distance to the trees in a mad sprint, bolo knives flashing in their hands. It was clear that the guerrillas planned to finish this fight up close and personal. Deke shuddered at the thought.

Directly to his right, he heard a wet chunk, a scream, and then silence. The guerrillas swarmed among the trees, seeking out and ending the enemy one by one. The fight was over in minutes. As the shooting died out, Deke and the others straightened up and looked around wearily, all of them exhausted as they started coming down from the sudden rush of adrenaline and coated in sweat.

One of the enemy soldiers had managed to stagger back into the clearing before he collapsed and died. Deke was surprised to see that the man was in rough shape. He looked too skinny, and his uniform was practically in tatters. Something about the condition of this soldier, and this remote collection of huts near the abandoned bunkers, just didn't add up. What were these Japanese doing out here, so far removed from the active fighting on Leyte?

"I'll bet that these are deserters," the lieutenant said, seeming to guess Deke's thoughts. "They were probably out here, waiting out the war. We just happened to stumble across them. I guess maybe not all the Japanese are determined to fight until the end."

There wasn't anybody left alive to interrogate.

"Too bad for them," Philly said.

Nonetheless, the short fight had not been without casualties. The rifle firing from the hut had claimed one of the guerrillas. Deke didn't know the man's name, but he was a fellow soldier all

the same. As he watched, the priest knelt and gave the man last
rites, even though he had already passed.

A quick search of the huts seemed to support Lieutenant
Steele's theory that this was a community of deserters. The
Japanese soldiers that they had come across until now seemed to
have adequate food and supplies—certainly they had plenty of
ammunition. Some were even relatively fresh troops, rushed to
the fight from elsewhere in the Japanese war effort. These men,
however, had very little. There was even some evidence that they
were trying to survive off the forest by hunting and eating small
game, although that was a challenging task.

Were these men already convinced of Japan's defeat, or were
they simply without hope? No one would ever know. Of course,
the soldiers had put up a fight against the patrol rather than
simply surrendering or running away, but maybe they'd felt as if
they had no choice. The war had reached the point where
survival was not a foregone conclusion after you surrendered to
the enemy. There was too much anger and loss on both sides for
that.

It was a shame, Deke thought. These men had tried to take
themselves out of the fight but hadn't quite made it out to the
other side. In another month or two, the men who had been
hiding out in this hamlet might have been able to walk out of
the forest and surrender once the fighting had ended and bitter
feelings toward prisoners had eased. Now they would never leave
this place.

Neither would the dead guerrilla. The other Filipinos used
their bolo knives to hack a shallow grave among the jungle roots.
Never mind the fact that those roots would soon grow back and
envelop his remains. He and the dead Japanese would remain
here until Judgment Day. Of course, no energy was wasted
burying the enemy dead.

The only consolation was that this place remained peaceful

and quiet when there wasn't a skirmish being fought. Already an orchestra of insect and bird noises was building. A tropical breeze stirred the tree fronds overhead.

Deke recognized the man but did not know his name. There wasn't even so much as a blanket that the man could be wrapped in. Instead, his arms were arranged neatly at his sides, and his hat was used to cover his face. His comrades looked glum but evidently had come to accept that this was the price of freedom that must be paid on occasion.

Father Francisco said a few prayers, and the grave was filled in; then a rough cross was lashed together out of two sticks and stuck into the ground.

"Let's move out," Lieutenant Steele said once the man was buried. He picked up his shotgun, which had been leaning against a stump. "I want to get as close to that POW camp as we can before nightfall."

CHAPTER FOURTEEN

DEKE LED the way as the patrol moved fast down the trail, making up for lost time. Danilo kept pace beside him, his eyes alert for any sign of the enemy. Philly tagged along in their wake, hurrying to keep up.

A few miles beyond the spot where the fight had taken place among the huts, the jungle path emptied onto a dirt road in the way that a creek merges with a larger stream. As the road gradually widened, they could see where tire tracks had been pressed into the road when it had been muddy after a rain, but the ruts had then dried into ridges, only to be flooded again by last night's rain. Because these ridges hadn't been disturbed, it didn't appear that the road received much traffic. A few weeds growing in the middle of the road also testified to that fact.

"I'd say that with this ride getting wider, we must be getting closer to something," Philly said. "I'll bet it's that POW camp."

"From the looks of this road, there's not a lot of coming and going," Deke replied.

Danilo held up a hand to indicate that they should all be quiet. Although they had been moving silently other than exchanging a few words now and then, the soldiers and guerrillas held their breath. To be detected at this point would mean giving up the element of surprise and losing every advantage.

They moved forward cautiously, weapons at the ready.

The trees thinned out, and they had their first glimpse of the Japanese POW camp.

The soldiers and guerrillas spread out and kept under cover, taking in the POW camp. The sight before them did little to put them at ease. What they saw was a compound that contained several low, squat buildings enclosed by a high fence strung together out of rusting, tangled wire. At one end stood a tall guard tower that presided over the whole affair.

The overall effect was of something crude and sinister, as if it had all been pieced together out of the surrounding forest, either by primitive man or the forgotten survivors of some apocalyptic event, and the jungle couldn't wait to take it back.

"I'll be damned," Philly muttered. "Will you look at that? They've got our boys penned up like monkeys at the zoo."

"You can be damn sure there's a machine gun in that tower," Deke whispered. "From up there, he can hit an ant if it looks at him sideways."

Philly raised his binoculars. "I think I see somebody in that guard tower. At least, I *think* I can see somebody. There's a lot of shade. The question is, Deke, can you pick him off if you have to?"

"Does the sun come up in the morning?"

Deke peered through his rifle scope and immediately felt less confident, despite his bold words. Sure enough, he could make out the barrel of a Nambu machine gun jutting from the tower. The platform at the top of the tower was surrounded by a low railing lashed together out of bamboo, which wouldn't offer the machine gunner much protection. However, it did provide enough cover to make it a difficult shot. Philly was correct that the interior of the platform was deeply shaded, so it was hard to make out any target.

Deke was sure that he could neutralize the machine gunner if he had to, but it might take a few shots. Meanwhile, the Nambu would be hammering away at targets below.

More troubling than the compound itself was what lay behind it. On the northwest side of the compound, beyond the fence, was a patch of open ground with several fresh graves marked by roughly made crosses. It seemed likely that this graveyard was the only way that anyone had managed to escape the confines of the camp.

To make matters worse, a quick count revealed that the contingent of camp guards was twice the size of their own patrol. They would have to watch the camp for a while to determine how many more guards might be off duty in the barracks shacks or even out supervising a work crew.

The way things were shaping up, this wasn't going to be an easy job.

The sight of the prisoners was tantalizing. On the other side of the fence, they could clearly see the men whom they were supposed to rescue. If they could just free those men, they could all go home. And yet the prisoners remained out of reach.

"Look at those poor bastards," muttered Philly, watching the prisoners through the binoculars. "They're nothing but skin and bones. I've seen skid row bums that were dressed better."

Deke didn't have much experience with skid row bums, but he had seen plenty of scarecrows guarding farm fields. To his mind's eye, the scarecrows were exactly what the prisoners resembled, right down to their tattered clothes flapping around sticklike arms and legs. A strong breeze might blow them over. In comparison, the Japanese guards looked beefy and well fed. Whatever food the enemy soldiers had at this point as the noose tightened around the Japanese, they were clearly reserving it for themselves.

Indeed, the handful of POWs they could see appeared thin and ragged. One thing for sure, Deke thought, they would not be able to rely much on the prisoners for help in overthrowing their Japanese guards.

He knew that Lieutenant Steele had been hopeful that the POWs would help to turn the tide once they joined the fight. However, the prisoners that they could see looked too weak to wrestle a kitten, let alone stage an uprising.

It was hard to believe that the decrepit men within the camp had once been proud American soldiers, marines, sailors, and airmen. They were truly shadows of their former selves thanks to their treatment at the hands of the Japanese.

"Goddamn bastards," Philly muttered.

He didn't have to explain—they all knew what he meant. Deke kept looking through the scope, feeling a slow burn of anger building. It was more than clear that the Japanese were starving the American POWs.

With an effort, he took his finger off the trigger. He lowered the rifle. There would be time later to exact a price from the captors. For now, the priority was to liberate the prisoners from this camp.

Fortunately there were no sentries on the road, and the Japanese seemed oblivious that anyone was watching the camp. The last thing that they seemed to fear was an attack from the outside. You couldn't blame them, considering that the camp was far off the beaten track. Between the fence and the machine gunner in the tower, all the Japanese efforts seemed intent on keeping the prisoners contained rather than on defense.

As they watched, a work party approached the camp, making their way across a clearing. The men were stripped down to loin-cloths in the Japanese style, the skin of their arms and shoulders tanned the color of dark leather by the tropical sun. These men were clearly shadows of their old selves, their bones showing in a way that was painful to look at. In fact, it was a wonder that some of them were still on their feet.

Each man had a pole across his shoulders, with a bucket hanging from each end of the pole. The buckets were loaded with rocks, a burden so heavy that many of the men staggered under the weight.

One of the guerrillas had spied previously on the camp and said something to Father Francisco, who relayed to the rest of the patrol that the men were hauling the rocks from a riverbed up the side of a steep jungle hill. According to the guerrilla's observations, the work crew went out at first light and labored until dark. It was believed that the rocks were going to be used to construct either a road or an airstrip.

No matter the intended use, it was backbreaking work.

One by one, under the watchful eye of a Japanese soldier who wielded a rifle with a bayonet, the prisoners in the work detail dumped out the contents of their buckets into a growing pile of rocks.

When one man did stumble, a Japanese sergeant stepped forward and beat him across the back with a cane, the way that a cruel farmer might beat a mule. All the while, the sergeant screamed at him in Japanese in a voice so loud that it carried all the way to the hidden patrol.

Deke couldn't understand a word of it, but Yoshio did.

"He is telling him to get up and work, or he will die," Yoshio interpreted.

It was unlikely that the prisoner understood the words, either, but he certainly understood the meaning. He struggled to get up, unsuccessfully. This seemed to further infuriate the guard, who rained yet more blows down on the prisoner with such force that Deke could hear them clearly as drumbeats.

He put the rifle to his shoulder. Mission be damned, it was time to put an end to that Japanese son of a bitch. He put his sights on the officer's throat.

Philly caught sight of what he was doing and muttered a warning, "Deke, don't do it. You'll get everybody killed, including us."

Deke wasn't sure that he cared as long as he could shoot that guard. The sergeant in his sights was broad shouldered and powerfully built, looking as if he could snap most of the prisoners in half if he wanted to. Deke ached to shoot that guard in the worst way. His finger touched the trigger.

Beside him, he felt Philly go tense and heard him say, "Aw, hell. Here we go."

But Deke held his fire.

He kept his finger on the trigger. Deep down he knew that Philly was right. He'd just have to be patient.

Another one of the prisoners had interceded in the beating, reaching down to help the fallen man. He received several blows from the cane for his trouble and what sounded like curses, but he was able to get the other prisoner back on his feet, and they both managed to reach the rock pile and dump their loads.

The sergeant was still shouting, and the guard with the rifle looked disappointed that he hadn't been able to shoot anybody. Judging by the number of graves in the boneyard, it was likely that he would get another chance sooner rather than later.

Deke shook his head. This was slave labor, pure and simple. Lieutenant Steele would have explained that it went against every rule set by the Geneva Convention. They already knew that the Japanese didn't care about that. The few prisoners taken by American forces were treated decently and not expected to work.

But worse than that, what the Japanese were doing was cruel, even vicious. Deke felt his anger sticking in the back of his throat as if he'd swallowed a bone.

It was hot and humid enough hiding out in the dappled shade offered by the jungle. Deke couldn't even imagine what it must be like to be working in the hot sun.

Reluctantly, he eased his finger off the trigger and lowered the rifle.

"I'll get you yet, you son of a bitch," he muttered.

* * *

THEY SETTLED down to wait and observe. There had been some hope that they could sweep in, quickly defeat the Japanese guards, rescue the prisoners, and be on their way.

No such luck. They could see now that those hopes had been overly optimistic. They were outnumbered by the garrison, and the camp appeared well defended. Also, they had not anticipated that the prisoners would be in such rough shape. Even after they were liberated, the journey back to Ormoc would be slow and difficult for these weakened, malnourished men.

"All right, men. It looks as if we can't just overwhelm the guards," Lieutenant Steele said. "We'll have to figure out another way to crack open this particular nut."

The lieutenant had called a powwow in the shade of a large Malabulak tree; the cotton-like fibers from the seed pods of these trees were used as the filling known as kapok in life jackets. Father Francisco listened intently to what the lieutenant had to say, then relayed the information to the Filipino guerrillas. Their blank faces did not reveal their thoughts once they were informed of the situation. They simply nodded in acceptance.

Deke appreciated the Filipino fighters' commitment to rescuing the prisoners, the bulk of which were Americans. After all, he supposed that these men all had homes and land that they would prefer to fight for, not to mention families to get back to, but here they were standing up to the Japanese in every way. They were damn good men and tough customers.

"I would almost say that at this point we should simply wait for the Japanese to be finished here on Leyte," Father Francisco said. "It can't be that much longer."

Steele shook his head. "That's a nice thought, Padre, but we don't have that much time. The Japanese might not be finished for weeks or months. They seem to have plenty of fight left in them."

"You make a good point, Lieutenant."

"Besides, you saw yourself what kind of treatment the prisoners are getting here. I'm not leaving those men in those conditions one hour longer than necessary. The Japanese have already put enough of them in that boneyard."

"Let me start shooting a few of them, Honcho," Deke urged. "I can even up the odds."

The lieutenant shook his head. "Much as I'd like to turn you loose, Deke, I just can't do that. If the Japanese think they are under attack, there's no telling what they might do to the POWs. I'm willing to bet that they don't plan on leaving any of the prisoners alive."

Deke nodded, as did everyone else. They had already been briefed by Major Flanders back at division HQ about the fate that had befallen POWs at other camps. Vengeful enemy guards had simply executed them rather than see them freed.

"Then what do we do, Honcho?" Philly asked.

"We watch, observe, and figure out a plan." The lieutenant paused. "Hopefully we'll figure something out by tomorrow morning at the latest. The longer that we sit out here in the woods, the better our chances of being detected. If that happens, I don't like to think about what the Japanese might do to the prisoners."

* * *

THEY SAT out the rest of the day, watching and waiting as Lieutenant Steele ordered. The prisoner-of-war camp seemed to be a forgotten outpost, because no one came or went. There were no trucks arriving with supplies, no messengers leaving. The camp commandant almost certainly possessed a radio of some sort to keep in touch with the rest of the Japanese forces, but there was not much activity beyond the work detail and calisthenics for the guards not overseeing the work detail. It was apparent that strict discipline was being maintained even at this remote camp.

Fortunately, the Japanese still didn't seem to have any inkling that there were enemy troops on their doorstep, although it was an open question how long that could last. For the moment, there didn't appear to be any extra activity, no guard posts along the fence, and no patrols came along the jungle road. The machine gunner in the watchtower seemed to be their main defense and lookout. One machine gunner armed with a Nambu was more than adequate.

Later in the day, there was weapons inspection for the garrison. They could see the man who must be the camp commandant, tall for a Japanese, going over his men's weapons and uniforms. He moved with a ramrod stiffness and appeared to have what looked like a bow and quiver slung across his back. This strange choice of weapons caught Deke's eye.

"What the hell?" Deke wondered, watching through his rifle scope. "I know for a fact that the Nips haven't run out of rifles."

The bow and arrows remained a puzzle. However, the commandant clearly took his duties seriously and ran a tight ship, which did not bode well for the mission.

Part of their frustration was that they had no way of communicating with the prisoners inside the compound. The POWs didn't know they were here. Ideally, there would have been some way to let them know that their situation was no longer helpless. The POWs might even have been able to help them from the inside and organize an escape. But for now there didn't seem to be any hope of that.

Once darkness arrived, they crept forward to test the fence up close. They were seeking a weak spot where they could snip through the wire, out of the direct line of sight of the machine gunner in the tower.

Philly reported back, "Honcho, that fence is tighter than a nun's knickers. Nobody is getting past that."

The priest's eyes widened at that metaphor.

"Apologies, Padre," Steele said. He turned back to Philly. "What else have you got? And leave the nuns out of it this time."

"You got it, Honcho. The fence looks rusty from a distance, but they've also got concertina wire all along the base that we'd have to crawl through. Honestly, if we had some sort of vehicle, our best bet would be to ram through the front gate."

"We're out of luck there, unless one of you has a tank in your back pocket that you're not telling me about," Steele said. "All right, we can't risk camping out here much longer. We've got to think of something, and fast."

Like the others, Deke had been busy getting the lay of the land. A plan was already beginning to take shape in Deke's mind, although he didn't like it the least little bit.

CHAPTER FIFTEEN

"No way," Lieutenant Steele said after hearing Deke's plan. "Absolutely not. And just in case I wasn't clear, no way in hell."

"I don't like it any better than you do, Honcho," Deke admitted. "But have you got any other ideas?"

"No, I don't," Steele admitted reluctantly. "It's still just about the worst plan I've ever heard, but goddammit, it's so idiotic that it just might work."

As commander of the guerrillas, Father Francisco had been invited to hear Deke's plan. He didn't like it, either, and made a suggestion of his own.

"We could toss a note over the fence," he said. The look on the priest's face indicated that he was grasping at straws. "Wouldn't that be easier?"

"I don't think so, Padre," Steele said. "What happens when one of the guards picks it up instead of one of the prisoners? The Japanese will know what we're up to and then start executing our people."

"You have a good point. Nonetheless . . ." The priest left the thought unfinished.

"Yeah, nonetheless," Steele agreed.

Deke's plan was simple but outlandish. He had proposed turning up at the prison gate and allowing himself to be captured. It sounded like madness, but it might be their best chance of getting a man on the inside. It seemed unlikely that the emaciated POWs could overpower the guards. However, Deke might be able to organize some sort of breakout, knowing that Patrol Easy and the guerrillas were waiting in the wings.

To that end, a plan was hatched to cut a hole in the perimeter fence just after midnight on the second night.

"I'd rather cut that hole in the fence sooner rather than later," Steele said. "But you're going to need some time to organize the breakout."

"Sounds about right," Deke said, although he was beginning to have his doubts. Did their entire escape plan actually revolve around simply cutting a hole in the fence and leaving the details of getting through that hole up to Deke?

"One thing for sure is that we're not going to leave you in there," Steele said. "One way or another, we'll get you out."

"If the Japanese shoot me outright from the get-go, you won't have to worry about it."

The lieutenant frowned. He didn't have a good response for that.

They talked it over some more. When he presented himself at the gate, it was decided that Deke's cover story would be that he had become separated from his patrol and had been wandering in the jungle for three days. Desperate and starving in the harsh forest environment, he had been willing to give himself up.

There were a couple of flaws in Deke's plan. The first—and it was a big one—was that the Japanese wouldn't believe him and would shoot him outright. The second flaw was that he might be kept separate from the other prisoners and not have a chance to communicate with them. Finally, it was possible that the appearance of a soldier at their gate would alert the Japanese that American troops were in the vicinity. They might double the guard in preparation for an attack, thus making escape harder.

"There are more holes in this plan than I've got in my socks," Lieutenant Steele said unhappily. He glared at Deke. "But if you're willing to give it a try, then so am I."

"I was afraid you might say that," Deke replied. He handed his rifle and bowie knife to Philly. "Take care of these for me, old buddy. If I don't come back, shoot some Japanese for me."

"You'll come back."

"I sure as hell hope so." Deke attempted a smile to set everyone's fears at ease, but it looked more like a grimace. "Those Japanese aren't going to know what hit them."

The midday sun was blazing down when Deke appeared at the gates of the prison compound.

The arrival of an American soldier at the prison gates caused consternation, to say the least. Deke didn't understand a word of it, but there was a lot of shouting, some of it directed at him. He couldn't understand any of it. He saw plenty of rifles pointed at him, but nobody was shooting—at least not yet.

He had arrived without a weapon and with his arms raised over his head in the universal gesture of surrender. He had to credit the sheer surprise at seeing an unarmed American with keeping him alive.

However, they weren't opening the gates. The Japanese guards kept looking suspiciously at the empty dirt road leading to the gates or at the empty trees in the distance. Maybe they thought that Deke was some sort of Trojan horse. Come to think of it, he was just that, at least in a sense.

Finally, the Japanese came up with an officer who spoke English. He wore round eyeglasses that gave him a studious appearance, like a militant schoolteacher.

"What do you want?" the officer demanded.

"Help me," Deke said, letting it all pour out. "Please. I can't take it out here anymore. I got separated from my unit, and I haven't had anything to eat in days. I want to surrender."

This was the story he had agreed upon with Lieutenant Steele. The Japanese officer looked him up and down skeptically. His gaze took in the scars on one side of Deke's face, and the officer's eyes briefly widened in surprise. It was a universal reaction, Deke thought, whether it came from a Japanese officer or a girl at a USO dance.

Deke certainly looked the part of a GI who had wandered the jungle for days. He carried no rifle or knife; he had no food or canteen. He'd already been plenty dirty, but he had rubbed even more dirt into his face and uniform.

At a gesture from the officer, the gate was opened just wide enough for a couple of soldiers to slip through.

They looked around nervously before hurrying through the gap and then dragging him inside. The gate was immediately shut again.

Before Deke even knew what was happening, his legs were kicked out from under him, and he was dumped on the bare dirt. When he tried to look up, one of the guards clipped him on the jaw with the butt of his rifle, and Deke fell again, his whole world spinning.

He was starting to think that this had been a very bad idea.

"You are a prisoner now," the officer said. He then said something in Japanese to the guards, which Deke surmised to be something like, *Drag him along and make sure he hits every bump on the way.*

Two guards shouldered their rifles and dragged him between them. They were a lot stronger than they looked. If Deke hadn't been a few inches taller than the men, he doubted that his feet would have touched the ground. While dragging him, they somehow managed to get in a few punches as well.

He was taken to what resembled a small, rough-hewn shed with a single door. The door was opened, Deke was thrown inside, and then the door was slammed shut.

There were no windows, so it was like being thrown down a well. The only light filtered through the cracks, so it took his eyes a while to adjust to the darkness. When they did, he found himself staring at four plain walls made of unpainted boards. In fact, the interior of the shed proved to be sweltering. The lack of light did not make it any cooler. The whole place smelled of dust, rot, and despair.

The inside of the door had no knob or latch of any kind. There was a solid floor of thick boards. He couldn't quite stand up all the way before his head hit the pitched roof. The roof was thatched with some sort of reedy material that had the musty smell of moldering straw, but it didn't have any give to it whatso-ever. The thatch did provide a home for a multitude of tropical insects that he could hear scurrying around inches from his face.

The shed hadn't looked all that sturdy from the outside, but Deke quickly determined that it was more than sturdy enough to hold him.

He put his back against the wall and slid down until he reached the floor, noting that his jaw ached from where he'd been hit with the rifle. That guard had whacked him a good one. He was sure that he'd have one helluva bruise.

Now what?

It turned out that he didn't have to wait long, although in the dark interior he had somewhat lost track of time. He was dragged out again, blinking in the blinding sun. The Japanese officer that he had started to nickname *Eyeglasses* in his mind was there with a couple of soldiers who took him firmly by the arms. Also present was a tough-looking noncommissioned officer who promptly punched Deke in the gut, knocking the wind out of him.

The sergeant grunted in satisfaction and said something in Japanese.

The bright sun in his eyes was causing more pain than the blow, but he managed to swivel his head around, doing his best to get a good look at the interior of the prison camp. There were no other prisoners to be seen. They had apparently been ordered to their barracks or were out on work detail, but several Japanese were present. Some stared in amazement at the man who had shown up at their gate; others laughed at the sight of such a pathetic American soldier as Deke was presenting himself to be.

One thing seemed clear, which was that the compound was not on high alert. Deke apparently was not seen as a threat, and his appearance had not set anyone on edge. He wasn't sure if he should be relieved or insulted.

This time around Deke was dragged into a much larger structure. His best guess was that he had been taken to the camp headquarters. This building had windows, at least. A Japanese battle flag on the wall and a framed portrait of what must be the Japanese emperor were the only decorations. The flag with its off-center meatball radiating the rays of the rising sun seemed oddly out of context, considering that he had mainly seen these flags waved as souvenirs by GIs. The sight of it in its natural state felt sinister.

Once again he was dumped unceremoniously on the floor of a large room. When he started to get up, he was shoved back to his knees. Apparently he would only be allowed to kneel.

For a while no one spoke. Deke noticed that the room was presided over by a single desk. Given the rustic surroundings, the desk was imposing and almost baronial, built of dark wood with ornate trim. He supposed that it had been liberated from some old plantation house and brought here as a spoil of war and a symbol of prestige, a statement about who was now the master of this domain.

Accompanying him to the room were the officer who had captured him, along with the stocky noncommissioned officer who had punched him. With a start Deke realized that this might be the same sergeant he had watched beating a prisoner with a cane. There were also a couple of soldiers, bayonets at the ready on the muzzles of their rifles. At one command from Eyeglasses, Deke was sure that the two soldiers would be more than happy to skewer him with those bayonets.

Behind the massive desk sat an officer who watched him with a gaze that resembled that of a cat—seemingly disinterested but predatory all the same. At any moment Deke feared that the man might pounce.

This must be the commandant. He appeared to be in his early forties, with strong shoulders evident even as he sat behind the desk. His hair was close cut and balding in the classic male pattern, making the bony ridges of his skull stand out like the backbone of a mule. With his face of stone, Deke had to admit that the man had an intimidating appearance.

This was the Japanese whom he had seen previously from a distance, armed with a bow and arrow. Glancing around, Deke spotted the bow and arrow in a corner, within easy reach of the man behind the desk. The bow was surprisingly tall, roughly Deke's own height. The wood looked smooth, well rubbed with oil or wax so that it gleamed. He was sure that a bow that size packed a wallop. There was a kind of resting power to it, like an unflexed muscle.

Deke couldn't help but think of the sniper that he had gone up against on Guam. That sniper had favored wearing a Samurai headband.

What was with these Japanese? Did they all figure that they were Samurai?

Deke nodded at the bow. "What do you hunt with that thing?"

Immediately Deke was swatted in the back of the head by the noncommissioned officer. The expression on the man's face was one of complete outrage.

The officer who had taken Deke into custody at the prison gate shouted angrily, "You do not question Colonel Yamagata!"

Deke just rubbed his head while the commandant assessed him. Finally the man said in English, "What are you doing here?"

"I got separated from my unit," Deke said. "Then I came across this place. I figured that it was either surrender or starve."

This response generated a fresh series of blows, again delivered by the sergeant, this time with a length of cane across Deke's shoulders and back.

The commandant asked him again, "What are you doing here?"

"Like I said, I got separated from my unit. I was lost until I came across your Ritz-Carlton here in the jungle."

Again, the cane came down. The commandant repeated his question. That was when Deke realized that he was being interrogated. Everyone else in the room seemed clear on that. Deke reckoned that he was just slow to catch on.

He was regretting his plan again for what seemed like the umpteenth time.

In any case, he gave the same answer that he had before. This only earned him another beating.

However, the commandant did not repeat the question in the aftermath. He only looked at Deke with a sneer and said, "You must not be much of a soldier if you chose surrender over an honorable death in the jungle."

"The way I figured it, what with how things are going for you Japs here on Leyte, I won't be your guest for very long."

That comment prompted another flurry of whacks from the

bamboo cane. Deke figured that he'd been asking for it that time. Some of the blows fell upon his shoulders, some across his back, and a few drifted to his buttocks and the backs of his legs —maybe that was just so they wouldn't feel left out.

Each strike hurt like hell, but he didn't do more than grimace. He refused to give these Japanese the satisfaction of hearing him cry out in pain.

The beating hurt, but he'd grown up with a stern pa who believed that the most direct route to the loving correction of one's son involved a leather belt with a big brass buckle. The leather strap stung, and the buckle left bruises. These lessons were most often delivered after Pa had consumed some amount of whiskey.

Consequently, Deke was no stranger to a beating. Also, his pa had been a whole hell of a lot stronger than this sergeant beating him now. He never had given his pa the satisfaction of whimpering, and he sure as hell wasn't going to do it now for these Japanese.

By the time he was done, the sergeant was panting from the effort.

The commandant looked on impassively, but Eyeglasses seemed a little uneasy. He appeared to be staring at something in the back of the room, as if trying to avoid watching the proceedings.

The commandant took up a new line of questioning. "What is your name?"

"Private Deacon Cole."

Whack went the cane across his shoulders.

"I will ask you again. What is your name?"

Deke's name didn't change, and neither did the beatings.

The interrogation, such as it was, continued off and on for two hours. As if to prove that it was all some sort of sick game, the whole thing paused long enough for one of the sentries to go out and come back in with a little bowl of rice and some water for Deke. While he ate, the commandant busied himself reading through papers on his desk. The other officer and the sergeant went out on the porch and smoked cigarettes; Deke could smell the tobacco smoke drifting in. They spoke in low voices and laughed, apparently sharing a joke.

Then the sergeant came back in, picked up his cane, and the whole business started all over again.

Considering the amount of energy expended, Deke wasn't sure that the enemy had learned a whole lot that was useful, but he had a personal moment of enlightenment. Looking at the bored-looking commandant behind his desk and then at the Japanese sergeant wielding the cane, Deke decided, *I'm gonna kill these sons of bitches the first chance I get.*

CHAPTER SIXTEEN

WHEN THE SUN started to go down, the Japanese apparently decided that they'd done enough hard work for one day by interrogating their newest prisoner. Taken from the headquarters building, Deke found himself half-dragged and half-carried—he needed it this time.

Instead of being returned to the shed, he was taken to the main prison barracks and tossed within. That much of the plan was working out. If he'd been locked inside the shed again, only to be interrogated yet more the next day, valuable time would have been lost. Also, Deke had to admit that he wasn't sure how much more beating he could take. Mentally he was fine, but he knew that his body had limits.

The barracks were full, the day's work party apparently having returned from their endless task of carrying buckets of rocks through the jungle.

Shakily, Deke got to his feet. He realized that even his teeth felt loose from all the rattling they'd taken.

"Easy, easy," said an airman in a tattered flight suit,

approaching him. "I know from personal experience that those bastards throw quite a welcome party."

"I reckon you wouldn't be wrong about that."

"How did you like the hot box?"

"Do you mean that little shed without the windows? For a minute there I had it confused with a fancy hotel."

"That's the one. Lovely place, right?"

The airman offered Deke a drink of water, and he nodded his appreciation.

"Drink up. We have plenty of water. All you can drink. That stands to reason—we dug the well, after all. It's just food that we don't have enough of."

"The Japanese seem to have plenty to eat."

"I guess they just decided not to share."

More men gathered around. "Where the hell did he come from?" someone asked.

"It's the invasion," another stick-thin soldier said. "Our boys have got to be close. Sometimes we can hear the artillery in the distance."

"Give him some air, fellas," said the soldier in the flight suit, whose voice rang with some authority. The ring around Deke loosened up.

The soldier who had spoken extended a hand toward Deke. "I'm Rex Faraday. Technically I'm Lieutenant Faraday, but the Japanese lump us all together, enlisted with the officers. We did have a captain when I first got here, but he caught a fever. He, uh, you know, didn't make it through. I'm currently the highest-ranking officer here, which puts me in charge of this menagerie."

The speech had served to give Deke the lay of the land, which he appreciated.

Deke shook the proffered hand. There was something about a handshake that was a refreshingly American gesture, even in the heart of a Japanese POW camp. The Japanese preferred to bow, which seemed fussy to Deke compared to an honest handshake.

"Deacon Cole," he said. "I usually go by Deke."

"Pleased to meet you."

Faraday was in his midtwenties, with sandy-blond hair that needed to be cut and several days' worth of light-colored stubble across his square jaw. It wasn't easy keeping to military grooming standards in these prison camp conditions, even for an officer. Faraday had the sort of straightforward good looks that Deke somehow associated with other men that he'd met from the Midwest. If you looked up "American" in the dictionary, you'd see a picture of somebody like Faraday.

The prisoners displayed a hodgepodge of clothing because they typically still wore whatever they'd been wearing when captured. It made it easy to tell which branch of the service each man had hailed from. Unlike the clean clothing issued to their own POWs, the Japanese didn't make that effort.

Faraday still wore his flight suit, though the top part had been left undone and tied around his waist in deference to the heat. He wore a muscle-type T-shirt that was starting to turn a dingy shade of grayish brown. Faraday was still showing some of the muscle that he would have developed in training, indicating that he had not been captive for very long.

"Let's get that shirt off and take a look at the damage."

"Do we have to?"

"Best to clean you up. If you get an infection in this place, it's as good as a death sentence. Besides, you are what passes for entertainment around here."

A semi-clean rag was brought, along with a basin of water and a sliver of soap, apparently a commodity so rare that it was almost treated with reverence. With an almost surprising gentleness, given the rough conditions and the low light levels in the barracks, Faraday wet the rag in soapy water and used it to clean the wounds across Deke's back.

It wasn't so easy to get the shirt off. In places where he had been cut by the cane, the fabric had become embedded in the dried blood. Deke exhaled sharply as the shirt finally peeled away. Faraday whistled. "Those sons of bitches really did a number on you."

"Don't worry, it's nothing I can't take."

Faraday suddenly stopped in his efforts. He had come to the hard ridges of scar tissue that Deke had carried since boyhood. "I don't think you're kidding. Where did you get all these scars?"

"Black bear," he said. "He wasn't near as gentle as that sergeant."

"A bear? Holy hell. No wonder those Japs didn't rattle you." Faraday didn't ask more about the scars from the bear, and Deke didn't elaborate. Faraday wrung out the bloody rag, wet it again, and went back to dabbing at Deke's back. "So what the hell are you doing out here? Has the advance really reached this far?"

"Here's the interesting part," Deke said.

"I'm all ears."

"There's plenty more where I came from," Deke said. "Well, there's enough, anyhow. The thing is, boys, I'm here to help get you out of this hellhole."

Several men were still gathered around, and the reactions on the faces nearby ranged from consternation to disbelief. One man broke down and cackled with laughter as if Deke had just told the funniest joke the man had ever heard.

But Faraday was eyeing Deke intently. In a gesture that was so quick and subtle that Deke wasn't entirely sure he had seen it, Faraday put a finger to his lips. Then he spoke loudly for the benefit of the crowd, "Everyone says that at first, and then we realize that the only way out of this place is by way of the grave-yard—or us finally winning the war."

"I suppose you're right," Deke agreed, just as loudly. "There's probably no way out."

"No, there's not."

Eventually the men crowded around Deke began to lose interest and drifted away as Deke was cleaned up. That was when Faraday took him aside. With him were a couple of other men that he introduced as Cooper and Venezia. They were as different as Mutt and Jeff, with Cooper being tall and broad as an oak, which was impressive given the conditions in which the prisoners lived, and Venezia being a fireplug of a man with dark Italian features.

"Do go on," Faraday said, quietly this time. "You were saying something about escaping from this place?"

"Sounds like you didn't want the people in the cheap seats to hear me the last time," Deke said. "You got a problem with rats in this place?"

"Unfortunately, both the two-legged kind and the four-legged kind," Faraday said. "The four-legged kind aren't bad eating if you can catch them. As for the two-legged variety, there are a few guys who will sell us out for an extra bowl of rice whenever they get wind of anything that the Japanese might be interested in knowing."

"Sounds like a rat problem, all right."

"It's also a matter of self-preservation," Faraday admitted. "If the Japanese get word of any kind of escape plot, because I'm the ranking officer, they'll drag me in to get the same treatment that you just got. Then they'll put me out in the yard and shoot me if they aren't happy with my answers. I might even get a blindfold if I'm lucky."

"All because of the rats."

Faraday shrugged. "You can't really blame them. Nobody starts out as a rat. Some of these guys are so hungry that they're not thinking straight. They've been here a long time. You just need to be aware of the rat problem. But not to worry. There are plenty of guys in here that you can trust. Most of them, as a matter of fact."

Looking around, Deke could see why some men might be desperate. A few were so skeletal that they were painful to look at, their eyes sunk deep into the hollows of their skulls. Others were so weak that they could barely stir from their bunks after their day of labor in the jungle. Deke was fairly certain that for these men, their next resting place was going to be that grave-yard beyond the prison fence.

He knew that he was too stubborn to ever make nice with the Japanese for a bowl of rice, but he could understand what Faraday meant about the hardships of being a POW wearing men down. Yesterday he would have called such men traitors. But he now had an inkling as to how the enemy treated the POWs. The sooner that everyone got out of here, the better.

"All right, here's the deal," Deke whispered. "I'm part of a patrol that was sent here to break everybody out. I let myself be captured so that we could get word to you boys on the inside. Tomorrow night just after midnight, the plan is for them to cut a hole in the fence, and we all skedaddle. We've got a little more than twenty-four hours."

"I don't think it's going to be quite as easy to walk out of here as you make it sound," Faraday pointed out. "Have you seen that guard tower with the machine gun?"

"They're going to cut the hole in the fence on the west side of these barracks. We figure there's just the smallest blind spot, or at least it will be hard for the machine gun to get a clear shot. If they have to, they can take out the guard tower, but they'd like to keep things quiet."

"Why take the chance? You've met Colonel Yamagata. He'll shoot every last one of us if he gets the excuse. He and that toady of his, Sergeant Matsueda. We call him Mr. Suey, but not to his face, believe me. The only one of the bunch that has a bone of decency in him is Lieutenant Osako."

"Eyeglasses?"

"Yeah, that's the one. He can be all right when he's by himself. But he can't go against his commanding officer, of course, and I think he's half-scared of Mr. Suey."

Deke was surprised. "You know all their names?"

"It's best to know your enemy," Faraday said. "Anyhow, why not just wait out the end of the war here on Leyte? It can't be more than a few weeks off."

"Maybe weeks, but maybe months. These Japanese are a tough nut to crack." Deke paused, not sure if he should continue.

Faraday and the others sensed his hesitation. "So what's the rest of the story? It sure seems like there's something that you don't want to tell me."

Deke hadn't been sure how much to tell Faraday, but he decided that the man deserved to know what he and the other POWs were up against. "We were sent here because the Japanese have been killing off their POWs in other camps rather than free them. The orders came right from the top, General MacArthur himself. He wants every last POW camp liberated before the Japanese can do something drastic."

"Killing our guys for no good reason? Bastards."

"Yeah."

"I can one hundred percent see the camp commandant here doing something like that. Let me tell you something about Colonel Yamagata and that bow of his. Every now and then he lines us all up in the prison yard and orders that the gate be opened. If any man wants to make a run for it, they're welcome to do it. They just have to outrun his arrows."

"Son of a bitch. Has anyone ever taken him up on it?"

"Sure, a few guys liked their chances. They didn't make it." A shadow crossed Faraday's face as he said this. "There were a few Filipino prisoners that weren't given a choice—they were told they had to make a run for it. They didn't make it either. I'm telling you, Colonel Yamagata is sadistic. He's a murderous bastard."

"What about you, Faraday? How long have you been in this place?"

"Just a couple of months. That's why I've still got some meat on my bones."

"What happened?"

"My plane got shot down. Only two of us got out. The pilot was sitting right next to me, but he was pinned in his seat. The other guy who got out was captured with me, but he was one of those who tried to make a run for the gate. Yamagata put an arrow through him."

"Holy hell. I'm sorry."

"That's war for you, I guess. There's nothing fair or right about it. The problem is that the Japanese hold all the cards. I'm sick and tired of it."

"All we've got to do is hold out until tomorrow night, and then we get everybody the hell out of here," Deke said.

"Twenty-four hours is like twenty-four years in this place," Faraday said. "The trick will be not to get caught between now and then."

"Shouldn't be a problem if the rats don't talk."

"I'm not that worried about the rats," Faraday said. "We'll keep this plan on a need-to-know basis right up until the last minute. No, I'm more worried about you. You've got that look in your eye."

"What look?" Deke wondered.

"The one that says you despise every Japanese you're looking at. You kind of squint at them like you've got them in the sights of a rifle. That makes them nervous."

"Huh." This was all news to Deke.

"It's no wonder they beat the hell out of you. Do us all a favor. If you want to last twenty-four hours, keep your head down."

For Deke, that wasn't going to be so easy.

CHAPTER SEVENTEEN

THE NEXT MORNING BEFORE DAWN, Deke was roused with the other prisoners to take part in a work crew. He had slept fitfully, to say the least. Being a prisoner of the Japanese was not conducive to a good night's sleep. Hopefully he would not be a prisoner for much longer.

He ached all over, but he did not complain. He just knew that he had to somehow survive this day and make it to midnight, when the escape from the prison compound would be set into motion.

To his surprise, there was no breakfast to speak of aside from more water. Faraday encouraged him to drink his fill. "It's best to have something in your belly, even if it's water."

"I didn't expect fried eggs, hash browns, and scrapple," Deke said. "But I'd settle for a scrap of bread."

"The Nips only feed us once a day," Faraday explained. "Don't expect much—we usually get a broth with just enough vegetables in it to turn the water a little green. A handful of rice now and then."

"Sounds delicious."

"I've seen men fight over it. It's not enough to keep a child alive, let alone a grown man."

It was fair to say that to the average American male who believed that nearly every meal should involve meat and potatoes of some kind, a Japanese diet would have seemed to be lacking even under normal circumstances. Most Japanese ate rice, vegetables, and fish. When they did have meat, it was only a small portion. After a traditional Japanese meal, most Americans would have been left wondering where they could find the nearest hamburger.

The men assembled in the prison yard, lining up for inspection. It was time for the morning head count. Bleary eyed and aching, Deke had no choice but to join them. The mood was not improved by the fact that the stink of the prison latrines clung to the humid morning air.

A couple of men were too weak to report for the roll call. For these men, under these conditions, Deke realized that there was little hope of recovery. There would be no medicine or nourishing food. Their next stop would likely be the boneyard out back. Escape from the prison camp seemed more urgent than ever.

Mr. Suey entered the prisoners' barracks to check on the weakened men, which involved kicking and punching them to ascertain that the men were not fit to work. Deke could hear the sergeant's blows landing from where he stood in the prison yard. He was starting to hate the Japanese sergeant even more, if that was possible.

By the time that the sun was poking through the treetops, the men were marching out of a smaller side gate to begin the day's labor. First, they had to retrieve the yokes with the empty buckets that were being used to haul rocks from the riverbed near the prison camp. A few men also picked up shovels. Deke eased one of the yokes across his shoulders, sucking in his breath at the pain that the touch of the wood prompted in his sore body.

He saw Mr. Suey watching him, a sadistic smile playing across the Japanese sergeant's lips, and tried not to let his own face betray any emotion. He kept Faraday's warning in mind about provoking the Japanese. He reminded himself that he had to get through only one day of this, while many others had been here for what must have felt like an eternity.

The day promised to be yet another hot and muggy one. Already the insects were waking up, adding their singsong racket to the vocalizations of the jungle birds. In contrast, the prisoners and even their guards were mostly silent, except for the shuffle of feet along the muddy trail.

The men made their way down the well-worn jungle path. They walked about a half mile, most of it downhill—which meant they would be moving uphill coming back. Finally, they reached the riverbank. The bank seemed to consist of a tangled mat of tree roots holding the soil in place. It was darker at this lower elevation, where the sun hadn't reached yet. The gurgle of running water threaded through the silence.

The so-called river was more of a stream, barely ten feet across, but the water ran over a bed of stones, each one about the size of a hefty potato. They set to work filling their buckets with the stones, then balancing the load across their shoulders for the trip back up the hill.

There was no talking allowed, so there was only the noise of stones clanging into the empty buckets and then clicking against each other. It was cooler along the stream and still shady, so it was not unpleasant.

The heat of the day promised to build, along with the swarms of insects. So far the only bugs that bothered the men were large, slow-moving mosquitoes. They were so fat with blood that when Deke slapped one, it left a crimson smear on his arm. Other men didn't have the energy to resist and simply let the mosquitoes feed.

According to the Geneva Convention, prisoners of war could not be expected to work on any projects that served the war effort directly. This rule was open to interpretation and had some gray areas. For example, German prisoners of war held in the United States usually labored on farms. In fact, most seemed glad to be out of the fight and enjoyed the work.

The local communities were often welcoming or at least accepting of the German POWs, knowing that they were usually ordinary men caught between a rock and a hard place when their nation went to war. Many of the prisoners were quite young. After the war, more than a few would even opt to stay.

But didn't raising crops and farmwork help the war effort in some way? Maybe that was a gray area, but they certainly would not have been put to work in munitions plants.

The Japanese had no such qualms about where or how Allied POWs were used. Often they were put to work building defenses against an Allied invasion. Their captors seemed to think that the more backbreaking the work was, the better. Hard labor was used as a kind of punishment or even to make sure that the prisoners were left exhausted and, therefore, without any energy to cause trouble.

Deke was no stranger to hard work, so he kept pace toiling alongside the others. The only bright spot in the shade along the river was a colorful tropical bird that flitted through the trees, as if taunting the prisoners with its own freedom.

As they gathered rocks from the riverbed, his back and shoulders felt sore, thanks to the beating that he'd taken at the hands of Mr. Suey. But as he worked and the day warmed up, he felt less stiff and was able to do as much work as anyone.

Deke didn't know why the hell they were hauling rocks. It seemed to be a pointless exercise or perhaps even foolishness on the part of the Japanese. There didn't seem to be any reason to pave a road in the jungle with stones. The stone-covered portion of the road couldn't have stretched more than a hundred feet from the gate—and there were many miles of dirt road to go. With the first big rain, it was likely that the stones would all be covered in mud or washed away.

Back home in the mountains, even the poorest dirt farmer would not have resorted to hauling rocks using a yoke and two buckets over his shoulders. Instead, he would have hitched up his horse or mule, or in the olden days an ox, and then he would've had the animal drag a sledge loaded with the rocks. However, there were no horses, mules, or oxen to be found in this remote corner of the jungle. Instead, they relied upon the prisoners' backs and shoulders. The prisoners had been turned into nothing more than beasts of burden.

The day wore on with only a few short breaks for water. As Faraday had indicated, there was no food given. Deke began to feel lightheaded, and it was no wonder. Hell, it was enough to make him miss C rations.

Then again, he had experienced hunger as a boy, and he knew that the best thing to do, even when you were lightheaded, was simply to push through and keep working. You would either find yourself feeling steady again or you would fall over. In this situation, the prisoners didn't have much choice but to keep working. When he had a chance, he drank more water.

Deke noticed that one of the stick-thin prisoners was really struggling under the load of the stones. He probably should have stayed in his bunk this morning, but he had gone out with the work crew. Now he had drawn the ire of Mr. Suey, who targeted the man with insults and was ready with the cane whenever the man stumbled, shouting what must be curses in Japanese. It was more than Deke could stand to watch.

The third time that the man stumbled, many of the stones

fell from the bucket. When it tipped over, Deke reached down to help the man put the stones back.

This seemed to infuriate Mr. Suey, who was immediately there with his cane, raining blows down on both Deke and the other prisoner.

Deke shrugged them off as if it had been only so much rain and tried to interpose himself between the struggling prisoner and Mr. Suey. The Japanese sergeant's anger heightened to the point where he began kicking Deke in addition to hitting him with the cane. It hurt like hell, especially when Mr. Suey put his boot up Deke's backside, but Deke wasn't going to give that son of a bitch the satisfaction of reacting to the pain.

Deke continued to ignore him and kept piling the rocks back into the bucket as if the sergeant did not even exist.

It was hard to say how things would have ended up. The sergeant was in such a state that he might have beaten them both to death. In fact, things appeared to be moving toward a more abrupt end, because the sergeant's hand reached for the pistol at his belt.

Suddenly there was the sharp bark of a command. The sergeant reined in his blows and glared at Deke. He seemed to have forgotten all about the other prisoner, who hunkered on all fours like a beaten dog, panting with the effort of simply not collapsing.

Deke looked up and realized that he had been saved by Eyeglasses. The Japanese officer was looking at the entire scene with disapproval. The younger man began to berate the sergeant in an angry stream of Japanese. It was clear that Eyeglasses had seen enough and thought that the sergeant was going too far. The sergeant hadn't quite come to attention, sending a not-so-subtle message that he had little respect for the officer. Finally, Eyeglasses turned on his heel and walked off in evident disgust.

Deke looked back at the sergeant, whose angry stare was

now fixed on Deke's face. He clearly blamed Deke for the chewing-out that he had received.

Deke knew better, but he couldn't back down from the sergeant's stare. The sergeant's face had turned red from his exertions in the tropical heat. His dark eyes were like bits of onyx, almost like the eyes of a shark. Deke's own glare was in marked contrast, because his own eyes were gray, more like cut glass, but equally unfathomable.

No words needed to be spoken. The one thing that was clear was that both men truly hated each other. The sergeant's hand drifted toward his pistol again, indicating that perhaps he no longer cared if he drew the ire of his officer if it meant putting the American POW in his place.

Faraday hurried over, keeping his head bowed as if in deference to the sergeant. He breathed a warning to Deke, "What the hell are you doing?"

"I reckon I've had enough of this joker," Deke muttered, not taking his eyes off Mr. Suey's.

"Look around you, man. There's not a whole lot that you can do about this situation. Keep your eye on the prize."

Deke knew that Faraday was right, but it didn't make things any easier. How he wished to get his hands around his rifle and get the Japanese sergeant in his sights.

He was sure that Mr. Suey felt the same way and would have likely shot him or beat him to death if the officer had not intervened. Next time, if Eyeglasses wasn't around to keep the lid on things, there was no telling what the sergeant might do. Deke understood that it was even more urgent than ever for them to escape the camp. Clearly Mr. Suey meant to kill him.

All the prisoners had seen what happened, and so the rest of the afternoon passed tensely. It was as if a brooding storm cloud hovered over them all. The other men had been here longer and had seen just how brutal the Japanese could be. They probably understood better than Deke that Mr. Suey was just biding his time.

Later in the day, the commandant himself appeared to check on the progress of the work. Colonel Yamagata arrived on foot, carrying his bow and quiver slung across his back, which Deke found to be an odd sight. Even more than other men, Deke understood that he had one foot in the past and was more than a little old-fashioned. But even he recognized that it was the twentieth century. There were airplanes and submarines, radio waves, and motion pictures. Yet here was a Japanese officer who armed himself with a bow and arrow. But instead of eccentric, Yamagata managed to appear menacing.

The colonel stopped to confer with Eyeglasses. Judging by the pointing that the commandant did and the earnest nodding from the subordinate officer, it appeared that Yamagata was making a few suggestions.

Meanwhile, the attention of some of the prisoners had been drawn to that brightly colored tropical bird sitting high up in a tree, some distance from where they were working in the streambed. Even a tired prisoner could be momentarily awed by the bird's bright plumage. Its feathers seemed to span all the colors of the rainbow. The bird appeared as a bright point in an otherwise tense and backbreaking day.

Deke didn't know what kind of bird it was, but if he was going to guess, he would say that it was a parrot. The bird even cried out a few times as if to say, *Look at me! Look at me!* A few of the prisoners even dared to pause in their work and lean on their shovels to gaze in wonder at the phenomenal creature.

The commandant apparently saw the bird as a distraction. Consequently, Colonel Yamagata was determined to deny the prisoners even that small pleasure.

He glared at the bird, then took the bow from his back, fitted an arrow to the string, and drew it back to his ear. It was an unfamiliar weapon to Deke, but he was impressed at seeing how deftly the colonel handled the bow. He also guessed that you had to be quite strong to draw a bow like that. The razor-sharp tip of his arrow did not waver as he held his aim steady. Clearly the commandant was very experienced with his weapon.

Deke took a moment to study the colonel. Before, he had only seen him sitting down, or standing from a distance. In his spotless uniform, the colonel had a rather commanding presence. He was well-built and taller than even some of the American prisoners. He was certainly better fed—where the majority of the POWs looked skeletal, Yamagata looked chunky by comparison.

Standing off to one side, the sergeant gazed at Yamagata with something like admiration in his dark, beady eyes. Deke noticed that the corners of Eyeglasses' mouth were turned down in a disapproving look. Like the men, he evidently admired the colorful bird.

Despite Yamagata's apparent skill with the bow and arrow, the bird made a difficult target. It was some distance away and high up in the tree, roughly the size of a large crow. Deke knew for a fact that there were plenty of GIs who couldn't have hit the bird with their rifles, much less a bow and arrow.

Deke figured the bird's chances were good, and that at best the colonel's arrow would just pass nearby and startle the creature. He caught himself holding his breath.

The colonel released the arrow with an audible twang. The arrow sang through the air, straight and true, so fast that it was hardly more than a streak.

The arrow struck the bird with an explosion of bright feathers. The bird dropped through the tree branches and disappeared. There was no doubt that the arrow had found its mark.

Deke had to admit that he was impressed by the colonel's ability. He was also disgusted. What was the point of killing a beautiful bird for no good reason? Deke's rule always had been that you ate what you killed. The colonel turned away, clearly without any intention of retrieving the bird or his arrow. He wore a satisfied smile.

The prisoners, however, were disappointed. It was as if the bird had been a symbol of freedom, the kind of freedom that they were not allowed, and the colonel had snuffed it out as if to deny them hope. The death of the bird had been symbolic in that regard.

Deke thought about the stories he'd heard claiming that the colonel had offered prisoners a chance to escape—or forced them to try—only to shoot them down with his bow. Until that moment, Deke had doubted that the stories were true. He now had no doubt that Colonel Yamagata possessed a wanton cruelty that made Deke hate him all the more.

The colonel returned up the trail, leaving the work crew under the direction of his subordinate officer. Eyeglasses appeared relieved once Yamagata had left—at least, he eased some of the ramrod posture that he had adopted in the colonel's presence. As for the sergeant, Deke did his best to stay out of his way.

It wasn't easy. Although the rest of the day passed quietly enough, it felt like they were all walking on eggshells around the volatile Mr. Suey. Again, he was like a storm waiting to break, and he kept casting venomous side glances at Deke. From time to time Faraday traded looks with Deke and gave him a quick, reassuring nod that was too subtle for their Japanese captors to notice. Both men knew that the hours ahead were crucial to the escape plan.

The incident with the commandant skewering the parrot with an arrow had also been unsettling in a different way. Once or twice Deke could have sworn that he heard the cry of the wounded bird from the trees, as if the arrow hadn't killed the poor creature outright and it was lingering somewhere in the forest shadows. An hour or two passed, and he did not hear the bird cry out again, but only the stillness of the jungle interrupted by the cacophony of insects and the rushing stream.

It was getting near dark when they finally brought in their last load of stones. Deke felt exhausted. He was still sore from the beating yesterday, and the fresh blows he had received today. He knew that as soon as he sat down or stopped moving, his body was going to register every ache. He was so soggy from all the heat that he felt like he could be wrung out like a washcloth. With each step that he took, his feet felt heavy as concrete blocks.

To make matters worse, his rumbling belly reminded him that he had not been fed yet today. Deke almost welcomed the thought of whatever thin soup the Japanese intended to serve up. It was a wonder that the prisoners were able to labor like this, day in and day out, without any real nourishment. No surprise that so many were just withering away to the point where they couldn't leave their bunks.

Deke was looking forward to whatever grub was served up and perhaps a few hours of rest before their escape plan was set in motion. However, that was not to be the case.

As the POWs reentered the prison compound and made their way toward the barracks, Mr. Suey was there to block Deke's path.

Here we go again. This is the last damn thing we need.

Trying to avoid another confrontation, Deke did the smart thing and kept his head down.

It did him no good. The Japanese sergeant shouted something that Deke couldn't understand, other than the angry tone.

But Eyeglasses was there to explain. With a sinking heart, Deke realized that what he had mistaken for humanity in the officer might only have been a difference of opinion about the methods used to discipline prisoners.

"You," he said. "You are going back in isolation. You have a bad attitude that must be corrected."

Nearby, Faraday had overheard. He and Deke exchanged a look. This had not been part of the plan. If Deke returned to the hot box, it might spoil their entire plan. Once again, Deke feared that his stubborn pride had gotten in the way.

Now what? He raised his eyebrows at Faraday but got only a blank stare in return. Apparently the man was at as much of a loss as Deke.

Surrounded by enemy soldiers, Deke had no choice but to allow himself to be herded into the cramped hut where he had first been held. This late in the day, it remained uncomfortably warm in there. The prisoners hadn't nicknamed in the "hot box" for nothing.

There was very little daylight left to seep through the cracks and gaps. The door closed, and he was plunged into almost total darkness.

Deke felt as if he had just been buried alive.

CHAPTER EIGHTEEN

TRAPPED in the dark confines of the hot box, Deke wondered what to do next. He wasn't one to panic or give up easily, but even he had to admit that his situation wasn't good. In just a few hours, he was supposed to be leading the POWs through a gap in the fence. How he was supposed to do that while imprisoned inside the hot box was anybody's guess.

It wasn't just his own fate that concerned him, but the lives of all those other men. Some were so thin and worn out that they clearly didn't have much more time.

However, he was locked up tighter than a nickel in a miser's fist.

For several minutes, he felt a rising panic, as if the walls of the cramped box were closing in on him, creeping closer in the darkness. He knew it was all in his head. He closed his eyes and forced himself to take deep, even breaths, mastering his mind until he felt the wave of panic recede.

When he opened his eyes, nothing had changed. He was still stuck in the hot box.

He reckoned that it was time to do something about it.

In his previous stay inside this place, which he had to remind himself had been only yesterday, he had given it only a cursory inspection. That stay had been relatively brief. With more time on his hands, he now made a more concerted effort to explore his surroundings.

This time he pushed against the walls, scratched at the boards covering the floor, even poked at the dense thatch to see if he could tunnel his way through the roof. Instead of finding a way out, he got a few fleabites and a face full of dust that irritated his already dry eyes. He was testing the limits of the place, hoping to find a weak spot somewhere, but the hot box was sturdier than it looked from the outside.

If he'd had his bowie knife, perhaps he could have levered some of the boards apart. But all that he had were his fingernails. Nevertheless, he stubbornly clawed at the edges of the boards until his fingernails were broken and even bleeding. It was a sign of his desperation that he kept going even as he began to leave bloody fingerprints on the dusty boards.

It was no use. It didn't help that he was damn near blind in the darkness, fumbling around like a mole.

He even tried the door in a last-ditch effort, but it was solid, without any give to it. Inside the cramped space, he couldn't build any momentum for a good run at it.

After what he guessed was an hour of desperate effort, trying everything that came to mind, it was time to face facts.

He wasn't going anywhere.

He realized that he had expended his last bit of energy in the futile effort to escape the hot box. Exhausted, he allowed himself to slump down against the wall and stretch out his legs in front of him, or at least as much as the cramped space allowed, once again feeling every ache and pain from the day.

Not only was he exhausted from the day's labors, but Mr. Suey had given him one hell of a beating.

Some hero you make, he thought, full of disgust for himself.

Deke wasn't used to being without options, so he sat there and brooded in the dark.

The only interruption came when a guard entered with a small bowl of food. Deke thought about rushing the guard, but the Japanese were one step ahead of him. Another guard stood right behind the one with the food, jabbing a rifle with a bayonet in Deke's direction. Any attempt to break out would only get him shot or stabbed. Deke slumped down again.

To his surprise, the officer that he had nicknamed Eyeglasses appeared. The man's actual name was Lieutenant Ryota Osako, a graduate of the elite Imperial Japanese Army Academy. Osako had been far more idealistic until being sent to Leyte to serve at this prison camp—he sometimes wondered if there had been a mix-up in his orders. Day by day, his idealism had been worn down by the dull duty. His goal now was simply to survive. But some ember of humanity still glowed within Osako, the spark of which had brought him here to the hot box.

Also, if he was going to be entirely honest, he hoped that by showing the prisoner some kindness, the man might reveal important information that Osako could then share with Colonel Yamagata, thus currying favor with the camp commandant. He couldn't help but suspect that the man was more than a simple prisoner.

None of these motivations would have mattered to Deke, who saw the Japanese officer as just another obstacle to getting out of this hellhole. Accompanying Lieutenant Osako was a soldier carrying a basin of water and a clean cloth.

Eyeglasses carried a lantern, which he brought close to Deke's face. The officer nodded at the soldier with the basin, who proceeded to wash the worst of the cuts and gouges on his face. Some had crusted over with dirt and dried blood, but the soldier worked to get them clean. Soon, the water in the basin turned pink, then red.

"You must learn not to provoke us," Eyeglasses said, speaking in slow but clear English. He spoke in a low voice, as if afraid that he would be overheard beyond the confines of the hot box. "Do as you are told, and no more harm will come to you."

"You call this harm? This is nothin'."

"We are not monsters," Eyeglasses said. "But prisoners must obey."

"I appreciate the advice," Deke said, surprised at how his voice creaked like a rusty hinge. "But what happens when you ain't around and your buddy the sergeant is in charge?"

Eyeglasses looked away. He didn't seem to have a good answer to that question. "Do as Sergeant Matsueda tells you."

"You must mean Mr. Suey."

The officer shifted uncomfortably. "You know who I mean."

From that response, it was abundantly clear that the commandant and his toady, Sergeant Matsueda, were running this show, even if the commandant's subordinate officer did not always agree with their actions. Deke supposed that providing a few words of warning and some rudimentary medical attention helped to ease this officer's conscience.

The medic set a clean corner of the bandage with something from a bottle and swabbed at Deke's cuts. Deke couldn't tell if it was iodine or sake, but either way, it sure did sting. He took that as a sign that the stuff was doing its job.

Eyeglasses nodded with satisfaction, seemingly glad that they were managing to clean Deke up.

"Tell me, why are you here?" the officer asked. "You do not seem like the sort of man who gets lost easily."

"Have you seen that jungle out there? I took a wrong turn."

The officer frowned, staring at Deke as if expecting him to

say more. Finally, he prompted, "A wrong turn that took you directly to our gate? This seems very curious."

But Deke wasn't interested in giving the Japanese officer additional information—or making him feel any better about himself. In Deke's book, this officer was just as bad as all the rest. "You do know that when this war is over and you've lost, they'll hang you just as high as the others for what has happened at this camp. General MacArthur has promised as much, and he's a man who keeps his word. Don't forget that he said he'd be back to the Philippines, and he meant it."

Eyeglasses glared at Deke, then said something in Japanese to the medic, speaking a few harsh words. The medic gathered up his bowl and bandages, then hurried out. Eyeglasses and the soldier with the bayonet left, leaving Deke to his evening meal.

As Faraday had promised, the meal was disappointing. When it had been delivered, the light from the open door had revealed a bowl that contained nothing more than tepid water with what looked like a few green leaves floating in it. He thought they might be the Japanese equivalent of turnip greens. He'd seen dishwater that looked more appetizing. His first thought was to dump it out, but he realized that to survive this place, and perhaps escape from it, he needed every last bit of energy.

There were no utensils, so Deke was left to lap up the watery broth like a dog and stuff the slimy greens into his mouth using his fingers. He ate quickly to avoid tasting it.

He thought that maybe he could use the bowl as a tool, but two guards returned to collect it, once again waving a bayonet in his face as if Deke were some sort of cornered wild animal.

Maybe they ain't too wrong, he thought.

Eyeglasses was not with them this time. Deke smirked at that. Perhaps the officer had been dissatisfied with Deke's unwillingness to appear thankful to the man for being just slightly less awful than the rest of the bunch.

Having finished what passed for a meal, he leaned back against the wall, willing himself not to fall asleep despite his exhaustion.

Out of sheer habit, he felt around for his rifle, which he was so used to having nearby. The feel of the smooth wood and steel in his hands was always reassuring. The rifle protected him but also gave him power. He reminded himself that he didn't have his rifle with him, which only made him feel more hollow and powerless.

The minutes passed, becoming hours. Without being able to see the sky, the stars, or the moon, he had no way of knowing the time. He hadn't worn a watch upon giving himself up at the prison gates, because the enemy would have seized it.

Patrol Easy and the guerrillas would be cutting through the fence at midnight.

He had pinned his hopes on Faraday to lead the escape.

It was just possible that Faraday would be able to get the other prisoners through the gap, but even if that happened, it was beginning to look like Deke would be left behind.

If that happened, the commandant and Mr. Suey would be none too happy with him, and Eyeglasses wouldn't be able to do a damn thing about it.

* * *

HIDDEN in the forest just beyond the perimeter of the fence, Lieutenant Steele watched the compound through binoculars, using his one good eye. He hadn't seen any unusual activity indicating that the Japanese suspected tonight's escape attempt. There did not appear to be any extra guards on patrol. Just about dark, he had watched two men climb up into the watchtower, and two others climb down.

In other words, it was business as usual.

The minutes leading to midnight crept past, filled with the night noises of the surrounding forest, which included singing insects and the occasional spine-curdling cry of some animal. Was the creature being hunted, or was it the hunter? It was hard to say. From time to time they heard muted laughter from the guard barracks.

Briefly, music drifted from the commandant's house, so low that it was hard to even recognize the tune. Maybe some kind of jazz? The thought of that Japanese bastard enjoying his evening while the prisoners suffered only added to Steele's anger.

He and the others would simply have to bide their time. With nothing else to do and hours on his hands, he thought about that word. *Bide*. Who had come up with that word, and what did it really mean, anyhow? Steele decided that if it meant nervously chewing gum and occasionally leaving his observation post in the brush outside the fence to prowl restlessly in the confines of the clearing, where the raiding party lay hidden, then he was biding, all right.

He looked around at the others, who were also passing the time as best as they could.

He had forbidden lights of any kind, as well as any smoking, lest the smell of tobacco smoke gave them away. The Japanese might not be expecting American raiders, but they were always on alert for attacks from Filipino guerrillas. The slightest clue might give them all away. Each extra hour that they hid here in the forest increased the risk exponentially, which was why the escape had to happen tonight.

So, he bided his time.

He had been reluctant to allow Deke to let himself be captured, fearful of his treatment at the hands of the Japanese, but it had seemed like the only option to get word to the prisoners and organize tonight's escape. In hindsight, he was sure that the plan would either seem brilliant—or completely idiotic, depending on how things turned out.

Deke had been the only one among the men who had been capable of working from the inside out. Philly and Rodeo were good men, but they didn't have the sand or the smarts to pull it off. Yoshio, or any of the guerrillas, for that matter, would likely have been killed outright as traitors. He couldn't go himself, because then there might be no one to lead the operation, dooming it to failure. So in the end, when Deke had presented his plan and volunteered himself, Steele had agreed.

Had it all been a mistake?

To make matters worse, he also was missing out on Deke's skill with a rifle. He would much rather have Deke targeting the watchtower through his scope, ready to take out the machine gunners if necessary. With Deke on the rifle, the machine-gun crew would have been dead the instant their fingers touched a trigger.

Instead, he had given that job to Philly. Philly was a good man, and he would do his best to get the job done if it came to it, but he wasn't half the marksman that Deke was.

He smiled, remembering how Deke had dropped that Japanese officer back on the fight at the ridge leading to Ormoc. The officer had been something of a heroic figure to his own troops, standing tall and waving his sword, directing the attack on the American position. That officer had thought the Americans couldn't shoot accurately from such a distance.

He'd been wrong about that. Deke had lined up his sights on a buttonhole in the officer's tunic and put a bullet right through it. It had been an incredible shot to make in the middle of a battle, with bullets zipping around the sniper's head and the furious cries of the attackers and the defenders ringing in his ears.

If the Japanese had been tough on Deke after he had surrendered, he had no doubt that the farm boy could take it. Deke was like one of those knots that you ran into when trying to split a piece of oak for firewood. As a leader of men, Steele knew well enough that stubbornness was a quality that could work against a man. However, applied in the right circumstances, sheer stubbornness was a gift without equal.

He had no doubts about Deke's ability in leading the prisoners out from the confines of the camp.

However, Steele wasn't aware of a major crack in their plan. In fact, it was more like a canyon than a crack.

What he had not seen as he kept his vigil, because it had grown too dark, was Deke being hurled inside the hot box. As far as he knew, Deke was with the other prisoners, waiting for the midnight hour to arrive so that he could lead them out of the compound.

Had he known the truth, Steele wouldn't have been biding his time.

He would have been praying.

CHAPTER NINETEEN

REX FARADAY HAD WATCHED as Deacon Cole was dragged away and thrown into the hot box.

It didn't bode well.

"That's the end of that," said Cooper, sidling up next to Faraday. "This is one hell of a mess. What are we going to do?"

"To hell if I know yet," Faraday replied truthfully.

Cooper just shook his head and walked away. Faraday kept his eyes outward, thinking through his next course of action. It was easier to know what to do in a plane crash, he thought, because at least you had trained for it. This was new territory.

Faraday was not feeling optimistic. He had seen strong-willed men locked in there for days at a time, only to emerge exhausted and broken. In any case, they didn't have days. The escape plan was set for tonight.

Deke certainly seemed like a tough customer—he hadn't been imprisoned long enough to be worn down. He still possessed strength and spirit. But it wasn't his willpower that was the issue so much as time.

Faraday considered that timeline. The escape was scheduled

for midnight tonight. When the hour for their deliverance arrived, it appeared likely that Deke was still going to be locked up. He was supposed to be their liaison between the POWs and the rescuers. If he was out of the picture, then who was going to lead them to safety?

He had warned Deke to keep his head down, but he had insisted on butting heads with Mr. Suey by standing up for a prisoner who was struggling to carry rocks from the stream.

Faraday couldn't blame him. Deke's actions were understandable, because the Japanese provoked that response in anyone with a sense of justice. The problem was that opposing Mr. Suey was a game that couldn't be won. The enemy held all the cards.

Now Deke was locked in the hot box, and their entire escape plan was in jeopardy.

Through a crack in the wall, Faraday watched the hot box long after the door to the prisoners' barracks had been closed and locked. By then it was starting to get dark, and the prison yard slowly fell into gloom.

He didn't know what he was hoping for, other than some sort of miraculous sign. He saw some activity as their captors brought Deke his evening meal, but then the door to the hot box closed again. Nothing stirred after that.

Having finished with their duties for the day, most of the guards had retired to their barracks. Aside from a pair of guards walking the perimeter each hour, the Japanese remained in their own barracks once the prisoners were locked in for the night. The only lights glowed from the windows of the commandant's house and the garrison barracks. The surrounding forest looked dark as the sea at night.

For the briefest time, he'd had some fleeting hope that they might all get out of this place. No more starvation diet. No more endless labor moving rocks from one pointless place to another.

No more Mr. Suey or Colonel Yamagata terrorizing them with his Samurai bow.

He realized that the idea of freedom had taken root so strongly in the last few hours that the thought of endless days of moving rocks and eating bowls of boiled weeds was almost more than he could take. The carrot had been dangled and taken away again.

Faraday sat back and considered his options. He needed to think this through.

He had a decision to make now that would decide all their fates, and he would have to make it largely on his own. Venezia and Cooper were the only men who knew about the escape plan. They had kept things close to the vest to avoid security leaks, considering that there were men who would rat them out for a single handful of cooked rice. Whatever Faraday decided, he knew that Venezia and Cooper could be counted on to go along with it.

No lights were allowed in the barracks, so they were kept like livestock in a darkened barn. Most had memorized the layout by now so that they could navigate in the dark. There was just enough remaining light to see the men around him. They looked worn out and beaten up. Their clothes were ragged. The air inside the barracks smelled of sweat and funk. Several men suffered from nagging coughs. The stifling heat made it difficult to relax or sleep.

If this wasn't hell, he didn't know what was.

He knew that the first step would be to get out of the barracks. Fortunately, their quarters weren't nearly as solidly built as the hot box. Months before, Cooper had told him how they had managed to find loose boards that could be opened in an emergency, such as a fire. The possibility of escape hadn't been considered. Faraday had yet to see these loose boards for himself, but he had been promised that they were there.

Looking around at his fellow POWs, he weighed their options yet again. He knew that this was their only chance. If he failed, they might all be killed. Faraday knew that his own life would certainly be forfeit, made an example of by that no-good colonel Yamagata. Maybe the commandant would tell him to make a run for it and then put an arrow through him, just like he'd done to Lucky.

But if he didn't try something, it would just be a more prolonged death, unless, as Deke had feared, the Japanese decided that no prisoners would ever be returned.

Faraday felt the weight of the decision that he needed to make weighing heavily on his shoulders. Should he gamble with all their lives or play it safe?

A smile came to his lips at that thought. No man who climbed aboard a bomber had ever played it safe. No man who picked up a rifle and fought for his country had ever played it safe. These were those same men. They were just tired and weak, but they deserved better.

He motioned Cooper and Venezia toward him.

"Listen up," he said. "We're doing this. We're getting out of this camp tonight—or we die trying."

"You can count on us," Cooper said. "In fact, I think I know how we can get started."

Faraday raised an eyebrow quizzically. "Is that so?"

"I told you before that I've got a few tricks up my sleeve. Let me show you what I mean."

Cooper led them to the back wall of the barracks and nudged a board with the battered toe of his combat boot.

Cooper explained that before Faraday's arrival in the camp, unknown to the Japanese, an enterprising prisoner had loosened two boards in the side of the barracks. The opening was just wide enough for a thin man to squeeze through.

Faraday was amazed. He'd heard Cooper mention this escape

route, but seeing was believing. "Has anybody ever tried getting out before?"

"Where would they go? To the USO dance?"

"Well, we've got somewhere to go tonight."

* * *

COLONEL YAMAGATA SAT at his desk, his uniform shirt unbuttoned in a nod to the heat and the fact that it was now dark out, past the official part of his day. He sat drinking sake, his Samurai archer's bow in the corner.

As a matter of fact, he was on his second rice wine, and he was beginning to feel the pleasant, mellowing effects of the strong liquor. He took a puff on his cigarette, the pungent tobacco smoke mingling with the lingering aroma of the modest meal he had just eaten, which had consisted of steamed rice with a little canned fish.

Recently he had been forced to reduce rations for his command, as their supplies were cut off due to the American invasion. Even after the evening meal, he still felt a little hungry. He'd also had to limit himself to four cigarettes a day.

He raised his glass and said to the empty room, "Kanpai!" *Bottoms up!*

Fortunately, he had enough sake to last for months. It was the one commodity that never seemed to be in short supply across the army, perhaps because of its ability to provide liquid courage as needed against overwhelming odds. Some even joked that the army ran on bullets, bombs, and booze.

His desk appeared neat and tidy. The only object seemingly out of place was a single arrow sitting on the surface of the desk. From time to time Yamagata stroked the edge of the razor-like tip with his thumb, admiring the sharpness of the arrowhead.

He knew from experience just how deadly an arrow could be

and longed for the chance to sink the tip into yet another target of flesh and bone. Only another archer would understand how that felt so satisfying on a primal level.

Yamagata shook off that thought for now. He was sure that he would have another chance to use his bow and arrow on more than a straw target soon enough. He leaned back in his chair until it creaked and sipped more rice wine. He had a good reason to be drinking more than usual lately.

Five days ago, he had received more bad news in a letter from home. Official news was largely censored, of course, but a trickle of information still managed to leak out. Unlike the phony government news that crowed about fake victories, the truth behind letters from home that somehow escaped the censors could not be denied.

His brother had written to say that American planes had dropped more bombs on Tokyo, setting off a firestorm in the ancient city of mostly wooden structures, killing thousands. Yamagata's elderly parents and a sister who lived with them had been among the victims, not to mention old friends and childhood neighbors. His brother was a schoolteacher, nimble with words, and his descriptions of the blackened corpses among the ruins had been disturbingly vivid.

He had grieved in his way, getting drunk on sake, ultimately comforted by the thought that his loved ones and old acquaintances had died for the glory of the Emperor.

There was nothing that Yamagata could do about the bombers. They were far beyond his reach. However, he knew that he could make the lives of the American POWs even more miserable. After all, some of them had been pilots or aircrew on the very bombers that had attacked Japan's home islands. He looked forward to making what was left of their lives a living hell. On the day that he had received the letter with that bitter news, he had vowed that one way or another, none of the American prisoners would ever return home.

Smiling at the thought, he turned up the volume on his radio, on which he managed to pick up a distant station in Manila playing ryūkōka, the style of music that was so popular in Japan. The song playing was "Tokyo Koushinkyoku," with sentimental lyrics sung by a sweet-voiced and lovely vocalist named Chiyako Sato, who typically performed while wearing traditional Japanese garb. What was not to like? Yamagata drank in the music much in the same way he was enjoying the sake and sighed deeply.

There was a knock at the door, and Yamagata responded gruffly, "Hai!" He was not happy about being interrupted during his rare downtime at the end of the day, and he didn't bother to disguise his annoyance.

Lieutenant Osako came in with Sergeant Matsueda. He did not much like Osako, whom he saw as something of a busybody. He also sensed that the younger officer did not approve of him, perhaps even saw Yamagata as something of a failure who had been sent to oversee a backwater post, although Osako had always been careful never to challenge the colonel's authority. For Osako, who was young, there was always the hope that he might be transferred elsewhere. For Yamagata, this camp would be his last post.

The colonel did not take his feet off his desk or turn down the radio, forcing Osako to talk over the music. He opened his eyes just enough to see that the lieutenant's neatly buttoned uniform appeared ready for the parade ground, even at this late hour of the day.

"Sir, you wanted to see us?" Osako asked.

"Lieutenant, it was nothing that could not wait until morning." Yamagata had indeed summoned the two men, but his intention had been to meet with them tomorrow. The tone of Yamagata's voice made his irritation clear. "I was going to say that the pace of bringing the stones from the streambed has been too slow. The road will never be paved at this rate. You must have the prisoners increase the pace, starting tomorrow morning."

"Hai!" The young lieutenant came to attention, knowing full well that he had essentially been reprimanded. At the same time, he had no idea how the prisoners could be made to work faster in their weakened state. Some of the men could barely stand. Perhaps he would have them work after dark, using lights?

"That is all," Yamagata said, finally opening his slitted eyes wide enough to give the lieutenant a baleful look. "Matsueda, you stay."

Once the young officer had turned on his heel and left, the colonel offered Matsueda a sake. He felt more comfortable with the sergeant, whose loyalties were clear. Yamagata knew that Matsueda would have followed him anywhere.

They drank for a few minutes in companionable silence, and then Matsueda cleared his throat meaningfully. He was the sort of old-fashioned sergeant who would never speak to an officer of Yamagata's rank unless spoken to first, which was something of a tradition in the Japanese army.

"Is there something on your mind, Matsueda? You may speak freely."

"Sir, I think that the new prisoner is causing trouble."

"I agree." It would be hard to mistake the look of contempt in the prisoner's eyes. Even a sound beating had failed to extinguish it. But the colonel knew well enough that other prisoners had arrived at the camp this way. Yamagata and Matsueda had taken pleasure in breaking them all.

However, this soldier seemed especially tough. All that Yamagata knew about this soldier was his name: *Deacon Cole*. These Americans had such curious names, but they were as empty of meaning to Yamagata as the vacant nest of some paper wasps.

He sensed that the soldier had not been entirely truthful as to how he had turned up at the prison gates.

"If the prisoners are behind in their work, as you warned Lieutenant Osako, then this man may only make the delay worse."

The commandant continued, "What do you suggest?"

"With your permission, I will have him left in the hot box."

"I have a better idea." Yamagata nodded at the bow and quiver of arrows in the corner. He had enjoyed shooting the colorful bird earlier that day, but that had only whetted his appetite for more. "In the morning, we shall assemble the prisoners and offer them the opportunity to escape, if they can outrun my arrow."

The sergeant smiled. The colonel had done this before, and none of the would-be escapees had made it through the gate before being pierced by a yard-long arrow. Then again, some of the so-called escapees had been Filipino slave laborers forced to make a run for it. From Yamagata's point of view, it had been entertaining nonetheless.

"He has a lot of spirit, but he does not seem like a fool. What if he does not want to try his luck?"

"We shall compel this new prisoner to make a run for it."

"How will you do that, sir? He seems very stubborn."

"I will tell him that if he does not run, then I will make someone else do it. Maybe two or three of the weakest ones. This Deacon Cole seems as if he would not let someone else run in his place."

The sergeant nodded knowingly. "That is a good idea, sir."

"In any case, it will be good sport."

Yamagata reached for the bottle of sake and topped off their glasses. The liquid in the bottle seemed to be diminishing rapidly.

They raised their glasses, and Yamagata said, "To the Emperor! *Kanpai!*"

Both men smacked their empty glasses down, grinning.

Yamagata glanced at the bow in the corner, and his gaze lingered with a mix of fondness and anticipation. He was looking forward to the morning.

CHAPTER TWENTY

AT EXACTLY TWO minutes before midnight, Patrol Easy and the
Filipino guerrillas sprang into action. Lieutenant Steele led them
out of their hiding place in the secluded clearing.

"Let's go," he whispered. "It's time to move out. Everybody
knows what to do. Philly? Yoshio?"

"We're on it, Honcho," Philly replied.

"Just remember that this isn't the OK Corral," Steele said.
"Don't shoot unless they shoot first. Got it?"

"Got it."

"All right, you two get into position."

The two snipers headed out. From outside the fence line,
Philly and Yoshio would be covering the guard tower.

Through observation, they had learned that a pair of guards
walked the interior of the fence line once each hour through the
night. The guards were typically half-asleep and probably
returned to their beds soon after completing their circuit. The
guards had just made their rounds and returned to the barracks,
leaving the coast clear.

The guard tower was the weakest link of their plan. The

problem was that if the machine gun in that tower opened fire before the prisoners had escaped through the fence, it would be disastrous. It would be Philly and Yoshio's job to take out the machine gunners if that happened.

By then, of course, the entire enemy garrison would be alerted by the gunfire, but at least the guards in the tower wouldn't be shooting at them.

Steele and Father Francisco had discussed sending Danilo into the tower at the outset of the escape attempt to neutralize the guards there, but they had ultimately decided that doing so was too risky. It would have meant crossing the open ground of the prison yard and climbing the ladder into the tower without alerting the enemy, and then neutralizing them quietly. That was a tall order, even for Danilo.

Instead, the plan was to cut a hole in the fence in the one blind spot in the guard tower's sight line, directly behind the prisoners' barracks. Success would rely on stealth and more than a little good luck.

Again, Steele would have preferred having Deke covering the tower instead of Philly and Yoshio, but his best marksman was currently a prisoner of the Japanese. The lieutenant hoped that wouldn't be the case for long.

That was their plan. Everything felt cobbled together, but there hadn't been time for anything more elaborate. It remained to be seen how it would all hold together. He recalled what General Eisenhower had famously stated about plans: "In preparing for battle I have always found that plans are useless, but planning is indispensable."

So far they really had been lucky. They had spent the better part of a day and a night under the very noses of the Japanese without being detected. That in itself was something of an accomplishment. Then again, it also spoke to the sheer density of the jungle and its ability to provide cover.

Steele had the unsettling thought that it would have been just as possible for an enemy outpost to be hidden nearby and to have gone undetected. Fortunately, there didn't seem to be any signs of one or any need for it. The Japanese were safely ensconced inside the perimeter of their prison camp.

The night favored them with a waning moon, with some high cloud cover. Just a few stars poked through the gauzy fabric of the dark tropical sky. The darkness would provide a good cloak for their actions tonight.

Steele looked toward Father Francisco. The priest and guerrilla leader appeared grim, but seemed to have his band of tough Filipino fighters well in hand. He felt reassured that they were a deadly bunch, armed to the teeth right down to the wicked bolo knives hanging at their belts or strapped across their backs. The guerrillas were veterans of many missions and waited calmly for Father Francisco to give them their orders.

Because Steele couldn't speak *el lenguaje*, he had to rely on the priest to communicate with the guerrillas.

"Are your men ready, Father?" Steele asked.

"We are ready," the priest said. "We have offered up our prayers. This night is now in God's hands."

"Then let's hope God is paying attention. Move out!"

The lieutenant carried a pair of wire cutters in one hand, his shotgun slung over his shoulder. Getting through the fence wouldn't be easy. He didn't want to rely on anyone else to get the job done.

Cautiously, he approached the perimeter fence. Although strung on rough poles made out of trees and sagging in places, the fence was deceptively strong, its patchwork appearance giving it layers that made it even more effective.

To make getting through the fence yet more difficult, the Japanese had set out rolls of barbed wire all along the exterior base of the fence. Weeds and thorny vines had grown up over that barbed wire, which had begun to rust in the damp climate. Still, the barbs were sharp enough, and he didn't relish the thought of being ripped open by the rusty wire. The jungle wasn't the place to get an infected wound or come down with lockjaw.

Steele crept forward and got to work with his clippers. In the darkness, he had to work by touch more than sight. Rodeo was right behind him, his hands wrapped in rags to protect them. As Steele clipped, Rodeo forced the wire and vines back to create a wider path. Crouched over, they were soon shoulder deep in the thick weeds. They could hear scurrying noises as small creatures, probably insects or rodents, got out of their way. From time to time they felt something crawling over them, which was more than a little unsettling in the dark.

"I hope to hell there's no snakes in here," Rodeo whispered.

"If those guards hear us, snakes will be the least of our worries. Now try to keep quiet."

Steele was correct that they had to work with as much stealth as possible. Then again, there was only so much one could do to clip quietly through the rusty wire, but the noise of the nighttime insects did much to cloak their advance through the tangled strands. The prisoner barracks blocked their view of the guard tower, allowing them to work in one of the few blind spots along the fence line.

After several minutes dealing with the twisty rolls of barbed wire and thorny vines, they reached the fence itself. Steele had rolled down his sleeves to protect his arms, but the cloth was now shredded in a couple of places.

The two guards had already made their rounds of the interior perimeter, so Steele quickly cut several strands of the fence, and with Rodeo's help they pulled the wire aside, creating a gap wide enough to pass through.

However, there was no one waiting for them on the other

side. They had expected Deke to be there, ready to lead the prisoners out. Instead, the prison yard was empty.

They heard the sound of muffled laughter, probably from the guard tower, and then a few words of Japanese. The guards were definitely awake and alert. Steele felt his pulse pounding even heavier than it had been.

"Where the hell are they?" Rodeo whispered.

"Give them a minute," he replied. "You know Deke. He'll be here."

Steele glanced at the faintly glowing hands of his watch, which showed him that it was now a few minutes after midnight. The rendezvous was behind schedule, and each minute that they lingered put them in greater danger of being discovered.

It was hard to see more than a few yards into the gloom. Taking a chance, Steele leaned forward and whispered as loudly as he dared, "Deke?"

There was no answer.

* * *

NOT MORE THAN one hundred yards away, Deke remained locked inside the hot box without any hope of escape. He had no way of knowing what time it was, but he knew that the minutes were ticking away, and along with them, any opportunity for the prisoners to break out.

The broken and bleeding nails of his hands were really beginning to ache, but he made one more attempt at finding the edge of a loose board in hopes of working his way free. After a few minutes, he gave up once again—not quite defeated, but certainly frustrated. He was trapped like a rat in a cage.

That was when he heard a sound outside. He listened more closely and made out shuffling footsteps approaching, then the sound of the latch being lifted off the door.

Deke rose, ready to leap for the opening. Bayonets or not, he knew that getting past the guard was his only hope of getting out of the hot box. He would either break free or die trying.

The door opened wider, and Deke crouched, tense as a coiled spring. In the darkness, he could see only a silhouette framed by the open doorway.

"Are you ready to get out of here?" asked a familiar voice in English.

Relief flooding through him, Deke realized it was Faraday. It looked as if he wouldn't have to throw himself against a bayonet after all.

"I'll be damned," Deke said. "You came for me."

"Lucky for us there aren't any guards posted on the hot box. You didn't really expect us to leave you behind, did you?"

"Then let's get the others and get the hell out of this place."

"That's the spirit." Faraday wrinkled his nose. "I almost forgot how much it stinks in here."

"Smells worse than a skunk's asshole," Deke agreed.

Deke exited the hot box. Although the night air was damp and humid, it was still considerably more comfortable than the confines of the hot box, and less stale.

"Where are the others?" Deke asked.

"Follow me."

Faraday hurried along, hunched over and moving quietly. Deke did his best to keep up, although he felt stiff from the beatings and the cramped quarters that he'd been held in. From time to time, he cast a nervous eye in the direction of the guard tower. So far they hadn't been seen or spotted.

Up ahead, Faraday slipped around the corner of the barracks and into the deeper shadows behind it.

The prisoner named Cooper was there, recognizable for his size, and Deke could see the white teeth of his feral smile in the gloom. "Here we go," he said.

Helping him was Venezia, the other POW who helped Faraday run the show. Like magic, first one board and then another were removed, creating a gap in the back wall of the barracks. It was just what Deke had hoped to do in the hot box, but to no avail. Clearly the barracks hadn't been built with the same scrutiny.

One by one, the POWs began to emerge through the gap. As they came out, the men gathered in the shadows. Although they remained utterly silent, there was a palpable air of both fear and excitement hovering around the group.

"What about your snitches?" Deke wondered. He knew that one warning cry would bring the Japanese guards running.

"Cooper had a quiet word with them. There are only a couple of weak links. He made it clear that it would be in their best interest to remember which side they were on. In other words, he promised to break their necks if they made a peep. He can be quite convincing when he wants to be."

Having seen the size of the POW and his Cheshire-cat grin, Deke was sure that Cooper wouldn't hesitate to make good on his threats. "I'll bet."

Soon the barracks were empty, and Faraday darted inside to make sure that no one was being left behind. "That's everybody," he said.

Some of the prisoners were so weak that they had to be supported by the other men, or even practically carried. Deke was surprised when Venezia, despite his short stature, hoisted a man onto his back and hauled him away in a fireman's carry. Deke knew that these weakened men would slow them down, but the idea of leaving them behind was unthinkable.

"Does anybody have a watch?" he asked. "What time is it?"

Faraday searched the crowd. One man had managed to keep his watch hidden from their captors. "Simpson?" he asked.

"Half past midnight," the man whispered back.

"Dammit, we're late," Deke said. "Let's go. Faraday, you know this ground better than I do, so you'd better lead the way."

Faraday nodded and headed out, but not before warning the group, "Try to stay in single file. Whatever you do, keep quiet, or the Japs will kill us all."

It was less than a couple hundred feet from the barracks to the fence line, but it felt like miles. Deke winced each time a man stumbled in the dark. Someone coughed, and Deke heard the laughter and conversation abruptly end in the guard tower. *Dammit all,* he thought.

There was nothing to do but move forward blindly into the dark, following Faraday.

Seconds later, he heard one of the sweetest sounds to grace his ears in days. It was the sound of someone whispering his name in the darkness ahead.

"Deke?"

He surged past Faraday and almost crashed right into Lieutenant Steele.

"It's about time," Honcho said.

"I ran into some trouble."

"Never mind, let's get everybody the hell out of here before the Japanese get wise to us."

This wasn't the time for introductions, so Faraday and Steele simply nodded at one another before Faraday slipped through the gap in the fence.

It was a precarious operation, considering that the sudden quiet from the guard tower seemed to indicate that the Japanese were on alert. Deke realized he was holding his breath.

One by one the POWs slipped through the gap in the wire toward freedom. Of course, this desperate gamble for freedom only increased the immediate peril that the prisoners were in.

There was no doubt that the escape attempt was putting all the POWs in incredible danger. The rules of war would clearly

have put the Japanese in the wrong if they had harmed coopera-
tive prisoners—not that those rules seemed to concern them all
that much. However, the escape attempt changed the equation
entirely. It was perfectly acceptable to shoot prisoners who were
trying to escape.

It was hard to know what fate would have awaited the POWs
as their Japanese captors became more desperate. One thing was
for sure as they went through the fence—to be caught now
would be a death sentence for each and every man.

There were only a handful of men waiting to make it through
the gap when the inevitable happened. One of the weakened
prisoners lost his balance and fell, landing in the tangled thorns
and barbed wire with an audible crash. The man couldn't help
but cry out in pain as the rusty barbs tore his flesh.

From the guard tower, a soldier shouted something unintelligible in Japanese.

"Hurry!" Deke whispered. He was still inside the fence line,
waiting with Faraday for the last man to make it through. Frustrated, Deke grabbed the last man by the back of his trousers
and practically hurled him through the fence.

That was when the machine gun finally opened up. The
tracers from the Nambu lit up the night. The machine gunner
did not have a clear line of fire because of the barracks, which
blocked his view of the hole in the fence, but that didn't stop
him from stitching the forest all around with bursts from the
machine gun.

They could have used a few more minutes for the POWs and
liberators to make their getaway into the forest. But they had
run out of time. The jig was up. All hell had broken loose.

From their position a hundred feet from the gap in the fence,
concealed in the forest beyond the perimeter, Philly and Yoshio
opened fire. They would be able to get off only a shot or two
before they were targeted by the Nambu.

Either they had gotten lucky, or one or the other of the men had finally displayed some real skill as a sniper, because the machine gun momentarily fell silent. The lull in the fire gave the Americans and Filipinos precious seconds to hide themselves deeper in the forest. With the last POW finally through the gap, Deke and Faraday slipped through themselves and ran like hell after the others.

"Go, go!" Steele shouted, the time for quiet having passed. All that mattered now was getting some distance between themselves and the Japanese before the garrison could organize a pursuit.

The soldiers fled up the jungle trail. It was hard going in the dark, with each of the soldiers trying to follow the dim blur of the man in front of him. There were no lights because that would have truly given their position away. Branches and vines bordering the trail slapped at them, blinding them even more. Deke shoved at the undergrowth that seemed to be clawing at them and trying to hold them back.

The machine gun opened back up, filling the night with the dreaded woodpecker-like *tap, tap, tap* of the deadly rhythmic gun. Now that they were clear of the prison compound, the POWs were no longer blocked from sight by the barracks. Tracers and bullets tore at the forest cover, shredding the leaves and branches so that they rained debris on the fleeing soldiers. Fortunately for them, the machine gunner was still shooting over their heads or into the surrounding jungle.

Now came the time for Father Francisco and his guerrillas to play their role. It was part of the strategy that the priest and the lieutenant had agreed upon. As the rest of the column fled, the priest led his men into the forest on both sides of the trail.

When the Japanese came after them, the guerrillas would have a surprise waiting.

"Everybody keep moving," Steele urged the weary POWs. "Move, move!"

His voice from the head of the column helped to provide a beacon for the POWs. Exhausted and weak though they were, they managed to trot down the trail, getting farther from the prison compound with every step.

However, the firing of the machine gun had alerted the rest of the Japanese garrison, who came spilling out of the guard barracks. Some were only half-dressed, but they all carried weapons. Some ran to fire up the generator so that the compound was soon bathed in electric light. A quick search revealed the hole in the fence and the route that the POWs and raiders had taken.

Through the midst of the pandemonium, Colonel Yamagata strode with his bow over one shoulder, making him an instantly recognizable figure.

As he came running from the prison barracks, Lieutenant Osako found the commandant and said excitedly, "Sir, the prisoners are all gone!"

Yamagata was shocked, but he did a good job of hiding his reaction from his men. To those watching, it almost seemed as if he had planned or somehow allowed this escape to take place. "They will not get far," he said. "They have no food, no weapons, and they are very weak."

"Yes, sir."

However, the commandant was curious about one thing. "What about the American soldier who was being held in the hot box? Is he still there?"

"I am sorry to report that he has escaped," Osako replied, fearing that he had forever stained himself in Yamagata's eyes as the bearer of bad news.

Sergeant Matsueda came running up. He ignored Osako and turned his attention on Colonel Yamagata. "Sir, we found the hole in the fence that they escaped through. With your permission, I will pursue them."

Yamagata nodded. The sergeant gathered a handful of trusted men and started down the trail after the fleeing enemy.

They did not get far. Father Francisco and his guerrillas were waiting for them. Several Japanese fell as the Filipinos opened fire.

Sergeant Matsueda did not leap to the ground like the others, but hurled a hand grenade in the direction that the muzzle flashes were coming from. He closed his eyes against the blinding flash, then smiled in satisfaction at the dying screams of more than one of the raiders. Before they could recover, he threw another grenade.

"On your feet, let's go!" he screamed at the men who had dived to the ground. He paused long enough to pull several of them upright, then plunged down the trail. More rifles cracked, but this time the Japanese were ready, and fired back. The forest gloom was soon punctuated by the bright rifle flashes.

Matsueda was surprised to find Colonel Yamagata at his side. The officer had appeared out of nowhere, apparently eager to join the pursuit. The commandant appeared oblivious to the rifle fire being exchanged, ignoring the crackle and zing of bullets in the darkness.

Yamagata drew his bow and fired an arrow at the silhouette of one of the Filipino guerrillas. Pierced by Yamagata's arrow, the guerrilla fell to his knees. A Japanese soldier ran up and finished the man, using his bayonet. Yamagata nodded with satisfaction.

Still, the Japanese were unable to push past the organized guerrilla defense that blocked the jungle trail. The two sides fought a hot and determined skirmish, the stabbing flames of muzzle flashes filling the night.

Yamagata's bow released again, the twang of the bowstring

lost in the sound of gunfire. Another one of the guerrilla's muzzle flashes winked out and went dark.

Still, Yamagata saw that he was losing too many men. The Japanese had walked right into an ambush set by the guerrillas. Although they outnumbered the enemy, their piecemeal attack was being cut to bits. In the dark, it was impossible to see whom they faced.

Yamagata issued orders to end the attack. "We will fall back to the compound," he said. "Most of the prisoners are too weak to get far. We will organize ourselves and pursue them at first light."

"I cannot believe they have all escaped," Matsueda said. "It must have something to do with that new prisoner. It was all part of some plan, and we fell for it."

"Do not trouble yourself, Sergeant. We will catch them tomorrow and put an end to these POWs and raiders. Perhaps it is for the best. If we no longer have prisoners to guard, then we can join those fighting to stop the American advance. We can be soldiers for a change!"

As the Japanese headed back to the prison compound, they were not pursued by the guerrillas, who must have been confident that they had stopped the Japanese. An uneasy quiet returned to the tropical night.

It seemed that the POWs and their liberators had gotten away, at least for now.

CHAPTER TWENTY-ONE

PATROL EASY and their guerrilla allies knew that there was no time to rest. They realized that the Japanese would not be giving up so easily. The enemy would surely regroup and give chase. The attack by the guerrillas had taken them by surprise and stopped the pursuit for now, but for how long?

Lieutenant Steele was well aware that the reprieve was only temporary.

Soon the entire garrison would be giving chase. The enemy would be well rested, better armed, and more numerous in terms of able-bodied fighting men. Steele and his patrol had been focused on liberating the prisoners, but not on fighting a running battle against the enemy. This was all turning out to be far more than they had bargained for.

Then again, what else was new?

"Keep moving, keep moving," the lieutenant urged, going down the slow-moving column. "Speed it up, boys. I've seen my grandma move faster."

Their snail's pace was frustrating. He resisted the urge to give the slower soldiers a shove to move them along. After all, some of them were so weak that they were barely able to keep upright. His heart went out to them, but at the same time, he really needed them to move faster.

The rear-guard action by Father Francisco and his guerrillas had indeed bought them some time, but they were losing precious minutes in the way that money slipped through the fingers of a drunken sailor.

Looking at the condition of the former POWs, it was easy to see why they weren't moving along the jungle trail more rapidly. Most were emaciated to the point where they appeared hollow eyed, almost skeletal. They literally did not have enough meat on their bones to give them the strength to keep walking. These had all been good men, good soldiers.

To see his fellow Americans in this condition simply made Steele feel fresh anger toward the Japanese. How could they have treated the POWs so poorly? He took it as a sign of the overall disdain that the Japanese had for Americans.

Then again, not all the liberated prisoners had been Americans. Along with a couple of Aussies, there were a few Filipino men who had survived the prisoner camp. Most had been low-level local officials or even farmers who had irritated the occupiers in some way and had consequently found themselves imprisoned.

Being an American prisoner was bad enough. The enemy had been extra brutal toward the Filipino prisoners. These men had survived a special kind of hell.

Deke had even witnessed some of that treatment in the camp.

"The Japanese see us as the enemy," Deke explained. "They see these Filipino prisoners as ungrateful or even as traitors, and they treated them accordingly."

Father Francisco had taken these Filipino prisoners under his wing. While he gave them food and water, the truth was that most really craved news of home. What had happened to their families and villages while they had been imprisoned? For most, the news had not been good. However, the priest did his best to ease their minds, possibly doling out a white lie from time to time or simply not telling the full story.

He was sure that he would be forgiven for not telling the whole truth, if it meant giving these men hope.

"Give us weapons," one of the former American prisoners said. "Hell, I'll go at 'em with a sharp stick if I have to."

He was not the only one who had expressed that sentiment. The former prisoners might be worn out and downtrodden, but there was no mistaking the murderous, vengeful gleam in their eyes.

"We haven't got any weapons to give you," Steele said truthfully. "We had to travel too light to bring extra weapons with us. The best weapon right now is just to get down this trail as fast as possible. Each step brings us closer to the cutting edge of the advance, which is the only place where we're really going to be safe."

"I guess the question is, Will we get that far before the Japanese catch us?" Philly wondered. He raised his voice to be heard up and down the column. "Honcho says to get your asses in gear!"

"That's enough, Philly," Steele said sharply. "These men are doing the best they can. Now go help them instead of shouting at them."

Admonished, Philly did as he was told and lent a shoulder to lean on for one of the former prisoners, whose foot was swaddled in a dirty bandage.

The column continued to wind its slow way down the jungle trail. Closer to the prison camp, there had been an actual road through the jungle. But it had narrowed again as they followed the same path that had brought them here; now it would lead them back the way that they had come. The footing grew more rugged as unseen roots and rocks tried to trip them in the dark.

The heat and humidity only compounded the difficulty. There was very little light in the canopy, the glow of the stars not reaching this far, so each man relied on following the form of the man in front of him. In some of the darker places, some men even reached out and held the shoulder of that man or the back of his belt. They all knew that if any of them wandered off the trail, it was unlikely that they would be seen again.

The only sound was the swishing of the leaves that they brushed against as the path narrowed. Once the column had moved through, the vegetation closed in again like a zipper, as if they had never passed through at all.

* * *

WELL BEFORE FIRST LIGHT, Colonel Yamagata had assembled the garrison in the prison yard. Without any actual prisoners, the place had an empty feeling. *They would just have to get used to it*, he thought.

He did not plan on returning with any of the POWs.

The escape would be a good excuse to carry out the plan that he had been considering for some time: total elimination of the POWs.

That was not to say that he wasn't angry about the escape. The fact that his entire contingent of prisoners had vanished into the nearby jungle certainly made him look like a fool.

"The men are ready, sir," Lieutenant Osako reported.

"Sergeant Matsueda and I will lead the column," Yamagata said. "You will bring up the rear of the column. The machine-gun squad will be under your command if it is needed. Is that understood?"

It was clear that Osako was disappointed about being in the rear echelon, but he knew there was no point in protesting. He gave a curt bow and said crisply, "Hai!"

He was leaving behind just a handful of men, mostly cooks and invalids who would not have been able to keep up. As he had indicated to Lieutenant Osako, he had even ordered the machine gun to be brought along. Who knew what they were up against in the forest?

He had no expectation of the raiders circling back to attack the compound. They had come for the prisoners, so now there was nothing here for them.

Sergeant Matsueda waited nearby, his Arisaka rifle slung over one shoulder and a machete in his hand. The sturdy man looked truly formidable.

Yamagata wore a pistol on his belt, but his main weapon was the bow that he carried. At first glance, a bow might seem to be a poor weapon against a rifle or pistol, but Yamagata knew better. He had hunted with a bow since boyhood, bringing down a variety of game.

His head ached a bit from the sake he had imbibed the night before, so he took a deep breath of fresh air, then another, hoping to clear his head. Otherwise, he felt strong and capable, even excited. He had not felt this way in many years, not since he was a boy going hunting in the mountains of Korea. At the time, that vassal nation served as a vast playground for Japanese sportsmen. He had hunted for days at a time in the rugged mountains and loved every minute of it.

There was no doubt that Yamagata had a great deal of experience as a hunter, in many types of terrain.

The bow made a good weapon at the close ranges in the jungle. It was also nearly silent.

There was also the fact that such a primitive weapon created a sense of fear and intimidation. Unlike a man hit by a bullet, a man shot with an arrow did not usually die instantly. Typically he would bleed to death, aware of the pain of an arrow buried inside him. Yamagata knew well enough how it worked, and even he shuddered at the thought.

He nodded at Sergeant Matsueda, who shouted the order to move out. The column marched through the gate.

Already the sun was beginning to rise over the distant ocean, the dawn light filtering through the forest. Mist clung to the tree trunks. The chattering of insects gradually increased with the light and heat.

In Japan, there was the belief that various minor gods or spirits inhabited the natural world, especially forests, mountains, and lakes. These were known as *yōkai*. Yamagata supposed that these foreign lands also had their demi-gods and spirits. Because he believed in the old ways, he said a silent prayer now to the *yōkai* of the forest, asking for success.

They were now on the hunt.

* * *

THE COLUMN MADE up of Patrol Easy, the Filipino guerrillas, and the former POWs had already been moving through the woods for hours when the first gray light of morning arrived. The forest around them was growing slightly brighter as the sun rose on another steamy tropical day.

Lieutenant Steele called for a halt, their first since the daring breakout. Gratefully, many of the men sank to the ground, too exhausted to talk, much less feel any excitement about having escaped from the POW camp.

"Share your rations, fellas," Lieutenant Steele said. "I know we haven't got much, but these boys need it more than we do."

Unfortunately, nobody had thought through how to feed the former prisoners by bringing extra rations on the raid. It had not even been a consideration when Major Flanders had briefed them for this mission. Steele supposed that the best they could do was reach American lines as quickly as possible.

However, it was clear that the lack of food was critical for men who were already on the razor's edge. They had no reserves of energy or extra calories to burn.

It was a rare soldier who wolfed down his C rations with gusto. After all, C rations were designed as a means of survival in the field and would never be confused with a home-cooked meal. However, the former prisoners devoured everything they could, right down to licking the cans clean, even the cans of the dreaded lima beans and ham.

"I hate to say it, but that was delicious," said Faraday, smacking his lips.

Deke laughed. "You must have been pretty damn hungry."

"You saw what the Japs fed us. It could hardly be called food."

"You mean that dishwater with weeds in it? You'd be right about that."

Deke had already introduced Steele and Faraday, the de facto commander and spokesman for the liberated prisoners.

The two officers conferred, with Faraday pushing to let the men rest for an hour.

"We don't have the time," Steele replied. "It will be a massacre if the Japanese catch up to us."

"How long do you think they can keep running without a rest? Some of these men haven't had solid food in months," Faraday countered. "They just ate. Now let them get a little sleep. When they wake up, you'll have soldiers again. That's all they need—some food and sleep. Well, some guns would help. These boys can't wait to get back at the enemy."

Steele conceded the point. The truth was that nobody had

gotten any sleep the night before. Even a short rest would do them all good. "One hour," he said.

Deke didn't need to be told twice. He was exhausted, and his body ached from all the punishment it had taken. He curled himself up into a ball and instantly fell asleep on the bare ground as if it had been a feather bed.

Steele and the rest of Patrol Easy kept an uneasy watch, half-expecting the sounds of pursuit to reach them at any moment. The hour passed all too quickly. But even that short rest, along with the food, had done the men a world of good. Many were still weak from their long ordeal, but at least they now had the attitude of soldiers once again.

However, for two of the former prisoners, escape had come too late. These were the men who, Deke recalled, had been too weak to go out on the work detail. When the orders came to move out, they did not stir. It was soon clear that they would never move again. Their final reserves had been used up in the escape from the prison camp.

"Poor bastards," Deke said.

"At least they died free," Faraday pointed out. "A fella can't ask for much more than that in this world."

* * *

THE COLUMN WAS SOON up and moving. They could have all used more food and more rest, but this was as much as they were going to get for now.

Deke had already reunited with Rodeo and Yoshio. As for Danilo, the man seemed to have disappeared.

"Have you got something for me?" Deke asked, once he had caught up to Philly.

"What, your rifle and knife?"

Deke had given them to Philly for safekeeping before surrendering himself to the Japanese. Being caught with a sniper's rifle wouldn't have done him any favors with the enemy.

"Yeah, my rifle and bowie knife."

"You know what, I traded them to one of the guerrillas for a jug of hooch."

"That's too bad for you," Deke said. "I would've just shot you or cut your head off, but now I reckon I'll have to carve your heart out with a spoon, slow and painful like."

"Relax, Corn Pone." Philly grinned and touched the rifle slung over his shoulder. He carried his own rifle in his hands. "I've got your rifle right here. Your knife too."

"It's about time," Deke said. "Got to admit, I felt kind of naked without Old Betsy."

Philly handed the weapons over. Deke was more than glad to hold the rifle once more. The smooth wood and cold steel were as familiar in his grasp as an old friend—or even a lover. He slipped the knife onto his belt and slid it around to his hip. He felt ready for action once again.

"Are you feeling OK?" Philly asked. "How was being a prisoner?"

"It wasn't great, I can tell you that much. But I was only there a short time. Some of these boys have been guests of the Japanese for months." Deke nodded at the man Philly was helping along the trail. "They weren't shown a whole lot of hospitality."

"No, it sure doesn't look like it," Philly agreed.

As it turned out, Deke had gotten his rifle and knife back none too soon. From the rear of the column, they heard shots being fired. Father Francisco and his guerrillas had once again taken the duty of being the rear guards, so the firing meant that the Japanese had caught up with them.

"Sounds like the fun is about to begin," Deke said, turning toward the sound of the shooting.

"Hey, where are you going?" Philly asked.

"You asked me how I was doing. Well, now, I've been kicked, beaten, and starved. Enough is enough." Deke gave a cold smile. "I reckon it's time for a little payback—with interest."

Deke didn't know it yet, but that payback wasn't going to be nearly as easy as he thought.

CHAPTER TWENTY-TWO

AT THE REAR of the column, Father Francisco and his Filipino fighters already had their hands full holding off the pursuers.

The dense vegetation worked in their favor, forcing the enemy to stay on the path. As a result, the enemy couldn't spread out to bring their full firepower to bear. The dense forest typically made flanking the guerrillas difficult—but as it turned out, not impossible. Meanwhile, the guerrillas' tactics brought the pursuit to a halt in the way that a cork stoppered a bottle.

The guerrillas were familiar with fighting in this way and had staggered themselves so that each man had a clear line of fire, some standing, some kneeling, enabling them to send a lot more lead in the direction of the enemy than they were receiving.

However, it was a mistake to underestimate the Japanese, who were experts in their own way at jungle warfare. While the main body of pursuers engaged the guerrillas on the trail, a handful led by Colonel Yamagata slipped into the forest.

The going was difficult, every step requiring them to force their way through the underbrush. Yamagata used his bow to push aside the brush, but it became tangled in some vines. He managed to pull it free. All around him, his men were having similar difficulties with their rifles. The problem was compounded by the fact that they were trying to move quietly and without being seen from the trail. Fortunately for them, the forest created such a thick screen he could hardly see the man to his right or left, though they were no more than ten feet away.

They managed to position themselves parallel to the trail, close enough to see the guerrillas pouring fire at his own men. Yamagata smiled. The Filipinos were about to get an unpleasant surprise.

He picked out a tunnel in the greenery that he could fire an arrow through. On the other end of the tunnel were a couple of Filipino fighters. They were totally unsuspecting targets. Even under the circumstances, Yamagata felt a little thrill go through him.

He nocked an arrow and released. The enemy fighter went down, his eyes wide with shock, an arrow jutting from the base of his neck.

Yamagata nocked another arrow. He reminded himself not to rush. Instead, he drew the arrow back and held it, feeling the full, coiled strength of the bow shivering like a straining muscle in his hand. Oblivious, the fighter pivoted to reload his rifle, presenting himself square on to Yamagata.

He released, and the arrow flashed through the tunnel of greenery.

The fighter that he had been aiming at remained standing. Yamagata grunted in disappointment, thinking at first that he had missed. Then he saw the fighter stare down at the copious amounts of blood now running through a hole in his torso. Yamagata realized that the arrow had struck with such force that it had gone right through the Filipino. He watched as the man coughed up blood and then sank to his knees.

Yamagata had no more clear targets through the undergrowth. He did not want to waste arrows that would be deflected by the twigs, leaves, and branches. He put down his bow and drew his pistol from the holster on his hip.

To his men hiding in the brush nearby, he gave the order to fire.

Their first volley was devastating, cutting down several of the Filipinos, who were taken by total surprise. His men worked their bolt-action rifles and fired again.

The element of surprise did not last long. After all, the guerrillas were experienced jungle fighters. They managed to hold back the Japanese advancing up the path while also dealing with the fact that they had been flanked.

Bullets tore through the greenery where the Japanese hid. Yamagata threw himself flat. Nearby he heard one or two of his men cry out as they were hit.

From the direction of the trail, he heard a shout as several of the guerrillas launched themselves into the forest, their long bolo knives flashing. It was more than evident how they planned to deal with any Japanese they caught.

Yamagata crawled away, figuring that his men would have to fend for themselves. In the thick brush, he didn't even know where they were—until he heard the scream of a soldier being dealt with by a razor-edged bolo knife.

Out of nowhere, an enemy fighter appeared a few feet away. Yamagata was practically on his belly, so he thought that the man might pass him by. But then the Filipino looked down and caught sight of him. Giving a grunt of surprise, the guerrilla lifted his arm to slash at Yamagata, but the colonel fired his pistol at nearly point-blank range. The bolo knife fell from the enemy fighter's grasp, and his body slumped into the undergrowth.

Yamagata kept crawling until the sounds of the struggle faded and he was confident that he was alone. Slowly, he got back to his feet. He had dragged his bow along with him. He took a moment to reload his pistol, just in case he still had to deal with any more of the guerrilla fighters.

But Yamagata did not circle back and return to his own troops. Instead, he pressed deeper into the forest, following what he hoped was a parallel course to the jungle trail that the American raiders were using as their line of retreat. He knew that his men were in capable hands with Sergeant Matsueda, and even, he reluctantly had to admit, with Lieutenant Osako. Those two would press the pursuit for now.

What Yamagata planned to do was get close enough to the trail to use his bow and arrow to pick off the raiders. He felt empowered by his success just now with the bow, which had been silent and deadly.

Colonel Yamagata was on the hunt, just as he had once done as a boy. Back then, he had pursued deer and wild boar, but the game he hunted now was far more enticing.

* * *

ON THE TRAIL, Father Francisco was busy directing his fighters with one breath and cursing the enemy with the next. He had long since stopped being conflicted about his ire toward the enemy. Of course he was careful not to use the Lord's name in vain, but he stuck with some of the American slang he had picked up. "Sons of bitches!" he shouted toward the jungle. The sight of the priest, dressed in his homespun brown robes, shaking his fist at the enemy and cursing, was equal parts comical and terrifying as he poured the wrath of God upon them.

Some of his men raced into the trees to deal with the soldiers that had flanked them, and he turned his attention to the dead and dying men on the trail.

"Madre de Dios!" Father Francisco cried out, taking in the horrifying sight of a man with an arrow jutting from his neck. It was bad enough to see a man die from a bullet, but seeing a man shot with an arrow was a new experience—one that the priest wished that he could have avoided.

The guerrilla had already gasped his last. The priest crossed himself, then knelt to give the man last rites and absolve him of sin.

"Exaudi nos, Domine sancte," he mumbled in Latin, using his thumb to trace the sign of the cross on the man's forehead. "Pater omnipotens, aeterne Deus." *Hear us, holy Lord, almighty Father, eternal God.* The intonations of the prayer managed to transcend the grisly scenes of combat in the midst of the dark jungle. Caught up in his prayers, the priest took no notice of the bullets cutting the air around him.

The presence of the priest was a comfort to the guerrillas and a motivating factor—the men knew that he would absolve them of sin and ease their way to the afterlife.

No sooner had Father Francisco finished with his duties than an arrow flashed past him, narrowly missing the priest. Out of the corner of his eye, he noticed the white blur of the arrow's fletching.

He raised his fist and shouted, "Sons of bitches!"

There were plenty of bullets tearing through the brush, but it seemed to be the arrows that the men feared the most. Such a brutal weapon had worn away some of their resolve. The guerrilla fighters retreated, slowly giving up ground. Step by step, the Japanese were rolling them back, forcing their way closer to the retreating POWs. If they could get past the hard shell of the guerrillas' rear guard, they could then rip into the soft underbelly of the column.

It was now a running battle along the forest path. For both the pursuers and the pursued, everything was at stake.

* * *

NOW THAT HE was armed again, Deke moved toward the rear of the column with Philly in tow. They both knew that their best hope lay in delaying the enemy that was closing in on them.

"It's a long way from here back to our lines," Philly noted. "We are definitely on our own. Any ideas?"

"Honcho is on the front porch, so we'll mind the back door," Deke said.

He felt eager for some measure of revenge against his captors, however short his "stay" with them had been. He ignored the fact that he was still sore and aching from his brief imprisonment. He couldn't even begin to imagine what it would have been like to be in their clutches for weeks or even months. Now that he had his rifle back, he figured that it was time for some good ol' American whomp-ass.

But the situation he found at the rear of the column quickly disabused him of that notion. He passed a badly wounded Filipino, and then another, both men making their way forward to join the main part of the column. There hadn't been that many guerrilla fighters to begin with—they were outnumbered by the Japanese garrison that was pursuing them, so that each loss of a fighter was felt keenly. The sound of gunfire seemed to be growing louder.

"I don't like the looks of this—or the sound of it, for that matter," Deke said.

"Me neither," Philly agreed.

They soon ran into Father Francisco, who was helping a wounded man up the trail. The priest appeared more unkempt than usual, with bits of leaves and twigs sticking to his cassock, his dark hair mussed. He even looked a bit wild eyed, like a horse that had caught the scent of a mountain lion.

"Padre, what's happening?" Deke asked.

"There are too many of them," he explained simply. "They got into the woods and flanked us. They are even shooting arrows."

"Arrows?" Deke knew all too well who had been firing those arrows.

The warrior-priest waved at the empty trail behind him to indicate that he was the last defender. "I will regroup my men farther up the trail, and we will hold them off as long as we can."

"All right, we'll see if we can buy you some time."

"Here they come," Philly said.

The priest hurried away. Deke had been hoping to set up an ambush of his own, but there was no time for that. No more than one hundred feet away, the leaves seemed to be stirring along the edges of the trail, although there wasn't any wind. Deke looked more closely. To his surprise, the forest itself appeared to be moving toward him. He saw that it was actually a group of Japanese who had camouflaged themselves using branches tied to their arms, tucked into their belts, and sticking from their helmets. They blended almost perfectly into the surrounding jungle, their movement being the only thing that gave them away.

"I'll be damned," he said. He was impressed, although he would have preferred to get Mr. Suey in his sights, rather than this traveling forest.

"You've got to hand it to those Nips," Philly said. "If we weren't expecting them, we'd never have seen them."

But Deke and Philly *had* seen them, which was too bad for the Japanese. "I've got the one on the right. You take the one on the left."

Deke put his rifle to his shoulder and lined up his sights on the nearest approaching enemy soldier. Philly did the same to the soldier sneaking along the left side of the trail. Both men fired within a split second of each other, dropping their targets, which appeared to be nothing more than a pile of twigs and branches once they fell to the floor of the path.

More Japanese returned fire. Bullets chewed up the leaves around Deke and Philly. They were far too exposed. To make matters worse, a burst of machine-gun fire ripped overhead. Both men threw themselves to the ground, knowing that the next burst wouldn't be so high. They had gotten lucky that time, although it was bad news that the Japanese had brought along a Nambu. The GIs and guerrillas had nothing to match it.

It was all too obvious now why Father Francisco and his guerrillas had been forced to retreat.

"We need to get the hell out of here," Deke whispered urgently. "We're in a tight spot."

"You don't need to tell me twice!"

They fired a couple more times, just to make the Japanese keep their own heads down, then leaped up and raced back the way they had come. Now and then they paused long enough to take a couple of potshots to hold up the Japanese advance.

All too soon they reached the rest of the group, bunched up now on the trail ahead. Father Francisco and the remainder of his guerrillas nervously scanned the forest, apparently still shaken by the surprise attack involving arrows. Their fellow members of Patrol Easy—Yoshio and Rodeo—looked haggard.

As for the former POWs, they were the very picture of exhaustion. Someone had given Faraday a pistol, and both Venezia and Cooper had bolo knives. A couple of the other men had picked up sticks to use as clubs. Otherwise, the group of former prisoners was not armed—and there were no weapons to give them.

Steele saw the predicament they were in and took charge.

"Deke, I want you and Philly back here. Pick off as many of the bastards as you can. Padre, you and your men will be the next line of defense."

"They have a machine gun," Philly pointed out.

"Yeah, I heard it. Look, we don't have any choice but to keep going. This might just be a running battle all the way back to our lines."

Deke knew they would never make it that far, not with the shape that the former prisoners were in. There were just too many miles to go. It seemed unfair, he thought grimly, for these men to have made it so far, only to be hunted down, virtually defenseless.

"Here they come again!" Philly warned.

Deke turned to face the Japanese once again. Down the length of the shadowy path, he could sense more than see movement. The enemy was creeping toward them. Deke held his fire, waiting for a good target.

He realized that there seemed to be no other option than the running battle that he dreaded. They could hold back the Japanese for a while, but if the enemy moved into the forest to flank them, the fight might be over all too soon. They simply didn't have enough men or weapons to adequately defend against an attack from multiple directions. Here on the trail, they were sitting ducks.

It was Danilo who saved them. He had appeared at the front of the column and was conferring with Steele. The lieutenant nodded, and Danilo waved at the GIs to follow him.

"This way!" Steele shouted.

CHAPTER TWENTY-THREE

"W HERE THE HELL ARE WE GOING?" Philly demanded, looking back nervously over his shoulder. "We sure can't outrun those Nips. Those little bastards must have wings on their feet."

"Hurry, hurry!" Danilo shouted.

Even while running flat out, Deke mused that Danilo never seemed to know any English until it suited him, and this seemed to be one of those times. Bringing up the rear, Deke paused now and then to take a shot at their pursuers. His heart was pounding from all the running, so it wasn't his most accurate shooting.

It had become his job to delay the enemy as much as possible to buy some time for the others. The Japanese were closing in on them rapidly, so he hoped that Danilo had something good up his sleeve.

Moments later he burst into the clearing with the old Japanese defenses, where they had sheltered the night of the storm during their journey out. Up ahead of him, men were already pouring into the bunker, taking up defensive positions facing the trail where the enemy would emerge from the forest.

Deke grinned. Danilo had done all right. Using the protection of the thick-walled bunker, even a handful of determined defenders could hold off a much larger force. The bunker was surrounded by a large clearing that offered a good field of fire. Crossing that clearing would be suicide—not that this ever seemed to stop the Japanese. Deke found a certain satisfaction in the irony of the Japanese bunker being used against them.

However, not everyone could fit within the bunker. Many of the Filipino fighters hunkered down in foxholes that had been dug around the bunker itself. These were men who preferred taking their chances out in the open over being confined in a bunker.

A few of the former POWs joined them. Those who had the energy to do so were adding whatever they could to the defenses, from logs to rocks. A few sandbags were dragged into new positions. The result could hardly be called a fortress, but it was better than nothing.

Not wasting any more time, Deke slipped inside the bunker. He took note of the armored door that was being left open for now to communicate with the men in the foxholes. The door was built of heavy boards with reinforcing bands of steel, almost like a medieval castle door. The steel was already rusting badly in the tropical conditions, leaving long streaks like dried blood splashed across the wood. The door wouldn't have been much use against heavy weapons, but it would be more than adequate to stop bullets.

For now the bunker would be the center of their defense. The bunker was really more of a rectangular "pillbox" in that it was not buried into a hillside but was freestanding. The Japanese must have built it here for an outpost to guard the jungle trail, but the enemy had abandoned this post in the middle of nowhere.

It had been designed with narrow horizontal firing slits set into all four sides. The slits were really intended for machine guns, but they would work well enough for riflemen as well.

"Padre, you and your men take those two sides," Lieutenant Steele ordered. "My boys will cover the other two sides."

"As you say," Father Francisco said. "Unfortunately, we are running low on ammunition."

"Then better make each shot count."

"I thought that I might pray."

"That might not be a bad idea," Steele agreed.

Although the ceiling was quite low, the bunker was surprisingly spacious even when crowded with so many men. The weakest POWs were immediately put into the two rough bunks. To Deke's nose once again came the vaguely fishy smell that he always seemed to associate with the Japanese. Although the bunker clearly had not been occupied by the enemy for quite some time, the smell still lingered.

Here in the jungle, concrete had not been used in the bunker's construction. Instead, the bunker was built of rammed earth, stone, and even logs cut from the forest. Nonetheless, it seemed sturdy enough to keep any attacker except maybe a tank at bay. Although he felt reassured, there was also the nagging thought that while none of the enemy was getting in, none of the defenders would be getting out as long as they were surrounded by the Japanese. They were trapped like rats in a box. Deke pushed that uncomfortable thought from his mind.

He took up a position alongside Philly. Yoshio and Rodeo covered the other firing slit. Father Francisco and the guerrillas had taken charge of the other firing slits.

"How are we doing for ammo?" the lieutenant asked.

"Getting low," Deke replied. He had used up a surprising number of bullets keeping the enemy at bay on the path.

"Same here," said Yoshio.

Father Francisco had already warned that the guerrillas'

ammo supply was getting low, which wasn't reassuring. It didn't help that the Americans and the Filipinos were largely armed with different weapons—several of the guerrillas still carried Arisaka rifles that had been liberated in one way or another from the Japanese.

The arrangement left the bulk of the former POWs in the foxholes ringing the bunker, nervously awaiting their fate. Faraday and Cooper were armed with pistols, which wouldn't do much good unless the Japanese came extremely close to the American position.

"We've got company," announced Deke, who was peering out at the clearing. He spotted the Japanese swarming down the path, spreading out and taking positions around the bunker.

"Listen up, everybody," Steele announced. "We are getting low on ammo. We need to make each shot count."

"How the hell are we getting out of here, Honcho?" Philly wanted to know. "The Japanese are going to have us surrounded."

"We would've been sitting ducks on that trail," the lieutenant responded. "Now we've got them right where we want them. We can whittle away at them while these men rest, and then once it's dark, we can slip away."

"Sounds good to me, Honcho," Philly said.

"Dammit, Philly, I wasn't asking your opinion. Now act like a sniper and shoot anybody that the enemy sends against us."

Deke decided that the lieutenant was being optimistic for the benefit of those listening. The look in his one good eye told a different story—Lieutenant Steele knew damn well that they were in a tight spot.

The Japanese attack began not with a fusillade of bullets, but with a single arrow. The arrow flashed through the air and arced down into one of the foxholes. A man screamed as the arrow pierced him.

Only then did the shooting begin.

Deke didn't fire blindly. He was waiting for one target in particular—well, make that two. He wanted to put a bullet through Mr. Suey and then through that bastard of a commandant. It was almost like a physical ache, an itch that needed to be scratched. Say what you wanted about war, but sometimes it did get personal.

"If anybody sees that son of a bitch with a bow and arrow, let me know," Deke said, turning and shouting to the others before giving his attention back to the firing slit in front of him.

Deke had to admit that he was impressed all over again by the commandant's archery skills. The bow had a longer range than Deke might have expected. Yamagata had managed to shoot one of the guerrillas without exposing himself. He was beginning to wonder if maybe he had underestimated the Japanese archer. On the face of it, a bow and arrow seemed to be a useless weapon against rifles and bullets, but there was just something so terrifying about it. Deke couldn't help but wonder if this was how his ancestors had felt, fighting the Indians while holed up in a wooden stockade with a long rifle.

As if to punctuate his thoughts, an arrow came right through one of the firing slits and buried itself in Rodeo's upper arm, the one that the butt of his rifle had been tucked into. Deke rushed over to Rodeo and pushed him to one side, hoping for a glimpse of Yamagata.

He spotted the archer at the far end of the clearing, where he had stepped away from the cover of the forest to fire his arrow. By the time that Deke acquired that spot in his rifle scope, Yamagata had vanished back into the trees.

Deke fired anyhow, hoping that he might get lucky and his bullet would find Yamagata in his jungle hiding place.

"What the hell, Deke?" Rodeo demanded indignantly. He clutched at his arm, clearly in pain.

"Sorry," Deke muttered. "I wanted a shot at that son of a bitch. The commandant of that Japanese camp likes to play with bows and arrows."

"Did you get him?"

"No," Deke said bitterly.

"I'd say the commandant does more than play with bows and arrows," Yoshio pointed out. He had come over to help Rodeo and was wrapping a rag around the base of the arrow. The tip had entered the fleshy part of Rodeo's biceps, but hadn't gone all the way through, leaving the full length of the arrow still jutting out. When Yoshio grasped the arrow, testing how firmly it was embedded, Rodeo yelped in pain.

"Hey, that's not a goddamn stick shift!"

"You can't fight with that arrow the way it is, and we cannot leave it buried in you. It will get infected," Yoshio said. "It must be removed."

"How the hell are you gonna do that?" Rodeo demanded.

"I have an idea."

Without any warning, he used the now bloody rag to get a good grip on the shaft of the arrow and shoved until the point came out the other side of Rodeo's biceps.

Rodeo screamed and made a fist, drawing back his good arm as if about to slug Yoshio. "You son of a bitch!"

Deke grabbed Rodeo's fist before he could punch Yoshio. "Hold on, Yoshio is right. It's got to come out."

Yoshio made the rest of his treatment plan clear by digging in his pack for the wire cutters they had used to get through the perimeter fence. He snipped off the tip of the arrow, then pulled the shaft backward, freeing it from Rodeo's arm. Once again, Rodeo howled.

Yoshio sprinkled some sulpha powder on the entry and exit wounds, then bound it tightly with the rag. Yoshio was the nearest thing they had to a medic, and once again he had demonstrated his medical skills. "There," he said, nodding with satisfaction. "Good as new."

"Good as new my ass," Rodeo replied. "I can tell you one thing. It's gonna hurt like hell to shoot this rifle. At least I'll get a Purple Heart out of it."

Honcho had overheard that last part. "Purple Heart? Hell, no. I hate to tell you this, Rodeo, but nobody would believe me if I put you in for a medal because you got shot with an arrow."

"Well, dammit all, then." Rodeo appeared genuinely disappointed. "That's not fair."

Yoshio grinned. "Maybe you will get shot next with an actual bullet and get yourself a medal after all."

"You're a regular barrel of laughs."

Another arrow came soaring in, picking off another one of the Filipino guerrillas in the foxholes. Deke noted that you could possibly get out of the way of an arrow—if you saw it was coming.

"Dammit, where the hell is he?" he muttered to himself once again. Through the scope, he was watching the spot where he had last seen Yamagata, but there was no sign of him. The arrow had come from an entirely different direction. Just liked a skilled sniper, Yamagata knew to move around.

Deke hurried to the firing slit on that side and scanned the edge of the forest, but there was no sign of the archer. Reluctantly, he had to admit that maybe the man was more talented than he had been willing to give him credit for. Neither had he seen any sign of Mr. Suey. Already the fight was not going the way that Deke had expected or hoped.

After all, a few arrows were terrifying weapons, but they were not the worst of it. The garrison troops had encircled the bunker and foxholes, pouring fire at them. The simple fact was that the Americans and Filipino fighters were outnumbered two or three to one. Their only advantage was the bunker, but even that wasn't completely impregnable. Bullets pinged constantly around the edges of the firing slits. Occasionally the Japanese bullets found their way inside.

From the interior of the bunker, one of the prisoners screamed as he was hit. The man had been little more than a bag of bones, and he collapsed and writhed on the dirt floor. Faraday bent over him, asking him where he was hit, but there was nothing that he could do. The man was beyond any kind of medical care. After a few awful moments, he finally lay still.

"Son-of-a-bitch Japs!" Faraday cursed.

In a rage, Faraday dashed to one of the firing slits and blasted away with the pistol that he'd been given earlier.

"You're wasting ammo," Deke pointed out.

"Maybe, but it sure as hell made me feel better."

Deke just nodded. He couldn't argue with that.

Out in the foxholes that made up the defensive perimeter, the Filipino fighters weren't faring much better.

Father Francisco did not possess a weapon because his religious vows would not allow it. However, he not only directed his defenders, but brought them water and spare ammo taken from the dead and dying after he had said his prayers over them. He was also tending to the wounded as best as he could.

From the bunker Deke could see the priest from time to time, dashing between foxholes at huge personal risk. Bullets kicked up the dirt all around him whenever he appeared in the open. Once or twice Deke could have sworn that he saw bullets pluck at the priest's robes. But the man himself remained unscathed.

Maybe God was protecting the man in some way, after all, Deke thought. Father Francisco had expressed earlier in the mission that he had begun to doubt his faith because of all the loss and suffering he had seen in the war. It was just possible that God had not lost faith in the priest.

Meanwhile, all that any of them could do was fight, hoping that they could pick off enough of the Japanese to even the odds.

"I wish to hell they would come at us in a banzai charge," Philly said.

"No such luck," Deke said.

It was a common misconception that the Japanese were all eager to throw away their lives in pointless banzai charges, but that was not the case. Those charges usually took place when the situation was so desperate that such tactics were a hopeless gamble. This was not the current situation. The Japanese could be stealthy adversaries. They were keeping to cover for the most part, wearing down the defenders. Deke had to hand it to Yamagata in that the man knew his business.

Another arrow whipped through the air, this time smacking against the rim of the firing slit and dropping harmlessly to the ground. Yamagata had missed, but what about the next time? That arrow had come awfully close.

Deke scanned the forest fringes for some sign of the archer, but he was too canny to show himself.

But from the woods, a new threat presented itself. There was a sudden *tap, tap, tap*. Almost instantaneously, a burst of slugs hit the side of the bunker all around the open firing pit in front of Deke and Philly. They instinctively ducked down.

The Japanese had a machine gun.

It had been bad enough to be pinned down by superior rifle fire and an arrow or two. This new development made things much worse.

"Well, don't that beat all," Deke said. "That machine gun changes things."

Philly gave him a look from below the rim of the firing slit, where they had both sheltered when the first volley from the Nambu had chewed up the wall of the pillbox. He said, "Corn Pone, that is probably the understatement of the year."

CHAPTER TWENTY-FOUR

WITH THE STEADY peck of the Nambu machine gun keeping them pinned down, the men inside the bunker and in the surrounding defensive foxholes were forced to stay low. Whenever the machine gun let up, they returned fire. The bunker door had been open for easier communication with the men in the foxholes beyond, but the lieutenant ordered it closed once the machine gun opened up.

One thing for sure was that both sides had reached a stalemate. The Americans weren't going anywhere. Meanwhile, the Japanese couldn't get at them. What happened next was anybody's guess, but time was not on the Americans' side.

"All they need to do is wait us out," Deke said, risking another look through the scope. Instantly the tangled vegetation on the far side of the clearing sprang closer to his eye. He didn't see any movement or targets, so held his fire. The running fight against the Japanese had used up more ammo than they had anticipated. Each shot needed to count.

"Yeah, we're low on ammo, water, and food," Philly agreed. "Plus, I hate to say it, but it's starting to stink in here."

"You got that right." Deke wrinkled his nose. With so many men forced to shelter inside the bunker, one corner had been designated as the latrine area. Aside from the firing slits, there wasn't much in the way of ventilation.

"So we sit here for how long?" Philly wondered.

"I don't see Colonel Yamagata as the patient type. He'll want to put an end to this sooner rather than later."

"You mean the Japanese are gonna try something to shake us loose?"

"Damn straight," Deke said.

Lieutenant Steele called for an ammo count.

"We have thirty rounds between us," Yoshio replied. He and Rodeo were paired up, covering one of the firing slits.

Deke and Philly counted out their clips. "About the same," Deke said.

"All right, I've got a dozen shells left," Steele said, referring to his twelve-gauge shotgun. "Father Francisco and his boys are in the same boat. I wish to hell that we'd brought more ammo."

Nobody needed to remind Steele that ammunition was heavy, and they had been traveling light on this raid. The goal had been to liberate the POWs, not engage in a running battle.

"That's not much ammo for a last stand," Philly said.

"Who the hell said anything about this being a last stand?" Steele demanded. "We came here to liberate these men and get them back to our lines, which is exactly what we are going to do."

"You got it, Honcho," Philly quickly agreed.

Deke knew that the lieutenant could make all the speeches that he wanted to, but their ability to achieve the mission goal was being severely limited by their firepower. Of course, the prisoners themselves didn't have a weapon among them. Deke also knew that Colonel Yamagata was no fool. He would have guessed the Americans' situation and would do something soon to force an outcome.

Also, much of the day had been lost to the stalemate. Already the sun was getting low through the treetops. It was hard to say whether nightfall would give an advantage to the Japanese or to the Americans, who might use darkness as cover to slip through the encircling enemy.

Deke didn't have to wait long before he was proved right about the Japanese taking action, although in this case, being correct gave him no pleasure. Through the scope, he detected movement at the edge of the forest where the attackers had taken cover. He let his breath out, waiting for a target.

"Here they come." Philly had seen it too.

All at once the Japanese burst from the forest and into the clearing. Deke counted a dozen men, all screaming their heads off and dashing toward the bunker with bayonets gleaming on the ends of their rifles. Most also had grenades strung around their necks. There was no doubt what they had in mind. They planned to get close enough to get some of those grenades through the firing slits. If that happened, the interior of the bunker would be a perfect detonation chamber for an explosive, the shrapnel causing terrible destruction. No, the Japanese couldn't be allowed to get that close.

On the plus side, the appearance of the men out in the open gave Deke and the other snipers plenty of targets, like serving up biscuits on a plate.

Or so he thought. Deke was just about to fire when the enemy's machine gun opened up, strafing the side of the bunker. Another burst raked the foxholes, sending the Filipino fighters scrambling for cover.

It was impossible not to duck your head down out of sheer reflex. When Deke put his head back up, the Japanese were already halfway across the clearing and closing fast.

"I want fire on the enemy now!" Steele screamed, a little unnecessarily. Following his own orders, he ran to the firing slit on the side facing the assault and poked his rifle through the opening.

Deke put his sights on the closest Japanese and fired. The man went down. He worked the bolt, picked out another target, and fired. He was shoulder to shoulder with the other snipers, and their deadly accurate fire was having a devastating effect on the enemy assault. Already half the attackers were gone.

Deke had the thought that the Japanese were damn stupid.

That was when there was a warning shout from the other side of the bunker.

"There's a bunch more of them coming up our backside," Faraday cried. He was facing the fresh wave of attackers with a useless pistol, having emptied his gun earlier in anger at the Japanese for one of their stray shots killing a POW inside the bunker. His plan seemed to be that he would simply use it as a club if the enemy got close enough.

"Deke, Philly, get over there, now!" the lieutenant shouted. "Rodeo, Yoshio, you cover this side with me."

Deke pushed past the knot of ex-POWs huddling in the center of the bunker to get at the firing slits on the other side. Faraday and Cooper were there, keeping an eye on the Japanese. They had no weapons, but it was clear from their expressions that they would punch at the Japanese through the firing slit if it came down to it.

"Get down before you get yourself shot," Deke growled, shoving Faraday aside to get a clear angle of fire.

It was immediately obvious to Deke that the initial charge across the clearing was nothing more than a feint, because on this side of the bunker, a half-dozen enemy soldiers approached silently, at a crouch. Several were loaded down with grenades. This facet of the bunker had the largest blind side because of the solid door set into the middle of the wall. The foxholes on this back side were empty, the Filipino fighters having been lured away to face the charging enemies.

Deke was sure that the grenades were intended to breach the door. Solid as it looked, if the Japanese piled enough grenades against the door, it might just splinter.

The Japanese soldier leading the sneak attack looked up. Deke caught a glimpse of his face, and a jolt of recognition went through him.

"I'll be damned if it ain't Mr. Suey," he muttered.

"That's him, all right," Faraday agreed. "Put a bullet through the middle of his ugly mug for me, will ya?"

"You got it."

"Who the hell is Mr. Suey?" Philly wondered.

"Nothing but the meanest Jap bastard you ever met," Faraday said. "Every guy here would like to get his hands on that son of a bitch and tear him to pieces."

Deke was trying to save them the trouble. He hadn't endured nearly as much at Suey's hands as the POWs had, but nonetheless, during his time in the hot box, he had dreamed about the moment when he got the enemy sergeant in his crosshairs.

But Suey wasn't making it easy. He ran at a crouch, moving fast, dodging right and left. Deke took his time aiming. He didn't want to wing Suey. He wanted to kill him.

His finger tightened on the trigger as Suey finally ran straight up the middle to cover the last few yards to the bunker.

Got you now.

Except at that moment someone shouted a warning from behind him. He felt Faraday grab him and pull him down. The next instant, the bunker was filled with an earsplitting blast, like being caught inside a tin can with a firecracker.

He turned to see that one of the Japanese attackers had

managed to shove a grenade through the firing slit on that side. It had detonated with devastating effect.

"I'm hit!" Rodeo shouted, reeling away from the firing slit, blood streaming from the side of his face.

Shrapnel from the grenade had also left several of the ex-POWs torn and bleeding, not to mention stunned and deafened.

Another grenade tumbled through the opening and rolled into the middle of the bunker.

"Look out!" Yoshio shouted.

Quick as lightning, Cooper launched himself across the bunker and pounced on the grenade like a cat on a mouse. The thing went off with a sickening *whunk* as Cooper's body absorbed the blast. There was no doubt that he had just traded several lives for his own.

Lieutenant Steele raised himself up and jammed his shotgun through the firing slit. The twelve-gauge made short work of whatever attackers had made it close enough to the bunker wall to get those grenades in.

The twin grenade blasts had pulled Deke's attention away from his own firing slit. When he looked again, Mr. Suey was no longer in sight, safely in the bunker's blind spot. Deke cursed, but there wasn't much he could do about it. He heard a thud on the other side of the door, leaving no doubt that the Japanese planned to blast their way through.

"Fire in the hole!" Deke shouted to warn the others.

But he didn't plan on letting the Japanese off the hook that easily. Taking a few steps back, he leveled his rifle at the thick door and fired.

Deke knew from experience that the Springfield fired a .30-06 round with enough power to punch through a six-inch tree trunk. More than one enemy soldier had found that out the hard way. He reckoned that his bullet could get through the door.

With any luck, one of those slugs would drill a hole right through Mr. Suey.

He got off three shots before the door blew.

The blast knocked Deke backward, clean off his feet. Splinters of the door flew inside through the roiling smoke. As the smoke cleared, it was evident that the door had remained in place, but it now hung askew like a tattered curtain.

The first Japanese that pushed his way into the bunker died when he was cut nearly in two by a blast from Lieutenant Steele's shotgun. Steele advanced on the blown door, pumping the shotgun and firing, screaming bloody murder all the while. Another enemy soldier came through the door and died.

Steele ran out of shells. Cursing, he grabbed hold of one end of the hot barrel, holding the shotgun like a baseball bat.

Somehow Deke managed to keep a grip on his rifle, although the blast that shattered the door had knocked him down. Ears ringing and dizzy, he got to his feet.

At that moment, it was Mr. Suey who came through the smoking, broken doorway. In one hand, he held a pistol. In the other, he held a grenade.

His sand-colored tunic was stained with blood, evidence that perhaps one of Deke's bullets through the door had winged him.

Mr. Suey held the grenade up triumphantly, shouting something unintelligible in Japanese. His eyes widened in recognition when he spotted Deke pointing the rifle at him.

"Aw, shut the hell up," Deke said, and shot him.

The impact of the bullet knocked Mr. Suey backward. He tumbled back out through the door, and the grenade went off. The blast knocked away a few more boards so that the broken door hung in its frame like a lopsided, gap-toothed smile.

A momentary quiet settled over the bunker and clearing as both sides tried to figure out what to do next.

Once again, the quiet did not last long. One of the former

prisoners decided that he'd had enough. He'd had enough of being hungry and thirsty. He'd had enough of fearing death at the hands of the enemy. After so many long months of cruel captivity, who could blame him? Freedom had seemed so close, only to be denied again at the hands of the enemy. Unable to take any more of it, the man simply snapped. The open door left by the grenade attack beckoned.

The man leaped up with a burst of energy that would have seemed impossible only minutes ago. After all, he was little more than skin and bones, what remained of his ragged uniform flapping around his skinny arms and legs.

Deke recognized him as one of the quieter captives who had kept his head down, seemingly intent on survival. The man's name was Truslow.

"I've had it!" Truslow shouted. "I'm getting out of here!"

To his credit, Faraday tried to stop him. He jumped up and tried to get between the man and the door. "Hold it, Truslow! Just hold it! Where the hell do you think you're going? We're surrounded!"

"I can't take it anymore!" Truslow shouted, then managed to dodge around Faraday and head for the door. Looking on, Deke and the others were too stunned to act.

A split second later, the man was out the doorway. He jumped over the heads of the startled Filipino fighters in the foxholes and began running for all he was worth across the open clearing.

The man's sudden appearance in the open seemed to have taken the enemy by surprise, because they held their fire.

Where Truslow hoped to escape to was hard to say, because the clearing really was ringed by Japanese troops hidden within the cover offered by the encroaching forest. His escape attempt was somewhat helped by the fact that it was starting to get dark, and the dusk was growing thicker. With any luck, his momentum might carry him clear through the enemy perimeter.

Alas, it was not to be. A lone figure stepped from the forest into the clearing. The figure was instantly recognizable as Colonel Yamagata because of the bow he brandished. He already had an arrow nocked. In the time it took to take a breath, Yamagata's powerful arm drew back the string and released an arrow.

The arrow's fletching made it visible like a white flash in the dusk as it sailed straight and true, burying itself in Truslow's chest cavity. Truslow threw his arms wide like a man beseeching the heavens, then tumbled to the ground, ending his run for freedom a few feet short of the edge of the clearing.

Yamagata. Deke had his rifle up once he had recovered his wits, but by then the archer had faded back among the trees.

"Dammit, dammit, dammit," Faraday was muttering, staring out through one of the firing slits at Truslow's lifeless figure in the distance. An enemy rifle cracked, and he was forced to duck down.

"That's it," Lieutenant Steele announced. He had positioned himself in front of the bunker door to block the exit, just in case anyone else got the idea to make a run for it. "One way or another, we are getting out of here."

CHAPTER TWENTY-FIVE

TRAPPED. It was how they all felt, Deke included, as they peered out through the firing slits at the ring of forest surrounding the bunker.

One hell of a place to make a last stand, Deke thought. Lieutenant Steele might not want to call it that, but that was what it was shaping up to be.

Our very own Alamo, he thought, *right here in the jungle.*

A weary quiet settled over the men in the bunker. Truslow's desperate bid for freedom had left them all shaken. His attempt had been doomed from the start, but they could all understand why he had at least tried. The truth was that they all felt the same way. Truslow simply hadn't been able to take it anymore.

Meanwhile, they were all just waiting for the next shoe to drop. It felt as if the Japanese held all the cards.

"How well did you know Truslow?" Deke asked Faraday, once an uneasy calm had returned.

Faraday shrugged. "You know, it's funny. I lived right alongside the man for months but didn't know that much about him. Hell, you could probably say the same about any of us."

"Sometimes it's best not to get to know the other fella too well."

"Honestly, we were all mostly too tired and worn out to chew the fat. I do know that he'd been a sailor who went in the drink when his ship went down. All I really knew about him aside from that was that he was married. He had a little girl back home somewhere in New Mexico. She'd been born while he was away, and he'd never even seen her. Imagine that? He said the Japanese took away the only picture he had of her and his wife when he was captured. Bastards."

"A sailor from New Mexico? Don't that beat all," Deke replied.

"Dammit, I should have been a little faster," Faraday said. "Maybe I could have stopped him. He wasn't in the right frame of mind."

"He went loco," Deke said, more to the point. "Can't blame him—and you sure as hell can't blame yourself. If anybody is to blame, it's me."

Faraday gave him a look, his eyes bright and almost feverish in what remained of the daylight. They had all been without enough food and water, and the effects were starting to show. "What the hell are you talking about?"

He and Deke were off to one side of the bunker, talking quietly. Although the former flyboy was an officer, that line between them had disappeared, if it had ever existed at all. What they had been through together in this short time had made them equals. It was true that they were very different, Deke with his country ways and Faraday with his officer's polish, but Deke had come to trust the man every bit as much as any member of Patrol Easy.

Steele had already announced that they would try to break through the enemy encirclement, so they just needed it to get darker. Then again, it came down to a coin toss whether the Japanese would launch another attack first.

"I feel responsible for each and every one of these men," Deke said. "I put them all at risk with this escape attempt. Hell, I promised them freedom, but maybe it's just not something that I can deliver."

"Don't say that," Faraday replied.

"I went in there thinking we were gonna kick some Japanese ass and take names later. Cut through them like a hot knife through butter. That was the plan, anyhow. I could tell that some of your boys weren't keen on it, and maybe they knew better. Who knows, in another few weeks, they might have been freed anyhow when the advance reached them."

Faraday shook his head. "I doubt it. You said yourself that maybe the enemy was looking to erase any evidence of the camps. That meant erasing their POWs. No, it's likely that we were on borrowed time."

"Look where it got us," Deke said. He wasn't one to give up easily, but he suddenly felt down and out. "Now we're trapped."

"So we'll die fighting. You saw what it was like in that camp. It was only a matter of time before those bastards worked us all to death—or worse."

"What are you planning on fighting the Japanese with?" Deke asked. After all, the former prisoners were unarmed.

Faraday looked away. He didn't have a good answer for that.

Deke had to admit that he hadn't felt so down in a long time. It was seeing Yamagata fire that arrow into Truslow so triumphantly that had set him on edge. He had hoped to get Yamagata in his sights by now, but the colonel had proved too elusive. Fortunately, the same couldn't be said of Mr. Suey. What was left of him now lay beyond the bunker door, attracting flies and ants.

Still, that small triumph hadn't been enough. Deke had the

nagging feeling that maybe they had won the battle but lost the war, so to speak.

Faraday moved closer and took hold of the front of Deke's uniform shirt, bunching it up in his fist. It was not a threatening gesture, but a way of making sure he had Deke's full attention. Deke tried to pull away, but Faraday wouldn't let him go. Given his current condition, Faraday had a surprising amount of strength.

"You listen to me, and listen good," Faraday said. "Not just anybody could have come into that camp and done what you did. Right away, you got under Mr. Suey's skin, and Yamagata's too. That showed me right away that you were the right man for the job."

"Some job I did—"

"Hold on. I'm not through yet." Faraday tightened his grip on Deke's shirt. "I've heard your buddies talk about what a great shot you are, and I saw some of that today. If anybody is going to take out that snake-eyed Yamagata, it's going to be you. Hell, you told me that you fought a bear and lived to talk about it. You got us this far, so don't give up now. I know I haven't pulled rank much with you, but that's an order, by the way."

"Yes, sir," Deke muttered.

Faraday let go of his shirt. Deke still wasn't entirely convinced, but Faraday had given him something to think about.

As they waited, the men of Patrol Easy shared around what was left of their food. Divided among so many, it didn't go far. That was all right—Deke didn't feel much like eating, anyway.

Next, Deke did what he always did in situations like this. He fieldstripped his rifle and gave it a thorough cleaning. He didn't need much light to see what he was doing. He knew every inch of the rifle as well as he knew the back of his hand or the contours of the scarred side of his face. There weren't too many bullets left to go down the rifled grooves of the barrel, but he knew that each one must count.

He found the activity itself calming. Bit by bit, the awful memory of seeing the arrow fly into Truslow faded.

When he had finished cleaning the rifle, he turned his attention to his knife. The hand-forged bowie knife was perfect for jungle combat and already razor sharp. Nonetheless, he took out a whetstone, spat on it, then steadily scraped the blade across it. This was a sound that had preceded combat going back to ancient times. In the end, these rituals of cleaning the rifle and sharpening the knife were as much about preparing one's mind as it was about preparing one's weapons.

After several minutes of working with the whetstone, Deke tested the edge of the blade with his thumb. It was so sharp that he could feel the steel wanting to cut him before his thumb was anywhere near it. What was sharper than a razor, he wondered? *This bowie knife, that's what.*

Not long after that, Father Francisco came in with one of the Filipino fighters, who turned out to speak a little English. The guerrilla had been wounded, and his arm was heavily bandaged. The priest had gone unscathed despite the heavy volume of Japanese fire that had been directed at the men in the outlying foxholes. It seemed to be a testament that someone up above was looking out for him.

"Padre, how are your men holding up?" Steele asked quietly, taking the priest to one corner of the bunker.

"We are low on ammunition," he said. "Also, we have no more food or water."

"Same here," Steele said. "That's why I propose that we try to get out of here. It won't be easy."

"We have no other choice," the priest said.

The only plan seemed to be to make a run for it by connecting with the trailhead and getting as far out ahead of the

Japanese as they could. Briefly, a diversion was considered, but quickly dismissed. It would be better if they could catch the Japanese off guard.

As plans went, it wasn't much of one. "Honestly, we don't need an elaborate plan," the lieutenant said. "What we need is a little luck."

"Perhaps I can help with that," Father Francisco said with a smile. Opening his arms in a welcoming gesture, he invited the men in the bunker to pray with him. A chorus of mumbled voices joined in. As the old saying went, there was no such thing as an atheist in a foxhole. The priest led some of the prayers in Spanish for the benefit of his guerrilla fighters, then switched to English for the Americans. Deke prayed along with them because he figured that the Lord above was more likely to pay attention with a priest leading the prayers.

"Thank you, Padre," Lieutenant Steele said. "Let's hope somebody upstairs was listening."

"He always listens," the priest said confidently, then slipped back out the door to rejoin his own men.

Deke peered out at the darkness, but there was no sign of the Japanese—not even a whisper. He had the disconcerting thought that they were listening back, wondering what the Americans would do next. The night itself wasn't exactly quiet, because it was filled with the sounds of insects and night birds. From time to time the screech of some larger animal made their skin crawl.

Fortunately for all of them, it was a dark night with just a sliver of waxing moon visible. High-flying clouds scuttled across the moon and stars, adding to the darkness. If it had been any brighter, Deke wouldn't have liked their chances. The odds weren't exactly in their favor, but at least the dark conditions of the jungle night favored them.

Around midnight, Steele quietly gave the order to move out.

"I'll take the lead," the lieutenant said. "Deke, I want you and Danilo to watch our backside. It will be your job to buy us some time once the Japanese come after us—and rest assured that they will. Whatever you do, don't fall behind, because there's nobody to come and get you."

"You got it, Honcho."

It was clear that this wasn't going to be easy. The former POWs were in rough shape. Their entire party was low on ammunition and supplies. But there was no point in sitting around and waiting for the inevitable while the Japanese figured out what to do next.

Steele looked around one last time, trying to give everyone a reassuring nod. Then he went out the door of the bunker and started across the clearing, crouching low. The men followed in a file, moving as quietly as possible.

Somebody stumbled, and there was the sound of a boot sole scuffing a rock. It seemed to carry forever through the stillness.

"Quiet!" Steele whispered, as loudly as he dared.

The rest of the men crept forward as quietly as possible. They all knew that if the machine gun opened fire, then they'd be cut to pieces. It was a huge gamble, but they really didn't have any choice.

CHAPTER TWENTY-SIX

DEKE GAVE DANILO A NOD, then started after the others filing out of the bunker. The open clearing wasn't more than a hundred yards across from the bunker at its center, but it felt like miles. By some miracle, most of the others had reached the other side before the first shot rang out.

With a certain amount of relief, he recognized the deep boom of Lieutenant Steele's shotgun. Whoever had been on the business end of that muzzle wouldn't be sending any more letters home to Tokyo.

"Run, dammit, run!" he heard Steele shout. "Once you're on the trail, don't stop for anything!"

Fortunately, the bulk of the men were almost across the clearing. As if by a sixth sense, Steele must have managed to find the entrance to the path in the dark. They were luckier still that the enemy machine gun wasn't brought into play immediately, allowing the rest of the group to get across.

Everyone except for Deke and Danilo, that was. Tracers lit up the night as the machine gun opened up, pecking at the bunker. Lucky for them, the machine gunner didn't seem to know where to direct his fire. Not bothering to crouch anymore, Deke sprinted for the cover of the jungle, Danilo right on his heels. He caught a glimpse of one of the Filipino fighters, no more than a ghostly shadow up ahead, gesturing to show him the entrance to the path. He saw the sprawled body of the dead Japanese soldier in time to jump over it, then was running down the trail.

He couldn't believe that they had given the encircling Japanese the slip. But then he had the thought that it hardly mattered. There was no way they could outrun the enemy. Once again, this was going to be a running battle that wouldn't end until they reached the American lines—or one side or the other was wiped out. Either way, it was a grim prospect.

Already he heard angry shouts behind him that were all too close. The enemy was giving chase, and already gaining on them. Ahead of him, the rest of the team was bunching up as the struggling ex-POWs slowed them down. Their rear-guard trio kept running into the man in front of them, probably the same fellow who had waved them toward the trail.

Deke cursed their slow pace, then reminded himself that these POWs were the whole reason they were here in the first place.

"This isn't looking good," Philly pointed out, once he had drifted back to join them. "Maybe we ought to have stayed in the bunker."

"We were trapped like rats in that place," Deke said. "No, thanks."

He slowed down long enough to turn and fire a couple of shots at the dim blur of movement behind him. He was painfully aware that he was almost out of ammunition. The three of them hung back for a moment, catching their breath and letting the rest of the column advance.

"I'm almost out," Deke said. "How about you?"

SAVAGE SNIPER

249

"I just put the last clip in my rifle. Next thing you know, we'll have to beat them off with sticks."

"Danilo? You got any ammo? Bullets?"

The tough Filipino seemed to comprehend the question well enough. He simply shook his head and patted the bolo knife hanging at his side. Deke nodded, understanding all too well that Danilo was already out of ammunition, although he still carried his captured Japanese rifle slung over one shoulder. Deke would have tried to go back and steal some ammo or guns off the Japanese, if he had dared.

"Let's go," Deke said. "We really don't have much choice except to make a run for it."

The three men started down the path, but all too soon they came across the others ahead of them. There was a small clearing where a large tree had blown down in a storm, leaving enough space for the ex-POWs to huddle. In the darkness, Deke could sense their exhaustion, even if he couldn't see it. He found Faraday helping a man who had twisted his ankle on a root jutting across the trail. Faraday was trying to wrap the ankle tightly with a strip of rag to give it support. Maybe the man could go a little farther.

"Why did you stop?" Deke asked. "Where the hell is the lieutenant?"

"He doesn't know we stopped. He thinks we're right behind him. He went on ahead with Rodeo and Yoshio, seeing if he could contact some of the advance units of our own boys," Faraday said. "Right after that, Mason here got tripped up by a root. I'm trying to get him back on his feet."

"You'd best hurry. The Japanese are right behind us."

No sooner had Deke spoken those words than a bullet snapped through the branches nearby, then another. The Japanese had seen them. Then to their surprise, an arrow zipped past, so close that Deke could hear the *thwip* it made cutting through the air. It meant that Colonel Yamagata was even closer. Deke raised his rifle, but there was no sign of the archer.

Danilo had seen the injured man and had used his bolo knife to cut a long staff from the branches of the deadfall, something that the soldier could use to take the weight off his injured ankle. The sooner he could hobble up the trail, the better.

The sight of the staff gave Deke an idea. He reached out and took it from Danilo. "Cut another," he said.

Danilo shrugged and started hacking at another tree limb with his bolo knife.

"Maybe he'll just take us all prisoner again," Faraday said.

"To hell with that," Deke said. "Here, take my rifle. It's only got three rounds left, but it's something. Philly, you and Danilo stay with Faraday."

"What about you?" Philly asked. He nodded at the staff in Deke's hands. "I was just joking about fighting the Japanese with sticks, you know."

"Don't worry about me," Deke said. "Kill as many of these Japs as you can. And for Jasper's sake, get these fellas moving."

Faraday got the men up and moving. He and Philly had the only operational weapons. Somewhere up ahead, if the lieutenant got lucky, he would run into the American advance.

Deke stepped off the trail and almost immediately found himself enveloped in the deep jungle. Rather than feeling cut off and alone, Deke felt himself reassured by the darkness. He was now a hunter, just like he had been as a boy in the mountains. He felt the hopelessness he had experienced earlier slip away. An ancient kind of power flowed through him, something so old that it was more like what a wolf or a bear felt than did a modern man. It was the power of the hunter.

He had left his rifle with Faraday. But he was far from defenseless. A cold smile played across his face, one that would have chilled a witness to the bone, although there was no one to see it.

The only light came from the sliver of moon, which created dappled pools of pale silver across the forest floor. Using one of these pools of moonlight to work by, first he laid out the staff on the forest floor. Then he drew his bowie knife, revealing the shining blade in the moonlight. This was the same style of knife that had been used by his ancestors to fight the Indians, the British, the Yankees—hell, maybe some distant Cole relation had even used it at the Alamo.

Working quickly, he bound the handle to the wooden staff using a length of twine that he'd been keeping in his pocket. It wasn't long enough, so he cut some vines and used those next. The vines were surprisingly tough and suitable to the task. The result was a spear that looked so primitive that a caveman might have used it—if a caveman happened to have a bowie knife. There was no telling how long the binding would last, but with any luck, he would need to use it only once.

Satisfied with his effort, he hefted the weapon. It felt natural in his hands.

Blade against bow, he thought.

The thought of a bow came to mind because it was Yamagata he wanted. He knew that if you wanted to kill a snake, you had to cut off its head. He had already killed Mr. Suey. If he could just eliminate Yamagata, he was sure that the Japanese pursuit would falter.

The only question that nagged at Deke was, What about Lieutenant Osako? Deke hadn't seen him, and for all he knew, the young officer had been left back at the prison compound. He decided that it didn't really matter, because Osako wouldn't have the backbone for pursuing the prisoners. No, it was Yamagata who was the snake's head.

Deke slipped through the trees, moving parallel to the jungle trail. He moved by instinct and by sound, listening for the occasional gunshots. There weren't many, which was a good sign—it meant that the Japanese had not caught up to the Americans yet.

He had no doubt that Yamagata would be at the head of the enemy column, leading his men. Deke moved through the forest with all the practiced silence of a natural-born hunter. He soon heard voices ahead, speaking Japanese. He had found the trail.

He crept closer. The Japanese had paused in their pursuit, probably wondering why the Americans had stopped. Were they planning to make another stand? Was it a trap? Knowing the enemy, they would not be stopped for long.

Deke was rewarded with a glimpse of Yamagata. The colonel stood alone in the moonlight, in the middle of the trail, scanning the path ahead for any sign of the Americans. Several of his men stood a respectful distance behind him. He held his bow in his hands, an arrow already nocked to the string, but the bow wasn't drawn back.

Now or never, Deke thought.

He stepped out of the forest directly into Yamagata's line of sight. Deke was close enough that he could see the whites of Yamagata's eyes widen in surprise. Whether he recognized Deke was impossible to say—it was likely that Deke was little more than a silhouette, although he still wore the distinctive bush hat.

Yamagata did not hesitate. Deke had to give him credit for that. Fast as a viper, the colonel drew back the bow and fired an arrow at the target that had presented itself.

Deke saw the flash of the arrow's white fletching as it came for him, fast as the blink of an eye. But Deke was ready for it and stepped to the left. The arrow slipped past him as quick and sinister as a striking snake, then buried itself into the tree that Deke had been standing in front of just an instant before.

Yamagata saw that he had missed and muttered something

that sounded like a curse. At the same time, he reached for another arrow and fitted it to the bowstring.

Now it was Deke's turn to move. He leveled the spear and launched himself at the colonel. The question was, Could he reach Yamagata in time? Deke would need to take five big steps to cover the distance. The colonel was an excellent shot with that bow, and he wouldn't miss again.

One step, two steps—

Yamagata drew back the bow, exposing the left side of his broad and powerful chest to Deke in the process.

Three steps, four—

Their eyes met in the moonlight. There was no doubt now that Yamagata recognized him. There was also no doubt that Deke was not going to get to take one more step before Yamagata released his arrow.

Deke launched himself the final distance, leaping across the space between them, spearpoint thrust dead ahead. At the same time, he screamed something that was part rebel yell, part pure animal snarl.

The jolt as the spear struck home was so hard that the momentum threw Deke off balance, and he fell, the wrappings securing the knife handle to the body of the spear ripping away in the process.

But it was enough. The tip of the spear caught Yamagata just under the rib cage. Freed of the staff, the knife blade knew its business and still managed to thrust toward the colonel's heart. An expression of surprise lit up Yamagata's face. He released the arrow, which whipped past Deke so close that the tip sliced open his ear.

Firing that arrow had been Yamagata's last act. Black in the moonlight, blood sheeted the front of his uniform as his heart beat its last. The colonel slumped to his knees; then with a final, almost puzzled look at Deke, he fell dead on the trail.

Deke stared down at him, his hands shaking, overcome by the awful savagery of what he had just done. He'd had no choice —it had come down to him or Yamagata.

There were still the rest of the Japanese soldiers to worry about. But they had been so startled by what they had seen that all they could do was stare at Deke and the colonel's body.

Deke didn't give them a chance to react. He reached out and retrieved his bowie knife from the colonel's rib cage, then slipped into the forest.

Only then did the shooting start, but Deke had already vanished like smoke.

CHAPTER TWENTY-SEVEN

Epilogue

DEKE REJOINED the rest of the column making its way along the trail through the jungle. Having raced ahead in hopes of encountering the American advance sooner rather than later, Lieutenant Steele had left Deke and Father Francisco in charge. Deke hoped that Steele returned soon with good news. They needed firepower to end the Japanese pursuit.

With both Mr. Suey and Colonel Yamagata out of the picture, Deke and the others prayed that the enemy might abandon the pursuit. But from behind them, they still heard shouts and the occasional potshot. The enemy had not given up and was still coming after them.

Any resemblance to a military operation on the part of the enemy had gone out the window. Instead, it was clear that the Japanese were bent on revenge. Based on the shouts and apparent taunts being hurled at them, the enemy sounded like an angry mob.

To make matters worse, no ammo had miraculously appeared. They were all down to just a few rounds. Also, they were still low on food and water. Father Francisco reported that his guerrilla fighters were no better off in terms of supplies.

"If nothing else, my men have their bolo knives," the priest said, then gave a knowing smile. "And God is on our side."

"That's good to know, Padre," Deke replied. "I reckon we can use the help. Meanwhile, have your boys give whatever ammo they have left to Danilo."

"Consider it done."

The former prisoners were doing the best they could but still moved at what felt like a snail's pace, barely staying ahead of the pursuers. They were all but drained of energy. Many of the men limped or leaned on makeshift crutches. Faraday was doing his best to urge them along, but there was only so much that he could do. With each passing minute, it became more worrisome that the former prisoners might fall back into the hands of the Japanese.

"They're still coming after us," Philly said. "Don't they know when to stop? Yoshio, you ought to shout at them to give up and see what happens."

"I could try, but 'give up' in Japanese is more of a curse word. It has very negative connotations."

"That's too bad for them. You know, I knew a girl who loved it when I gave her connotations," Philly said.

"Save your yappin' for the Japanese, why don't you," Deke said irritably.

Deke turned to look with concern down the trail behind them. He could only guess that leadership of the pursuit had fallen to Lieutenant Osako, who would be the ranking officer at this point. Deke had not counted on Osako to be quite so diligent in his duties or so determined. Perhaps he had underestimated the man.

"Everybody keep moving," Deke said. "It's the best we can do."

He had gotten his rifle back from Faraday, although he had just three rounds remaining. That was better than nothing. It took just one bullet to make a difference.

Growing up, there had been times when he'd had just one bullet and had been expected to come back with something for the supper pot. For the Cole family and for most others during the Great Depression era in the mountains, buying a whole box of bullets at once would have been an extravagance. The general store several miles from their farm sold bullets and shotgun shells individually for a few pennies each. Sometimes even those pennies were hard to come by. Hard cash was a scarce commodity. Nobody wasted a shot back then, and Deke didn't plan on doing that now. The way he saw it, three bullets meant three dead Japanese.

He and Danilo slipped toward the rear of the column and hung back there in the brush at the side of the trail. From their position, they awaited the appearance of the Japanese. They had chosen a bend in the path as their hiding place, giving them a long view down the trail. As soon as the enemy came into sight, they would have a clear shot at them. Deke doubted that they would have to wait long.

The priest had seen to it that Danilo had a few more rounds for his rifle, but how many? Deke used three fingers to tap his own rifle. Danilo nodded and held up four fingers. He knew well enough that Danilo would also make each shot count.

Around them, the forest seemed to be holding its breath. Trees of varying heights fenced them in, some soaring skyward and others groping up through the shaded canopy, desperate for a bit of sunlight. Slender vines curled among broad leaves. A few droplets of water fell, making a patter on the broad brim of his bush hat. He welcomed the cover that the jungle provided, but at the same time, there was always something sinister about it, as if old spirits dwelled among the shadows.

Back home he had encountered mountain forests that felt the same way.

There were also threats that were all too real. He watched a spider the size of his hand groping its way along a branch. An insect nibbled at the exposed back of his neck, but Deke ignored it, all his attention focused on the space where he expected the first enemy soldiers to appear.

The enemy did not disappoint. A couple of soldiers hurried along the trail, hot on the heels of the Americans.

Deke nodded at Danilo. Both men stepped into the center of the path and fired, dropping two enemy soldiers. Then they melted back into the forest. There was a flurry of shots from the enemy that passed harmlessly overhead. Better yet, the Japanese had temporarily halted, evidently worried that they were walking into an ambush. If more enemy soldiers did want to show themselves and get shot, he and Danilo would be happy to oblige.

Deke thought it was a damn shame that they didn't have more ammo. He and Danilo might have held off the enemy indefinitely, just two men against many. That was the power of a sniper.

However, a sniper needed bullets to be effective. Another Japanese soldier crept forward, and Deke dropped him. One bullet left. He would have to make it count. Danilo gave him a look of concern that needed no translation. Once they were out of ammo, then what?

Deke put the rifle to his shoulder and his eye to the telescopic sight, so that the kaleidoscope of the jungle patterns and colors sprang closer. Another Japanese soldier came into view, and it was almost too easy to put his crosshairs on the man's throat and drop him. Beside him, Danilo also fired, worked the bolt, fired again.

They were officially out of ammo, and there were still too many Japanese hot on their trail. Deke wasn't about to abandon his rifle, so he slung it across his back and drew his bowie knife. Beside him, Danilo did the same, the man's long bolo knife making an evil hiss as it came free of the scabbard. Maybe they could get in among the trees and spring out at the enemy, taking them by surprise. With any luck, they might even be able to get ahold of a couple of Japanese rifles.

Fortunately it didn't come to that. They heard a shout from up the trail, in the direction of their own men. For once it was not a warning shout but a whoop of what might have been joy. Then they heard several voices cheering. The enemy behind them was temporarily stalled thanks to the telling effect of their final shots, so he and Danilo hurried to catch up with the others.

They soon found the reason for the shouting and cheering. The tide was finally turning in their favor. Lieutenant Steele had returned, leading a contingent of US troops. One of them even carried a Browning Automatic Weapon, or BAR—just the thing to halt the advancing enemy in their tracks.

"We heard that you boys might need a little help," one of the soldiers said. "You came to the right place."

"There's a mess of Japanese right on our heels," Deke said. "They're stirred up angry as hornets."

"Not a problem," another soldier said, hefting the BAR. "Let's rack 'em and stack 'em, boys."

"I like the sound of that."

"You say these fellas on your trail were the camp guards?"

"Yeah."

"Bastards," the BAR gunner said, looking around at the rail-thin former prisoners dressed in their ragged uniforms. "We'll take care of 'em, believe me."

But as the troops moved into position, they were greeted with the deadly *tap, tap, tap* of the Nambu machine gun. Deke thought that the Japanese must have figured out from the cheering that they were no longer dealing with just the raiders and escaped prisoners. Consequently, they had set up their machine gun. Anyone coming down that jungle path in their direction would be mowed down.

A couple of medics were treating the worst cases among the ex-POWs. Lieutenant Steele was doling out rations but cautioning the men not to overeat. "Just take a few bites," he warned them. "I don't think your systems can handle much more than that."

Hard as it was for the men not to gorge themselves, they did their best. Faraday moved among them, making sure that nobody ate too much.

"Holy cow, look at these guys," one of the GIs said. "They look like scarecrows. The least that the Nips could have done is feed them. It's not right."

Deke didn't disagree, but he was more interested in bullets than biscuits. "Give me some ammo," he said.

The GI handed him a couple of clips. Then Deke ran in the direction of the firing, ready to join the fight.

However, he had a better idea than running headlong into deadly bursts from the Nambu. Instead, he slipped off the trail and moved through the forest parallel to it, hoping to surprise the machine gunner.

Unfortunately for Deke, some of the Japanese had the same idea. He came face-to-face with an enemy soldier who was doing just the same thing in the opposite direction. Startled, the enemy soldier made the fatal mistake of shouting something at Deke. Whether the enemy soldier was shouting a curse or a command to surrender, he'd never know, because Deke leveled his rifle and shot him. Then he pressed on through the trees.

From the sounds on the trail, he knew that he'd come even with the machine-gun position. He crept forward and fired at the figure crouching behind the gun, just visible through the trees. The firing abruptly stopped, giving the GIs on the trail the opening they needed. They advanced on the Japanese position, clearing the way with hand grenades and bursts from the BAR. Deke kept his head down while the BAR gunner sprayed the trail, the burst shredding leaves and twigs along with any enemy soldiers who had dared to show themselves.

Seconds later, the fight was over, and GIs swarmed the area around the machine gun. Deke stepped out of the woods and saw that one of the Japanese was still alive. To his surprise, he realized that it was Lieutenant Osako. He had not recognized him at first because the man's eyeglasses had been knocked askew.

A GI leveled his weapon at the Japanese officer and was about to pull the trigger, but Deke pushed the muzzle aside. "Hold on," he said. "We want this one alive."

The lieutenant was wounded, down on his knees, looking up at the American soldiers. He clearly recognized Deke. "I remember you," he said. "Deacon Cole."

"I reckon the tables have turned, Osako. You're our prisoner now."

The Japanese officer shook his head. "No, I cannot surrender," he said, sounding resigned. "Honor does not allow it."

Instead of putting his hands up, Osako reached for the pistol in the holster on his belt. The GI to Deke's left cursed and swung his weapon at Osako again, clearly intending to put an end to matters before the enemy officer could draw his pistol.

Deke was faster. In one smooth motion, he took a step forward, and at the same time, reversed his rifle and clubbed Osako on the side of the head. Knocked out, the Japanese slumped to the forest floor.

"Consider yourself captured," Deke said.

* * *

THE FIGHT for Leyte was far from over, but it was becoming more apparent that the Japanese had lost the battle. At least, it was apparent to everyone but the Japanese. Starting with the initial landing near Palo and then the second landing to seize Ormoc, their forces had been pushed back from the coastal areas and forced to make a last stand in the hills and forests. As always, the Japanese simply refused to give up and surrender. Instead, they were going to make the Americans pay dearly with their lives.

It was more than a little frightening to think of the massive fight that would be necessary to capture Japan itself. If they fought so hard for every inch of islands such as Guadalcanal, Guam, and Leyte, what would it mean when the fight came to the Japanese home islands of Honshu, Hokkaido, Shikoku, and Kyushu?

But for now that worry was down the road and far away. Patrol Easy reveled in the fact that they and Father Francisco's guerrilla fighters had managed to liberate the POW camp.

Once they returned to American lines, there were photographers to document the arrival of the newly freed men. Even Major Flanders was there to welcome them and oversee the photo op. However, upon seeing the condition that the former prisoners were in, he had shooed away the photographers, keeping just one to document the poor physical condition of the liberated soldiers. He made it clear that the photographs would not be for publication.

"Folks back home don't need to see that," he said. "It certainly won't help the war effort. But dammit, these photos might just be evidence once this war is over."

More medics arrived to help treat the former prisoners, some so weak that they had to be carried away in stretchers. As for the others, it was announced that they would be sent to the fleet to recover their strength. There would be ample food for them and medical care. An air attack or even a submarine strike against the ships remained a threat, but it still seemed better than taking their chances on the open beach.

Deke managed to catch up with Faraday before he shipped out.

"I just want to thank you for all that you've done," Faraday said. "It's not just any guy who would surrender himself to the Japanese in order to help us break out."

"It seemed like a good idea at the time," Deke said.

Faraday gave him a wry grin. "At least you got a taste of what it was like to be in that place."

"I could have done without that."

"I just wish we could have captured Colonel Yamagata and Mr. Suey to give them a taste of their own medicine. I would have loved to see them in a POW compound."

"Don't worry, they got what they had coming to them."

"I suppose so," Faraday said; then he joined the line waiting to board a launch that would carry the former POWs far from Leyte.

Deke was sorry to see Faraday go, but he was glad that Faraday and the others would be given a chance to recuperate far from the combat still taking place on Leyte.

A few Japanese prisoners—precious few—had also been taken. Lieutenant Osako was now among those men. They were kept in a big stockade that had been erected for that purpose, but there was shelter from the sun and rain. Even more than that, the prisoners were fed and not forced to perform slave labor. It was all a marked contrast to the cruel conditions that the Americans had faced while being held prisoner. Yoshio had been roped into interviewing several of the higher-ranking officers who had been captured.

From a distance, Deke had caught a glimpse of Lieutenant Osako staring in wonder at the hordes of men and supplies that now occupied the beachhead, with more arriving all the time. He and the other Japanese could have no doubt now that an American victory was a foregone conclusion. For a change the symbolic Japanese sun on their battle flag might have been setting—at least on Leyte.

Patrol Easy got a full day of sleeping and eating, but there was to be no real rest for the weary. By the next afternoon, they found themselves headed back into the forest. As it turned out, there were still plenty of Japanese to fight. There were even rumors that they might be sent to Manila next, where instead of the forest, they would be fighting across city streets.

"Aw, I was just gettin' comfortable, Honcho," Philly complained.

"Sounds like the army has another job for us," Deke said. "What's it gonna be?"

"Don't know yet," the lieutenant admitted. "But I will tell you one thing, which is that you'd better bring your rifle. You're going to need it."

NOTE TO READERS

Thank you for reading the continued adventures of Deacon Cole and Patrol Easy. Once again, many of their actions on Leyte are based on the 77th Infantry Division, following their route after the capture of Ormoc and the push toward Palompon. If you would like to know more, please get a copy of *Ours to Hold It High: The History of the 77th Infantry Division in World War II* by Max Myers. I hope that my story honors these actual men and events in some small way.

There are some bits of history here that that are worth mentioning. First, the name of Faraday's plane, *Blind Date*, comes from an actual aircraft lost during a bombing mission to Tokyo on May 23, 1945. The people of the Philippines, especially guerrilla forces, were important allies during the campaign. They were considered US nationals until the Philippines became an independent nation on July 4, 1946. The rescue mission and the POW camp are fictionalized for the story, but are inspired by the cruel conditions in real-life. General MacArthur really did issue a warning about the treatment of POWs shortly after landing on Leyte and several Japanese officers were punished accordingly after the war.

It almost goes without saying that some of the language and attitudes on these pages are appropriate to the World War II setting but are avoided today. Japan is now one of our great democratic allies in a challenging world order.

Finally, thank you to the usual team that has helped bring these books to reality, including Aidan, Mary, Mike, Deny, advance readers Dano, Charles, and Paul, the talented narrator Scott Bennett, Streetlight Graphics, Intracoastal Media, and Castle Walls Editing. There are many others too numerous to mention whose support and help over the years are deeply appreciated—including you, dear reader. Writing a book is a leap of faith where you just try to do your best to tell the story. To quote Deacon Cole, "I reckon that I get lucky now and then. Like my daddy used to say, you can't hit any of the targets you don't shoot at. In other words, you have to take your chances now and then."

— DH

ABOUT THE AUTHOR

David Healey lives in Maryland, where he worked as a journalist for more than twenty years. He is an author member of the International Thriller Writers.

Check in with him on Facebook at
https://www.facebook.com/david.healey.books